C000226603

Cherry Smyth

Hold Still

Holland Park Press London

Published by Holland Park Press 2013

Copyright © Cherry Smyth 2013

First Edition

A CIP catalogue record for this book is
available from The British Library.

ISBN 978-1-907320-36-1

Cover designed by Reactive Graphics

Printed and bound by CPI Group (UK) Ltd,
Croydon, CR0 4YY

www.hollandparkpress.co.uk

Hold Still is set in 1860s London and Paris, and is a fictional account of a short period in the life of Joanna Hiffernan, the muse and model of both James Whistler and Gustave Courbet.

Cherry Smyth has created an enthralling picture of what must have been a remarkable woman. How did a young girl, just seventeen when she met Jim Whistler, admittedly with beautiful red hair, and a vivid personality, inspire talented painters to create wonderful paintings such as: Whistler's *Symphony in White, No.1: The White Girl* and Courbet's *La Belle Irlandaise?*

Hold Still tells the story from Jo's point of view. Her father instils in her a sense of self and Jo grows up to be a free spirit, a suffragette avant la lettre. Jo draws you in on her journey and her growing sense of her own artistic identity.

The novel offers a wonderful insight into the artistic process; the rivalry and at the same time the supportive camaraderie. At the heart of the story is love, which shapes Jo's life: *She loves him looking at her, feels as if she is made for his gaze, is made anew in it.*

You get a fresh understanding of how women in Victorian society were supposed to behave. Jo tackles this head on, and it is this courage that enables her to progress from seemingly being used as an artist's model, to turn this into the break she needs to make her way in life.

Read *Hold Still* for an interpretation of Courbet's notorious *The Origin of the World's* genesis, with a highly plausible explanation of the absent head and face of the model.

Contents

I

Wapping, 1861

The studio is quiet and still. Jo undresses behind the maroon curtain and wraps a sheet of green silk around her, tying it over one shoulder like a toga. She is sleepy, her limbs as heavy as thick felt. Or is it her mind that is filled with felt, weighing her down, as if by a strange dream the meaning of which has not yet emerged? She bends over and untangles her red hair, adding volume. Yesterday she was Ariadne, draped in blue and white robes with a loose red satin scarf twisting over her collar bone. Today she will be Minerva, seated on a stool holding a spear, balancing one foot on the rung. A big fire blazes in the hearth. Wood not coal. She prefers its more companionable smell. There is also heat from the ring of gas-burners closely packed together overhead. The students are drifting in, setting up their easels, murmuring and lighting their cigarettes. Her mother no longer accompanies her to each sitting. The screaming rows are over. Jo had to promise – cross her heart and hope to die – that she would not pose nude.

She settles on the stool on the platform at the extreme end of the room. The walls are lined with charcoal and watercolour winners. Her eye always finds the drawing of a sleigh moving through snow, its passengers bundled in blankets, the dogs pressing homeward. Or perhaps their journey is away from home, the long road ahead, unseen in the whiteness. She can never quite decide. This morning they are heading out, their food still warm in their bellies, their eyes straining for the new view, the unmapped vista, words like 'tundra' and 'the steppes' beckoning.

Around her is the hush of lazy industry that Jo loves. Studios have a kind of dirty spaciousness – all those angles pushing out of young men's dreams. This atmosphere of yearning opens and tightens her chest at the same time. She wants it the way she wants the first roast chestnut of autumn, a smell you can eat. Stuff yourself with. Her father would take them down to Greenwich Park on the river when he still ran a tug, her and her sister, to kick through the spiky green pods looking for fruit splitting out of the casings. The ground was spongy with them and they pricked their fingers trying to prise them apart. There was nothing her Da loved more than food that cost him no money. 'See that, Jo. What would that steal from you in Portobello, eh daughter?' She remembers big brown river trout from Essex, white mushroom skulls by the basketful from Epping, gory blackberries from Hampstead Heath. Those expeditions of plenty. Their proud scavenging. Her father's delight in saving a few bob.

She can hear one of the students say her name. *Joanna Hiffernan.* She must have written her name more times than anyone, her father watching. That's H.I.F.F.E.R.N.A.N., not Heffernan, which is more common, or Houlihan. No, Hiffernan grew out of the sound of rocks, the sea and the hard scrabble soil of County Clare. Many slight shifts of the tongue had adapted the Gaelic name for 'the people of the shining hair', or 'the people skilled with horses' or some such – people that Jo would invoke when asked, *where are you from?* She could tell by the tone of the question that some wanted it to be a slap in the face, meaning get the hell back there, while others used it more as a probe, as in *which part of the country* and for *how long,* and *who were your people's people?* Every story begins with a bigger story wrapped up inside it.

Jo looks around the room, scratches her wrist. Soon she will have to keep her head straight and still. All of the students in the studio are men. Some have been expelled from art schools for wanting to draw the nude, places like the Royal Academy where students have to sketch antique sculptures for three years before they are allowed to set eyes on a female model. Last year Jo heard that thirty-eight women had signed a petition for permission to study live models with Academy teachers. The Academy had let in one female artist by mistake after she had signed her submitted drawings with only her initial. Good for her, Jo had thought at the time. Then others could follow. She envisages her signature: J. Hiffernan. Joseph? Jack?

How elaborate can a capital 'J' be? She learnt it can carry animals. And fish. And serpents. Could extend its trunk the length of a page and curl its dragon head along the top. Her father showed her a copy of the golden pages from the Book of Kells, had her mimic the intricacies of the lettering, the fantastical creatures with the head of an eagle and body of a deerhound.

'They saved civilisation,' she remembers him saying, his voice rising, his speech-voice coming into him like sea air, opening his chest. 'When the Roman Empire fell and libraries were ransacked, destroyed and burned to the ground, they had great books, great learning. Where?'

'Inside the monks, Da.' She parroted the rote.

'The Irish monks, daughter dear! I'll tell you this and I'll tell you for nothing, they rescued knowledge. Kept it safely transcribed and hidden. And beautiful writing makes beautiful thinking. Even up those "ffs". That's it. Good.' His face is still rubicund with passion and excess. To Jo, it is the colour of love.

She sees herself dipping the nib, running a snake along the edge of the page, patterning its skin in coiling knots. He would give her spine a gentle poke and she would sit up straighter. 'As a twig is bent, so it will grow.' She was six and still believed everything her father said. He had it all mapped out for her: she might have the luck of looks, he told her, but she would also learn a trade; she would work as a botanical illustrator somewhere like Kew. She would be commissioned by a great empress to detail every plant in her vast gardens. She would make voyages he never made in his squat little river tug.

She remembered travelling her nib up the wrist of her left arm, drawing a lily and blowing on the inky trail. She held it up for him. He winked. He always encouraged both her talent and her contrariness. It amused him, made up for the lack of a son to entertain him. Then one by one, she added ants, their busy legs clinging to the stem. A mound of ants gathered at the head of the flower until the petals were dotted black. She was dreamy with satisfaction. The lily would never look the same on paper, would not flutter as she made and unmade a fist, the tendons jumping. She kept every drawing in a small leather trunk held shut with two straps. She would sit on it and hide it under her skirts if anyone came in. She wanted a drawing no one could destroy. A drawing that lived with her.

Jo had left school early. Most girls did. She helped her mother to bring in the washing and fought acres of white tablecloths and sheets – the cliffs of suds and the flapping, drying cloth hanging all over the house, like white dividing walls she could not draw on. She scribbled and scrawled on anything flat and smooth. Her father sold her drawings outside Mass. They were the spitting image of people in the congregation. He thought her hand could be her fortune, but her mother knew it would be her hair. What couldn't she catch with her lovely long copper-coloured hair?

The London sky sheathes the skylights in intermittent cloud. Jo watches a white billow float overhead like a massive imperial galleon, its sails tipped in sunlight. She would like to paint the brighter edges, a study of the sun that is always there. Why is it so hard to remember on overcast days? She wonders if her mother will ever get better, why no doctor can say what is wrong with her, why her belly is bloated and her cheeks dented as if nourishment can no longer reach them. Two frayed cirrus merge and part, leaving a gorge of blue. Her father had taught her the names of clouds, how to read the changing weather by the wind above the river.

Conversations fragment and fade across the room. 'The new RA show – an absolute load of rot!'

'I agree! Utter piffle!'

'I saw Millais' illustrations in *The Cornhill Magazine* – that's hardly art, is it?'

'Anyone know of cheap lodgings?'

'He's moved back from Scotland, I hear.'

The voices are not fully engaged, but rumble, low and perfunctory, back and forth. They only half-listen. All their senses are occupied by the eye and its message to the hand. Stan McGovern, a stout man with delicate wavering hands, passes through the room, tapping on students' drawings, on their wrists, on their backs. 'No talking, gentlemen, please. Go back and look at Rubens, like I said, Halliday. You've given her the ankles of a heifer. Here, like this.' Jo is listening and learning.

She looks ahead. A young man is staring at her. He has an eyeglass attached to one eye, which makes him look lopsided and a tiny bit peculiar. But still dashing. His hand is moving behind the easel but he is not supervising it. His feet are shifting in light-toed dance-steps. He is short and thin but the way he stares, his bearing and his movements make him appear larger; his behaviour and figure seem to spread out into the room like a force. It could be to do with the low-crowned, wide-brimmed hat he is wearing over his black curly hair and the red necktie and the fat, shapely moustache. He does not look English. She finds that her eyes keep returning to his face. Concentration makes his brow stern, his thick eyebrows knitted. He lights a cigarette, steadies for a moment and turns to his drawing. She feels a kind of relief. No, it is loss, masked as relief. Now he is squinting at her with only the briefest of glances, moving his head like a tern tripping along the edge of the tide. The drawing is the living thing he is interested in. She knows he is working on the finer features of her face and tries to stare him out, meet his presence with hers, become the brain in her body and make him connect with it. She wants to send out the signal: *Look, mister, I'm not just dairy and narrow ankles and flaming red hair.* She knows it is the kind of shade that turns heads – more like a metal than something human. Perhaps that is why people want to touch it – or tear it out. It has its own fire that a mere girl must have stolen to possess. She can almost hear them thinking, this girl, she burns. She is a trail of bright flame. Not just her hair, but her pool-blue eyes. Large and unaccountably sad, they say, although some would guess, if they ever looked back far enough, that the sorrow came from the hunger, the hunger that her family ran away from, carried in them, as they had once carried the cell of her.

Then, before anyone else, this man, this hopping pixie of a chap, rolls up his drawing, turns and leaves. The energy in the room lulls. Jo was certain he would loiter, sidle up and try to speak to her, and she was ready to be aloof, give him a line about never walking out with a student. She has been cheated and is desperate to move, get off the stool, stomp her feet and rub her thighs. Pins and needles torment her hands. She could chuck this bloody spear at someone. The rich boy with a stiff, fake-looking beard who cannot draw and attends every session – he would do for starters. Who was that damn elf-man? The hippity-hop of him. Then, pouf, gone in a puff of smoke.

Jo is at the centre of nine pairs of eyes, pinned by invisible threads like a lady Gulliver, and yet she is nowhere, she needs to piss and her stomach is growling. The sun comes out and she knows by the windowed shadow on the parquet that it is not yet noon. The clock is on the wall behind her. Anyway, Stan forgot to wind it and it has stopped at twenty-two minutes past seven.

Jo collects her pay from Stan, walks down Rathbone Place and crosses Oxford Street, side-stepping the steaming manure. She swings her umbrella to a song in her head, which becomes sung on her lips without her realising it. *My mother won't mind, and my father won't slight you for your lack of kind.* The afternoon has brightened and the March air is touched with the tingly smell of new growth. Yellow catkins hang off the trees in Soho Square. Poor King Charles is iced in bird droppings, his face drooping and disconsolate. She plans to go home via the haberdasher's in Covent Garden to buy some bands of fur for her new mantle. Her crinoline jerks and pivots from her waist as she walks along. She passes an Italian café on Greek Street where three young men are sitting outside at tables on the pavement, joking and waving their arms. One waves at her. It is him. The vanishing student.

He motions her to join them. *'Mademoiselle!'* He bows theatrically. 'I'm Jim Whistler.' He sounds American and French, all put on.

'Joanna Hiffernan.' Her hand darts out too quick, a nervous fish. Jim removes a burgundy glove with fastidious care.

'Enchanté.' He introduces his friends. 'Meet Henri Fantin-Latour, who we call Fantin, and this is Alphonse Legros, who is Alphonse. Don't ask me why. Our petite *Société de Trois,'* he says grinning. 'I met Fantin in the Louvre when we were both doing knock-off copies of the Great Masters to sell on the street. We're all on the same road – '

'– the road from Holland,' Fantin finishes his sentence. 'So says Degas.'

Alphonse stays silent, seems shy or disconcerted.

'And where's the road heading to?' Jo asks. 'Paris?'

They all raise their teacups and cheer.

'To framing and fame! Do sit down.' Jim pulls up another chair, dusts its seat with his sleeve. 'Do you draw or paint yourself?'

'Doesn't everyone?' Jo says. She is surprised and reassured that he does not say where he knows her from. She wants to say that she drew before she could talk. She drew images that were seen and those that were not. When they first gave her a pencil, she was off, skating away across the surface of the paper as if she had been waiting all of her short life for this missing part of herself to be restored. Finally she could put all the pictures that cluttered and crowded everywhere she looked on to a surface where they stabilised and took solid form. It felt like exhaling after holding her breath for a long time.

'Be warned, an artist's career always begins tomorrow,' Jim says.

'Unless you're Courbet,' says Alphonse. 'The Salon accepts everything he paints.'

'Yes, Alphonse, but Courbet has fifteen years on us,' Jim says. 'We are all of our time, the test is to be ahead of it.'

'And live long enough to know.' Alphonse laughs and adjusts his waistcoat as if it is too tight.

'Yes, we will, provided that some unruly critic doesn't asphyxiate us with slander and derision!' says Jim. 'That infernal fool at the *Telegraph that* – '

'*Les hommes! Les hommes!*' Fantin interrupts, shaking his head. 'Do you know, Jo, that Courbet once brought a live ox into his atelier? The place was full of runaways from the Ecole des Beaux-Arts. Sadly, it only lasted for four months because Courbet wrecked the place and the landlord wouldn't renew his lease, but I learnt more than I'd learnt in four years at art school.'

'*I cannot permit any relationship between professor and pupil to exist...*' Jim begins in a heavy French accent.

'*I, Courbet, have no pupils...there can be no schools...*' Alphonse continues with an air of pomp. '*Only painters, collaborators...*'

Fantin has commandeered another cup and saucer and pours Jo some tea. 'Milk?'

'Lots, thank you.'

'Milky tea for a milk-white girl,' Jim whispers, a smile on his face. He holds a match to Alphonse's cigarette, then with a flourish lights his own and shakes out the flame when it threatens his fingertips.

'Cheshire cat,' she whispers back and looks away but she is enthralled, hooked into their camaraderie, their utter self-regard and seriousness beneath the dusting of wit and raillery. They all act as if they are well-dressed swells but up close, their clothes are shabby, almost shapeless with wear.

The tea tastes as if someone has extinguished a cigar in it. She can barely finish it. Much later she will learn its name: *lapsang souchong*. She will repeat it to herself as if it is a password to an underground passageway that will lead down to a hidden world. *Lapsang souchong.*

The winter dark has crept back like a cat from the afternoons and the lamplighters are out a little later each evening. A couple of bluetits are feeding on the white blossom of a plum tree. Jo savours the walk home to Calthorpe Street in Clerkenwell, saving on the fare and thinking about the *Société de Trois*. She wanted to inhale their mood as you inhale a cigarette. She could go dizzy on those chaps, one of those chaps.

She carries a tray of tea and biscuits – the new Garibaldi biscuits that can sometimes tempt her mother – up to her bedroom. The room has the sour, unwashed smell of sickness. Her father is reading aloud from the *Manchester Guardian*. 'The two-day strike continues at Three Mills House in Bow. You know that mill that used to mill flour and now only distils gin? Didn't some nephew of yours work there, Kitty?'

'Second cousin. Saw one young lad sucked down into a thresher and another squeezed to death on the water wheel. Michael Harrington. On my mother's side. West Cork people. We must invite him over when I am well again, D.V.'

Jo's mother looks frail but her blue eyes burn with eagerness. Her long dark hair is silvered at the temples but she is still a handsome woman. Jo slides the tray on to her lap.

'People rally round at first, but now no-one comes,' her mother says quietly.

'And after the umpteen pots of soup you've made for all and sundry. Listen, Jo, I'll start on the spuds. Scrub or peel?'

'Scrub is grand, Da. Thanks.' Her father slips out.

'You're bonny today, *acushla.*' Her mother's hand cups her cheek. 'The sun blessed us with its presence this afternoon.'

Tension rides across Jo's neck and shoulders. Ah yes, she was a patient nurse, attentive, thoughtful and particular, at first, but when the illness continued, she lost heart, lost faith in her ability to nurse and wanted her mother well again. She swallows and smiles, hoping she looks hopeful enough. 'Do you feel brighter, Mammy? Not too much pain?'

'Not at all. Better than yesterday.'

'I see.' Jo is disquieted. She is being dismissed, not considered worthy of the truth. Yesterday, her mother had assured her that she was not in pain. She had always been impeccable with the truth and demanded it of her family. Jo cannot stand this version of her. Something inside her is closing off, a small valve of feeling tightening as if she is slowly preparing herself for the time when her mother will not be there. Her tone is a tad more curt than usual, her smile a touch more false. It occurs to her as

17

she sits on the edge of the bed that in losing her mother, she is losing some of herself. She gets up, draws the curtains against the dimming day and straightens the candlewick at the foot of the bed, saying to herself, 'I will be a better nurse, I will be a better nurse.' Her arms are awkward, her gestures jerky. She makes more movements than the actions require. When she is upset, she no longer knows where her body ends and objects begin. There is only a thin grace in her.

'Just be my friend, Jo,' her mother says softly as if she can read her mind.

Jo goes to her, chastened, and takes her hand.

'I'm sorry, my dear one. I'm so – '

'Sing to me, child. Something merry.'

As Jo begins to sing all the resentment melts and disappears. She is present again, wholly there. This is the best of what she can give, a simple, sure element, like a potion that cures everything. Her mother rests her head back, shuts her eyes, her fingers slowly tapping time as she hums along. As the song cures her mother, it is curing Jo.

Their mother does not come down for meals. Jo joins Bridget in the kitchen. She is cooking lamb chops, parsnips and mash with a gleaming lake of gravy. They have dinner in the evening if Jo is working.

'Let me tell you who I met today.' Jo takes her sister's arm.

'First, stir that pear compote for Mam.'

'A man who acts as though he's making himself up as he goes along. A walking fabrication.'

'Sounds slippery. Can you sieve it now, please? Here.' Bridget moves utensils effortlessly from one part of the counter to another, stirring and serving as if she had five hands.

'You are the great goddess, Kali. She of the many arms.'

'I remember. Shiva's missus. We saw a painting at the British Museum last year. Sprinkle some cinnamon on top. Has he got a job?'

'Oh, probably not. He's a painter.'

'All pretensions and no pennies.'

18

'That's the one.'

'And his name?'

Bridget laughs when Jo tells her and begins to whistle faintly. Jo flicks the tea towel at her. Bridget is as unlike Jo as it is possible to be. A tall, willowy girl with long straight fair hair and skin that takes the sun. She is practical and steady, helps their father with the calligraphy business that he started when his wife became ill. She has courted a regular boy who she has loved since they were both thirteen. They are saving for marriage. Bridget is someone who has chosen to say yes to what is expected and it has all turned out well. And she will always say yes, thinks Jo without rancour. But to Jo, yes is a wall. She will not have it, hold it or cherish it. Yes has only given her grief. The yes she gave was thrown back. Now she builds on no, creates her own round stone tower to see out over the wall.

'Be careful, Jo.'

'I know. I know.' Jo spins on her toes, raises her arms up as if in supplication. 'But dear God, Bridge, if I'm any more careful I'll be joining the Sisters of Mercy.'

Their father never speaks when he eats. He pours himself a bottle of stout, passes the glass to his two daughters for a customary sip.

'Keep you stout and strong. Good for the blood. That's what your mother had after she gave birth. A glass of the black stuff.'

Jo can see that only his face is brave. Sometimes his hands tremble with the fear of what he might lose. He used to boast that they had spent barely any time apart in eighteen years. He would tell everyone how his Kitty had anchored his daydreams and held him back from the cliff of his own rash mistakes, how they had come to London in 1844, when Jo was one year old, on Kitty's insistence, just before famine decimated Ireland. The Great Hunger had wiped out many of their relatives and scattered others to cities all over the New World.

Her father had taught Jo and Bridget calligraphy in the evenings. A profession, he thought. How to write exquisitely. Calligraphy that could be taught to fine ladies who needed to

19

impress with their correspondence. The money from his pupils sent Jo to a Miss Morelli in Primrose Hill for drawing lessons. Jo went there three times a week until she discovered that she could draw better than the mistress of that fine art. The best thing she gave her was the story of Artemisia Gentileschi, told to her by a nun in her convent school in Italy. Miss Morelli's round brown eyes widened and her voice rose and quavered when she described how as a young girl Gentileschi was taught to paint by her father until her talent excelled his and she needed a better tutor. Then, almost in a whisper, she explained how the tutor, a painter named Tassi, raped her and when he refused to marry her, Gentileschi and her father took him to court. In Renaissance Rome in 1612. Jo longed to see one of her paintings for herself. She collected their names and dates and learnt them. *Susannah and the Elders, 1610.*

Jo's father had entered a picture of hers of Epping Forest into a painting competition in Finsbury Town Hall, the year before, where it won first prize. The judge, an art historian called Matthew Hill, wanted to buy it. He was a stern, brisk man who leant forward in a way that made Jo think of a peahen. A lonely peahen, all poky face and brown sloping tweed back. He said that he had never seen such power of colouring and truth of eye and offered her work as a copyist. She worked for him for two days a week and would spend hours in the Dulwich Picture Gallery and the National Gallery providing materials for Mr Hill's research and for inclusion in his books. 'Learn a little French for its elegance,' he advised, 'but do not read too much poetry yet.' One day he appeared with a pocketful of stones he had found in Regent's Park. 'Draw these, Jo, and if you get these right, you will be able to draw anything.'

Once he had taken her to the National Gallery to see a Titian exhibition. He stood before the painting *Noli Me Tangere,* his hands clasped behind his back, tipped in towards it and said, 'Come close. Lose yourself in the paint. Forget the figures.' She leant in until all she could see were the long brushstrokes and smooth round daubs of abrupt colour. He moved back and she shadowed him.

'What's the first colour you must learn to use?' he asked.

'White,' she said, looking at the robes swathing both figures.

'No, my dear, red,' he said. 'Always red. For any people, anywhere in the world, red is the first colour they find a name for. The colour of blood, of birth, of fertility and of danger.'

She studied the red of Mary Magdalen's shawl as Mr Hill explained how Titian used Venetian Red as the underpainting for many of his paintings and often dabbed his finger with a drop of red to heighten a surface.

'What's the second colour they needed a name for?' she asked.

'You tell me.'

She looked back at the painting, at the foliage, the land. 'It must be green.'

'Correct. Then yellow. Colours of growth and harvest. Have you ever noticed how sunlight on grass makes it appear yellow?'

Suddenly as she looked back at the painting, the colours took on distinct temperatures – burning, warm, tepid, cool – like skin or even food.

She walked out into Trafalgar Square and its dense flock of straggly pigeons feeling as if her body had been satisfied by an elaborate and exquisite meal, her head light. Her eyes began to select areas of light and shade, lit on a flash of apple red, then picked out cheek red, woollen red and metal red. Her stride seemed longer, more alert, and for that moment everything that the city could reveal was revealed.

Mr Hill helped her to collect all the images of Judith he could find. She kept a folded drawing of Judith in her pocket, drawn after Gentileschi's *Judith Beheading Holofernes,* and she showed it to her mother just to hear her gasp. 'What type of a girl is that?'

'She's in the Bible, Mam.'

Judith, the beautiful widow. Judith who came out of mourning, put on her gladdest rags, her sparkliest jewels, her blackest kohl and slipped into the enemy camp, into the tent of Holofernes himself. There she glimmered and shone like sun on oil and danced for the enemy king, her face shimmering, not showing, her belly moving under a tease of veils, displaying her people's secret rites of dance, a game of hide and seek, until he sought nothing hidden and tore it all from her, and took her. And he ravaged her. Jo chose that word. Because of its savagery, its rage, its ravines of destruction – what a man can do to a woman. And when he had had his fill, filled Judith with himself, she let him slump against her and she cradled his head to make it easier. She had strong arms. She had made herself strong in readiness. She could run fast and fight as dirty as a man.

In the play in Jo's head, she was Judith and then she was Artemisia. She was standing up in the Italian court defending her body, her right to be a painter, her right to not be trespassed. Judith's raised, muscled arm was Jo's arm. Artemisia's hand lifting the paintbrush to the canvas in her fine self-portrait was her hand. Jo's mouth was her scabbard, her tongue her sword. She used her sword to tease and terrify men, to make them collapse laughing, admire her beyond her body and her long wavy hair. She would watch their eyes change, from devouring her to finding her hard to swallow. They spat her out and she tossed her hair and left them, turned to stone. She drew the lot of them with their bald, bold stares, their slightly parted lips, their creeping tongue: the priest, the schoolteacher, the butcher, the uncle, the postmaster, the stranger on the omnibus. Never her father. He stayed soft. And sometimes she would catch his gaze on her – a sort of proud bewilderment that she existed and he had had some hand in that and there would be a split second when she could feel his blood was hers. She tried to draw this look but she never got it right. Maybe it would take her a lifetime. Or maybe some love cannot be drawn. Nor could it be forced. Take heed, Anthony Mark Mulligan...

'Let's see who's at the studio tomorrow,' Bridget stage-whispers across the table.

'It's nothing, hush now.' Jo starts to clear the empty plates.

'What's this? What's this? A new chum, is it? A boyo?' Jo's father pokes her ribs as she passes.

'I knew it! I absolutely knew it. Your smile is two foot wide today. All down your front!'

'Agh, Da, you make no sense,' Jo says.

He runs his palm over his bald pate. 'I can fathom more than you think, daughter.'

This morning Jo as Psyche is lying on a couch, her bare back to the studio, a patterned wool shawl covering her lower torso and behind. She likes this position. She can read, although her left elbow gets cramp from holding up her head. She is reading Dante's *Inferno*, imagining drawing the torch men – those souls buried upside down, their feet on fire – the flames dying out and bursting forth again. She has learnt how to turn the pages with one hand without budging her right shoulder. Jim was not there when she last looked. She does not know if he has arrived late. She tries to sense if his eyes are focused on her, listen for his hippity-hop. It is excruciating. But, she tells herself, she is not being stung by wasps and hornets; no maggots or worms live off her blood. It is a fine spring day, her body is tip-top, her skin clear and her hair newly washed and thick and tied up in a white ribbon. She flicks the pages back to a line of Virgil's that she wanted to memorise. *The more a thing is perfect, the more it feels of pleasure and pain.* Yes, this is perfect, being in the delay before sweetness. Knowing something new is approaching enlivens her senses. This excitement makes her feel lavish then languid and part of her knows it is based on something imaginary and is therefore more complete, more sustaining than any flawed reality to come. Even if it never comes, this is pleasure, she thinks to herself. Like Dante, she has emerged from the dark woods. She imagines sending out a beam of invisible light that only Jim can see. It can travel across oceans and scale mountains. She concentrates on emitting it, then receiving a response bounced back from somewhere in this vast city, her body trying to tune in, as if every pore could be trained to detect it. If we can communicate with the dead through table-turning, she thinks, how much easier it must be to channel the living. He is there. He is there. If she turns around he will be there.

The bells of St Giles-in-the-Fields chime noon and she lies back, pulls the shawl up to cover herself and stretches her arms over her head. Her body is more ample today and her lower back tender. Her breasts and her belly are bigger than usual, her temper shorter. She will begin to bleed soon. This makes her hungrier as if she could take every living thing into herself, with the devouring appetite of seven brothers.

She sits up and looks around. Jim is not there. William Fox, the rich chap, smiles too broadly, beckons her to come and see his wretched drawing. She is bored, flat and angry as if she had spilt coffee down her clean, white bodice. She gets dressed clumsily. Her white cotton stocking has torn on a toenail – another hole to darn. There are three centipedes of stitching already on that foot. Why is it always the right foot? They were not new, but she hates it when things wear out, the ha'pennies slipping through the holes, ha'pennies that could pay towards more drawing classes and paints. She has worn a new bonnet for nothing. She has spit and polished her boots for no one. She has dressed for Sunday on a Tuesday, a common day, with common light and common men.

A ring of men standing outside the Duke of York on the corner of Rathbone Place whistle as Jo walks past. She turns into Charlotte Street to visit the vegetable market on the way home. Coal smoke makes the air oppressive and cloying, the sky dark. As she crosses Goodge Street into Chenies Street, she passes a sweep's cart, its brushes ranged like black cymbals at various heights. A young boy lies asleep on a pile of dustsheets beside it, his face sooty. She can imagine his long, airless climb up the chimney shaft, his chest heaving, throat rasping, and yearns to gather him up, take him home, wash him by the fire and dress him in new breeches and a fresh white shirt. The desire to grasp him is so physical that she looks about to check that it is not evident to the passers-by: the bespectacled man in the top hat, the peeler with his slow walk, the two

24

women walking arm-in-arm, baskets of brown eggs at their elbows. She cuts through Russell Square gardens, the circular flowerbeds of pansies blurring in her vision. She can hear the ruckus of children from the Foundling Hospital gardens. As she walks past the grand houses with their enormous windows overlooking Mecklenburgh Square she thinks of the long night in the attic. Bridget was holding her hand. There was a flannel in her mouth. She lay on a bed of old, shoddy curtains, her body nothing but a red tunnel of pain. The trunk that contained her mother's wedding dress and pieces of lace regarded her with its stolid, familial demeanour. She bit on the flannel as the agony twisted down through her pelvis. She remembers telling herself that if she looked through the skylight, focused on the evening star, became its white light, surrounded by the vastness of space, she would survive.

She did survive, she tells herself as she marches the anger off. She survived Anthony Mark Mulligan, went to planet Mars and back for him, armed with its red-green flicker. He may have come from the most well-off family in the parish, his father's drapery almost his, but Jo soon felt caged by his smooth scissoring words, his handsome buttery face, his pleading teeth. He picked bits off her he liked, or loved, he said, all the usual face of it, her eyes, her skin, her lovely hair – or did he say 'tresses'? – how she hated that word – and then he snipped and cut at her as if she was a bolt of fabric – she was too loud, snip, too raucous, snip, too boisterous, snip snip, too mouthy, rip it wide apart, and her bonnets were too big or too small or too cheap. Jo said no. And she meant it. She took her bawdy beak and decided that marriage was one thing she could do without. But it was too late. They had to get engaged. She was fifteen, feeling more like twenty-five. The door locked by everyone else.

Now, she promises herself, as she reaches home, she will have a man who keeps all the doors open. She puts away the groceries in the pantry. The last of her father's morning pupils have left. He is cooking the only meal he knows how: Welsh rarebit. He scoops mustard on to the plate. The cheese has slightly burnt. She opens the window, wipes down the surfaces which are dotted and dashed with crumbs, a streak of butter and shavings of Cheddar. She tries to remember if the kitchen table still lifes she has seen showed any of the mess of preparing, of eating. A painter's name comes to her: Luis Meléndez. The cracked-open walnut shells, the stacked boxes of quince jelly, the pile of soft orange oranges. The last of the afternoon sunlight is hitting the cream jug on the windowsill. She places the butter dish next to it. Then the bone-handled knife. She would paint the way the shadows fall on the white surface if she had the time. A portrait of the kitchen without her mother. It never looks quite as spick and span when she and Bridget have tidied and cleaned it as if it knows neither of them fully belong there. She sweeps and mops the floor, her eyes checking the changing apricot light.

After dinner her father sits in an armchair and lights his pipe. She wants to sit on his lap, be twelve, tug on his whiskers, ask him the question she always asked: 'Old walrusman, do you ever dream of the waves and the deep?' to hear his reply: 'Yes, my ruby, I do. I always will. And when I go, I shall return to live each day I missed by the sea.' She remembers him as an endlessly tall tree planted in the middle of the front room. She would hold his hands and begin to walk her feet up the long trunk of his legs until he would flip her over and she would somersault back to the floor and begin again.

She sits down and starts to read a book of Blake's poetry that her parents had given her for her seventeenth birthday. Her restlessness eases.

Three days later, Jo is leaving the studio, her umbrella up against the rain when she sees him. He is standing under a lamppost with a newspaper unfolded over a beribboned hat.

'Hello there, I need shelter!' he calls.

She motions him to come and he tucks himself under the brolly. It is easier if she takes his arm. He makes it feel natural, not forward. Perhaps because he has drawn her, watched her intently, it seems as though something has already passed between them. They fit, even if she is taller. She wants to ask

26

where he has been but there is no need. He is there, her arm in his. He is busy chattering, throwing in words in French she only half comprehends.

'Trouble is, *ma jolie amie,* I'm not a furniture dealer. But I'm made to act like one. How is it? *C'est absurde. Vraiment. Je suis un peintre!* But now I do have the filthy lucre to be able to invite you to luncheon with me at the Café Regency. Just as long as I don't have to sell Matthew.'

'Who's Matthew?'

'A fat-haired brush. It once belonged to Sir William Boxall. His portrait of me was exhibited at the RA in 1849, you know. The year my dear papa shuffled off his mortal coil and I was packed off to boarding school in Bristol. From Vasilievsky Island to the West Country. The Neva to the Avon.'

'That's nearly a palindrome!' Jo laughs. She has to shorten her stride.

'My whole life has been a palindrome. No more Winter Palace Gardens for me. Rote, rote, rote and reprimands and rules. Do you know there are right ways and wrong ways to reach a correct answer? My methods were always considered wrong, even though I got the right answer. Sheer putrefaction!'

They make their way through the moving wave of black umbrellas along Regent Street. They look like beetles ducking and diving and rising and dipping, giving way and pushing through regardless. Jim guides Jo into the café and she shakes off her brolly. He leads her upstairs and weaves towards a table that is just being vacated at the window overlooking the street. He tips his hat at every table and the diners look confused and bemused. This concerns him not in the least. Only a few appear to know him. He pauses and bows to them too extravagantly, forgetting Jo is there. Only when they are seated, does Jo notice how beautiful his hands are. Elegant, long fingers making the shapes of his ideas, chasing a word, flitting and folding and unfolding as if he needs their visual language to complement his voice.

'You're always drawing,' she says, imitating his gestures.

27

'My hands? I know. They itch for it. I'm sorry. Is it terribly distracting?'

His brown eyes are intense and lively.

'It's lovely. They're birds.'

'Big geese, honking?'

'Swifts. Building nests.'

'Don't they use spittle?'

'I believe so.'

'Oh Lord, I wasn't spitting in my excitement to be with such a gorgeous girl, was I?'

'Not at all,' she smiles and cannot help blushing.

'When I was first given a pencil – I was under three – I began to draw everything that had been stored in my head until then. *Eh voilà!* It was as if I had finally been given a means to speak.'

'You discovered your hand had been missing a sixth digit?'

'You know! Of course you do.'

It is fifteen minutes before they open the menus. The prices make Jo blench. Jim orders the most expensive dish, involving lobster, Dijon mustard and Normandy cream and Jo chooses grilled Dover sole, spinach and *gratin Dauphinois*.

The cuffs of his shirt are frayed. At one moment he absent-mindedly nips off a loose thread with his teeth. He catches her noticing. 'Did I really do that?' His grin is impish. She laughs.

'I've left my manners in Wapping, where they're sorely needed.'

'If only we could sell them.'

'Oh, the rich think they can. In dreadful paintings in abhorrent exhibitions.'

'Manners are nothing without essence.'

'Did your father teach you that?'

Jo reddens again, less willingly this time.

'No, Mr Hill.'

'Matthew Hill, the art historian?'

'Yes.'

'Have you attended his lectures at St Martin's?'

'One or two. I work for him. As a copyist.'

'That's great practice, I dare say.'

She is slipping down the rungs in the ladder of class that she thought she had assailed so nimbly, so convincingly, exhausted by trying to keep up with him. Jim looks pained for her, pours her more water, spilling some on the tablecloth. As she dabs the corners of her mouth with her serviette, all her gestures seem magnified, howling with significance and flawed etiquette.

'Well, my mother taught me about renunciation. To avoid it at all costs. She's tragically religious.'

'What form does this tragedy take?'

'I was required to recite a verse from Psalms before breakfast.'

'Imposed grace never works, does it?'

'You're quite right. A lovely way to put it. And this' – he flails his hands down his body – 'artist business she detests with utter hatred. Her dear and manly boy should become a lucrative railroad engineer at the earliest opportunity.'

'You must be selling something. That's a fine suit.'

'Out of hock, *ma chérie,* just for today.' He laughs. 'And these shoes – don't tell a soul – I picked up from a hotel corridor somewhere in Paris in the middle of the night. Our everyday existence must be a work of genius! That's our bohemian credo. From Henry Murger. He's just died, the poor fellow, and had the most gigantic funeral in Paris. I'd have given anything to have been there.'

'Who was he? An artist?'

'A novelist who made everyone want to be an artist. He wrote *Scènes de la vie de Bohème.* I'll lend you my copy if you guard it with your life. It's the funniest thing you'll ever read. The antics of four writers and artists without a sou between them. Ah, Rodolphe and Mimi and their broken and fantastic existence await you!'

'I don't read much French, I'm afraid.'

'You will. You must. There's one scene where the bailiffs come for all Mademoiselle Musette's furniture, which they set down in her courtyard. She simply unrolls her carpet and holds her salon on the chairs outside.'

29

He stares too long at everything and everyone in the room, commenting on their abundance or absence of style, the chandeliers, the gilt mirrors, the particular shade of the turquoise walls, the Levantine paintings of veiled dark-skinned women and turbaned men on camelback, sacks full of orange and yellow spices – an abomination! 'If these were scenes of Borough Market or Petticoat Lane no one would look at them, let alone hang them. They're just as colourful. Come down to Borough at dawn one morning and you'll see. These people are frightened of the life on their own street corners but foreign corners fascinate them endlessly.'

Throughout the lunch, their eyes are grazing each other, selecting details of exposed skin, imagining the hidden flesh, trying to keep their gaze impersonal and inconsequential but Jo can sense fascination working its way around them and through them, beginning to bind them in invisible bonds. She can hear the horses pass in the street below, the newspaper sellers flogging the latest edition of the *Standard*. She wants to cool off from the heat of Jim's gaze by looking outside, studying the window displays; watching the ladies in the latest fashions under the awnings, sheltering from the rain; the sodden barrow boys wending their way through the hubbub of traffic; nannies with their perambulators battling the throng; gents hailing hansom cabs to take them west to Knightsbridge; and children begging, their feet bare and blackened, their clothes in tatters. She is in the gods, everything unfolding within a scene that she is both viewing and participating in, as if watched by someone else from afar. She is certain that she will never forget the charge of this moment, connected to the centre of all possible worlds, her heart rocketing upwards. If only there was a way to pause the action on this stage, to freeze it for a few moments to allow her to appreciate every sensation, savour the imperceptible shifts her body is making to enter the mirror he is holding up to her.

Now Jim is talking of Paris, of nights in the Pigalle and days in the Louvre, or in various ateliers, and her body tautens: she is too ill-educated and ill-travelled to keep pace with all he has seen, all he knows. She falls down to earth, full of self-reproach, her feet in stony soil.

Suddenly she hears herself saying that she has to leave, explains that she is expected at home. She is bluffing, stammering, sliding off the high balcony into the pit. His face sheds its animation.

'Oh, I've detained you too long. You should have said.' He sparkles with chivalry. She wishes he would take her hand. She is babbling excuses, yet cannot seem to stand up to go. He is ordering the bill. She wants to leave before it arrives with its astronomical total that could doubtless feed her family for a week. She is putting on her bonnet. He stands and extends his palm. She rests her hand lightly in his, afraid of its heat, but he presses it to his lips. He comes close and whispers in her ear, 'Your hair is magnificent. That fiery copper. I know all the chaps must tell you so. That's why I didn't.'

'Thank you.' She fumbles with the cords of her drawstring purse. 'Not for the compliment or for its withholding, but because you told me that you withheld it.'

'Does it bore you awfully? Our predictability?'

'No, I – I mean, I'm not a stone statue, you know.'

'Come to Hampton Court on Saturday with me and *la Société*. We're taking a boat ride.'

She hesitates.

'Please do, Joanna.'

It's the first time he's said her name. The sound of it in his accent makes it unfamiliar, woos her.

'It's Jo. I will.'

'Excellent!' He claps his hands. 'Meet me at the north pier of Westminster Bridge at 10am. Bring a sketchpad.'

Her mother is asleep when Jo gets home. The fire is flickering low and she shuffles and pokes the embers and banks it up with fresh coal and a layer of slack. The room is filled with the strong crisp scent of the lavender that Bridget has sewn into a pillow to help her mother sleep. Jo fetches her sketchpad and begins to draw her mother's face. It is calm and pale but appears a

31

distance away as if under water, with something transparent between them. She seems older when she sleeps as though all the vitality required to fight the pain has subsided, her bones appearing more pronounced. For the sketch to be true, Jo knows that it can never be shown to anyone. If her mother's honesty is failing, so Jo's must strengthen. She concentrates intensely as if the truest likeness could capture and sustain her mother's life-force, ward off disease and decay, and guard her. After a few minutes, Jo realises that drawing makes it easier for her to really look. It provides a screen for her worst fears.

She remembers as a young girl at the window looking out at the fog and begging her mother to take her out into the muted street. She would run ahead, her hands outstretched trying to grasp the damp white plume, but it always kept a yard or two in front, and she kept chasing until she looked back and could see nothing but the pale airy substance all around her like the soft lint lining of an enormous pocket. She loved knowing that her mother was near but invisible, that further down the street was their house, snug in the muffled, opaque morning. Then her mother called her and she ran back attached to the thread of her voice.

Jo cannot speak to Bridget about the lunch with Jim. She tries to mention it casually, but her eyes well up. In her rush to leave, she realised that she had forgotten to thank him properly. Bridget puts down her darning. 'What is it, my pet? Mr Whistler isn't whistling?'

'He is. I can't – I can only – '

'Go slowly. You've seen him again, I take it?'

Jo nods.

'But why not happy, then?'

'Too happy,' Jo murmurs. She needs his world too much and is aware that his world does not have any need for her at all, that one step into it is an irrevocable one. They will try to force the door shut to her. She insists to herself that she will not be caught in another false promise.

'There's nothing like darning to settle the mind.' Bridget is only half in jest. 'Small repairs mend unseen holes.'

'I don't give a toss for darning. Needles make my life tiny – a nothing!' Jo sighs and clenches at the air. 'I want to box something!' She hates the small parlour, the slow limp of evening.

'Now, now...'

Bridget may not say no, but she could certainly say maybe not.

'You sound like a Catechism,' Jo hears herself snorting.

Bridget does not say anything.

'And how can you possibly see in this infernal light? It's dimmer than a church in here.' Jo takes a deep breath and tells herself that she ought to stop before she wrecks Bridget's china shop. As she picks up her father's nightshirt to darn, she can see that her sister has drifted free. She has said nothing but an absent look fills her face, not cold exactly, but tepid. She is breathing more heavily through her nose and for the briefest moment Jo can see her struggle with performing her acquiescence. These moments scare Jo. Bridget is momentarily unreachable and younger sisters must be reached.

Bridget gets up and leaves the room. Jo sweats in frustrated turmoil. Should she race after her? Why are relatives so desperately hard to relate to? Bridget comes back with a lit oil lamp and sets it on the small table at Jo's side.

'You're right. It's dark as Hades.'

'Oh God, and I make it double hell for you, dear sis.' Jo is almost crying. 'Forgive me.'

'Settle yourself, love.' Bridget's hand settles briefly on Jo's crown and strokes her hair. 'You're all stirred up and I know it isn't about me.'

Saturday is fine with a swift westerly breeze and a cloudless sky. Jo has told her parents that she and her school friend Milly Jones are taking a walk in Hyde Park, maybe renting a boat on the Serpentine. She hears Big Ben strike. A man hurrying over the bridge checks his watch. Couples are strolling along the river. Jim arrives, very spruced up in a Scottish tweed cap and a blue and green plaid cape. Fantin and Alphonse wear tatty grey suits, black capes and black top hats that have seen better days.

'That's a beautiful red,' Jim says. 'It suits you.' Jo's dress is a fraction too snug and she cannot inhale fully in it but it is her best. She also chose a straw bonnet with a claret trim, hoping that the weather would stay dry.

The men are groggy from having played billiards and dominos at an inn at Vauxhall the previous night. Fantin teases Jim for not being able to see, playing blind.

'I blame the cider,' says Jim. 'A habit from a well-spent youth. Besides, I recommend the half-seen. Impressions are often richer than total clarity. Don't you agree, Jo?'

'Well, yes,' she says, gazing at the river. 'A tree's reflection in a pond is infinitely more compelling than the tree itself.' She is channelling Mr Hill and he is not even dead yet.

Jim takes something out of his pocket and without saying anything, gives it to her: a pocket-sized, English-French dictionary.

'It's secondhand but the latest edition.'

'You shouldn't have. Thank you. That's very kind.' Jo opens it at random and wishes she could learn simply by looking.

'Five words a day, starting with *Bonjour Mademoiselle Jo,*' Jim says.

'*Comme vous êtes belle,*' Alphonse says.

'*Merci,*' she says.

Fantin and Jim grin. Jo selects several words and tries to speak the French translation. The men echo her and correct the pronunciation: 'Cauldron: *la marmite;* poppy: *le coquelicot;* truly: *vraiment;* wardrobe: *l'armoire.*' She regrets not having learnt every French word Mr Hill ever used.

As they step on to the boat, Jo looks upstream to where the river curves out of sight. She wonders if the gift clutched in her hand is the ticket for a journey that begins with this trip and could take her to France, to Paris, to some new definition of herself. She is as alive and raring to go as a leveret.

The boat moves swiftly upriver, under the bridges and out past the factories, tanneries and wharves to the leafy houses whose lawns roll down as if to drink from the water. They are all fascinated by the way the boatman rigs the sails and swings the boom across the boat as the wind changes. Jo notices the deftness of his feet, the way he can sense the headwind before they can. She tries to remember what her father taught her about currents. They pass fields of cattle and sheep and great oak and elm woods further west. Jo passes around a flask of tea and a tin of homemade scones to welcome applause. 'It's the first time I've eaten since yesterday lunchtime.' Jim rubs his hands.

They moor at the pier at Hampton Court. Fantin and Alphonse begin to sketch the Palace Gardens from the river. Jim brings out his monocle on a thin black cord and adjusts it to his eye to sketch the boatman who rolls up his sleeves to better display his tattoos, his hand posed on the tiller. Jo is the last to bring out her sketchpad, chalk and pencils. She wants to sketch the cherry tree in blossom on the riverbank and the shower of petals on the surface of the water. She starts slowly, crosses out and starts again. She watches Jim working. It is the quietest, stillest she has ever seen him. He has the oddest method of composition: first the hands mid-air, then the suspended face, then the disconnected feet as if at random. It is only when he comes to fill in the full outline of the body that Jo sees that his proportion and perspective are flawless and, she decides, the face itself is exquisite. The weathered boatman's lines seem dignified rather than disquieting – Jim has drawn them like rigging, keeping the features in line; the eyes, empathetic but canny. It has no sentimentality and yet is utterly touching. Like Jim, it has a frankness she finds enthralling.

Jo begins to draw. Her hand is still intractable, an iron hand – she presses too hard, breaks the lead, starts again and looks up and down until she begins to experience the weightless absorption of the activity itself and loses the world around her. The measuring outlines and the shading build until the scene on the bank no longer matters – it was simply the path to this kind of deliberate dreaming. Then, after a while, she is outside it again, aware of the boat, the movement of the swell, the robin's song, the clear sweet air, the auditioning aspect of the three young men.

Jim is standing behind her, his hand on her shoulder.

'Wonderful, Jo. It looks as if it's about to sneeze. And what if it did? Then what?'

She puts back her head and laughs. He is right, it is too static, held in. A sneeze would bring sudden movement, transition, loosened petals, chaos in the air and on the river.

'May I?' Jim asks for the sketchpad. 'Like this, perhaps.'

He is sketching over her sketch in thicker, surer strokes and a blast of indignation surges through her. The cheek of him.

But as she watches, all of a sudden the tree has breath, the petals shivering, the air animated and pink with them. He hands it back to her.

'Good grief. Thank you. I think...' Jo is overcome. She is as proud as if she had just perfected the drawing herself. Like Fantin had said of Courbet, Jim has taught her more in thirty seconds than in as many months at Miss Morelli's drawing classes. She was so intent on memorising every mark he made that she no longer had any connection with the sketch as her possession.

'But you became the cherry tree!' she says. 'I could see it, feel it.'

'And it became me too. It's no good one way, you know. Interdependency. *C'est ça.*'

Fantin is laughing knowingly. Alphonse is sullen, his eyes suspicious, covetous. Of Jim? Of her? She cannot tell. He broods, Bluebeard-like, shaggy and dark. He will not show his drawing to anyone. Fantin tries to coax him, then snatches the pad. Alphonse over-reacts, shouts at him and snatches it back, stowing it under his jacket. He buttons it up with emphasis, tugs at its hem as if his clothes are not right for his body or his body is not right for the image he has of it in his mind. Mister Glowering, Jo christens him silently.

36

'I want to show you something. Come, Jo,' Jim helps her to stand up and manoeuvre her crinoline over the rim of the boat and they walk along the riverbank. A duck swims past followed by five goslings covered in golden fuzz. Jo thinks that finally they will visit the Privy Gardens or the Maze, but he leads her towards a small copse of birches. He runs his fingers over their white flaking bark. He leans against a tree, 'Look.' He is trying not to smile, to seduce her instead with his solemnity, his doe-eyes. It works. She takes a step closer.

'This is what I wanted to show you...' He takes her by the shoulders, turns her back to him and pulls her in against him, '... the world from the point of view of a lonely birch tree. Everyone rushes by to see the entertaining Palace Gardens, the tiltyard walls, the Maze, and no-one stops here where there is still untouched wilderness.'

She laughs and looks up at the new leaves fluttering above them, at the grassy spread of the copse, the umbrella ferns, the shadows of the trunks lying in stark lines across them. There is a cluster of purple and white crocuses pushing through the undergrowth. She can feel his breath on her neck and closes her eyes. Her head is heavy, her knees trembling. She leans her head back as he kisses her neck.

'Ah Jo, you are a real beauty. I've wanted you since the first moment I laid eyes on you.'

His hands are clasped around her waist. She lays her hands on his. They do not move. Then he runs his fingers gently up her wrists, exploring the texture and temperature of her skin, under her sleeves and along her forearms. She remembers the young girl drawing on her inner wrist and it seems as though he is drawing her into a new skin.

'It drove me crazy that day at the studio, seeing all those idiots make a shambles of your beautiful body.' His voice is thick and sweet and touches her everywhere his eyes touched that day. He moves his hips against hers and lets out an involuntary sound from the back of his throat.

She tries to turn around but he holds her firm.

'If I kiss you now, I won't be able to stop.'

'Please, Jim.' She is struggling in his arms, twisting her torso to turn to him, to be kissed. The current charging between them makes her hot then shivery. Then without warning her desire is overtaken by a rage. She prises his hands apart and off her body and swings round to face him. She glares so hard that he looks frightened and she bursts out laughing. As she turns and takes a step to go, a moment of infinite sadness passes through her and she unexpectedly turns back and kisses him on the mouth.

They sway against the tree, falling and holding each other up. They get lost in the taste, the smell and the sensation of the other's mouth, opening, breaking down, finishing old loves and beginning a new one, as if summoning it from the earth, the trees, the sky. Jo burns with a rush of power. Every physical delight she has ever experienced has accumulated to feed and free this kiss. Finally they pull apart, dizzied and silent.

As they walk back towards the boat, they do not speak or touch. She hears a twig snap, a flap of pigeon wings that almost sounds like the whinny of a horse. She looks back and can make out a dark shape in the thicket. Her intuition tells her that it is Alphonse, even though her eyes cannot distinguish any human form. Her entire body begins to redden and she darts a look at Jim, feels trapped in a wider net, searching his face for complicity. Panic agitates her belly. She is too open, too vulnerable. She cannot inhale a full breath, longs to get home and loosen her stays. Jim is walking ahead, climbing over the stern of the boat, turning to smile at her, reach for her hand. Is every pleasure swiftly dealt a blow of pain? She has a great urge to leave, find her own way home. She refuses to take his hand, managing to get into the boat by herself. Interdependent, indeed! Hand-in-glove, more like. The cads.

Fantin gives her a smile. Mister Glowering is not there. She has a clam face, a clam mouth. Even the surface of the river seems double-edged: a serene leaf-green disguising a swift undertow and malicious eddies. She grips the edge of the boat, too aware that she cannot swim. She closes her eyes and waits.

Alphonse emerges from the thicket and pretends to hurry towards them. It is the first time she has seen him smile. She knows it is fake. 'I heard a nightingale, thought I could sketch it.'

'Let's go, I'm starving,' Jim says. He gives no sign of what she feared. His behaviour is unchanged. He gives her a long, steady look, the sort of look that says it can never have enough of looking. As the boat begins to rock away from the bank, she is more at ease again.

They meet at Wapping the following weekend. The wharves are alive with business even though it is Sunday. Longshoremen are heading home, bags slung over their shoulders; under-dressed women slouch in dull doorways trying not to look weary. Jo follows the lines of masts and rigging that stretch the width of the river, as grey as pig-iron. Sailors sit on deck, playing cards, repairing sails, smoking and talking; fishermen clamber ashore, their faces worn and tanned, their boots glinting with fish scales; two barges lie askew on the mud strewn with rusted debris waiting for high tide; and above and around it all the thick animal odours from the glue factory and the tanneries linger in the still air.

'I can see why you love it,' she says. It was the life her father also loved. But unlike Jim, he had lived it, worked it.

'Everyone uptown thinks it's squalid, but it's where life and hope and trade and dreams all mingle. It's a soup made from a pungent stock.' He stops outside a ramshackle tenement. 'These are my lodgings.'

She follows him up the narrow wooden stairs to the top of the building, leaving the clamour of the docks behind. She is aware of the heel-to-toe contact on each step, marking the climb. He unlocks the door. She takes one look around and bursts out laughing. All over the bare whitewashed walls are thick charcoal drawings of furniture: a wardrobe, a table, three chairs and a bookcase. There is merely a bed, a washstand and ewer and one chair left. Piles of books line the two windowsills and totter in stacks on the floor.

39

'I told you, I had to countenance furniture sales. But I'm expecting a draft from America this week.' He sidesteps a heap of papers. Jo bends down and leafs through the many sketches and etchings of the wharves and the intense industry of the river from the barges and police boats, to the old women selling matches and fishermen selling bloaters strung together on string. She forgets her fears when she is looking at his work, forgets her body's nervous memory.

'These are good, Jim.' They are better than anything she has seen at Rathbone Place.

'*La Tamise,*' he says. 'How I love her! I love her because she's always different and I hate her because she's never the same.'

'This is exceptional.' She holds up an etching. 'The figures in the fog – I don't know how you managed to have them vanishing just as you make them out.'

'London fog rescues me. When everyone hurries home to be out of it, that's when I venture out.'

She lowers her voice and croaks, 'The Fog Vampire. He'll suck your fog.'

'Can I offer you some tea?' He stokes the fire and shovels on more coal. 'There are some cups somewhere. On an imaginary shelf.'

'As long as it's not cigar-breath tea. Yes, that would be lovely.'

He hands her an empty cup and saucer.

'You won't vanish just as I make you out, will you?' he asks, moving closer.

'You will never make me out.' She mimes stirring in some imaginary sugar and sipping hot invisible tea without dropping her gaze. 'Delicious. So warming.'

'Plenty of milk as you like it.' His eyes rove over her face down to her chest.

'Hmmmm...'

His fingers begin to caress her cheek and she moves her face with his hand in a dance. He touches her neck, her collarbone.

'Have you ever thought – ?'

through her. This is the poetry she had dreamt having sex to be, knew from poets it could be.

'If ever any beauty I did see, which I desired, and got, 'twas but a dream of thee,' he says.

'You make one little room an everywhere.'

There is silence. The rest of Donne's poem seems to be completed in the air around them. It has never made such perfect sense to her.

'How do I get to have you?' He turns to look at her, tender and amazed as someone coming out of a long time spent in darkness. 'You are beyond wonderful.'

'You take me beyond...beyond.'

He combs his hands through his hair, pushing the curls away from his eyes. He gives her a curiously bashful smile.

'Thank you, Jo.'

Jim has heated the kettle on the fire and filled an enamel basin with warm water. Jo stands holding up her hair while he washes her, moulding her belly, her round hips as though she was soft clay. She has not stood naked in front of a man before. She likes the fullness of her body, feels calm, cosy even, and satisfied. They get dressed slowly, reaching to give each other quick, light touches as they get accustomed to being separate. Their clothes rub heavily against their skin which has become sensitive to the air itself. She weaves her hair into a single plait. They walk along the river to the Rose Tavern where they order beef pie and two pints of ale and eat as if they have not eaten for days. Everything tastes sensational. Jo has never experienced such magnanimity towards every living being. A small aftershock of pleasure ripples through her sex, and her face and neck flush. Jim is smoking, chatting, laughing, his mouth chewing words in excitement. They begin to exchange the encoded glances and the shorthand gestures that she has seen all new lovers exchange, that are common to all couples and unique to each one. She has entered a fiction, more bountiful than any she has ever read.

43

As they move on to the roofed terrace, a large sailing barge passes upriver. The late afternoon sun has tinged the water tangerine. 'The sun is making gold-dust of your hair,' he says, bringing out his sketchpad. She has forgotten to bring hers. She must be like Jim and carry it everywhere, be ready for every opportunity. He draws as he talks, eager and open as a child. She loves him looking at her, feels as if she is made for his gaze, is made anew in it. She wonders how she can trust him so completely so quickly, want to tell him everything she has ever thought, ever feared or enjoyed. And yet at the same time, it is as though he can see it all already, has heard it, knows it deeply and this transparency makes her light and clear, like a glass of muddy water that is allowed to settle.

'Come tomorrow afternoon – I've an idea! My God, Murger was right: "Start a passion and ideas will come to you". Just look at that superb bowsprit of another boat passing. And the criss-cross of ropes and pulleys tugging the perspective this way and that.'

Her arm is stretched out along the railing, her face serious. 'Not tomorrow, Jim, the day after.'

'The day after? That's an eternity.'

'Is that a pout?'

He exaggerates the expression, jutting out his chin. 'You've no idea how long I've waited for you.'

'My mother's unwell. She needs me.'

'The lonely birch will pine.'

'Diabolical puns will not persuade me. I will come on Tuesday afternoon. I work for Mr Hill on Tuesday morning.'

'Marry me on Tuesday morning!'

'I don't believe in marriage.' The words seemed to come of their own volition and they gave her a shock – a good shock.

'Ouch. That's me put in my place.' He takes her hand. 'I'm sorry. Is your mother very sick?'

'She is so fatigued she rarely leaves her bed.'

She watches men aboard a red-funnelled ship unloading sacks of grain into a warehouse across the river. A lanky man in moleskins carries a long tar brush and bucket along the quay.

She does not want to return to her family version of reality, but to dwell in Jim's world of ideas, enthusiasms and desire. Jim waves at a pretty young woman passing by. Her face is kittenish, her eyes flirtatious. She looks at him quizzically but he ignores her unspoken question. A ship blasts its whistle to clear its path towards the docks.

'I want to paint you right here, wearing black. I'll ask Alphonse to pose beside you. I've a scene in mind. But I'll warn him to not mention any of it to Courbet.'

'Oh.' She has an immediate vision of the dark crescents under Mister Glowering's eyes. She looks away. The girl is dawdling at the corner, watching them. She is a starved kitten, Jo realises. Stick-thin and poorly dressed, she is someone who will never lose a look of neglect.

He senses her strangeness. 'Jo?'

It is her turn to pout. She scowls and lifts her shawl, her gloves and purse. 'It's nothing. I will learn to share you.'

II

Symphony in White No. 1: The White Girl, 1862

The room is dimly lit. The audience rustle and titter as they settle into the chairs that form two wide semi-circles in the large, sumptuous drawing room. The seats are covered in exquisite hand-embroidered Balkan fabrics. Two young men wearing loincloths emerge from the gloom carrying flaming torches that flicker across the paintings on the walls, animating the portraits of the Ionides family and flitting over Aegean seascapes with their small white churches on hilltops and olive trees stretching down to the bright turquoise sea. Jim and Luke Ionides follow, kitted out in Grecian costume, belts of golden disks hung around their waists. Luke appears handsome, Jim mildly comic, his legs spindly.

'All hail the brother wounded at Delphi,' Luke announces, 'for he led our great armies to victory.' He swings out his arm. 'And seduced their women with his Hellenic charm.'

'Have you not heard the news, my King?' Jim says. 'They have seized Troy. I knew it did not augur well when they rolled in that gigantic wooden horse.'

'Never look a gift horse in the mouth!' Fantin shouts from the audience.

Everyone laughs. Luke's laurel crown slips over his eyes and the leather thong of Jim's sandal comes undone and he staggers towards Luke, half-dragging his left foot. Jo catches two women nodding in her direction, whispering behind their fans. Their eyes pop like a toad's, then slit like a snake's. Jo is tempted to stick out her tongue. Instead she waves ostentatiously, and others turn to see who she is greeting and if they will greet her in return. There are two plays unfolding simultaneously in the room that drips with costly perfume, powder and too many manners. Jo is enjoying watching the performance of the two women, who cannot be seen to snub her directly, and grant her a tiny tilt of their heads and a weak smile.

47

'A pox on you and all your puny broods,' Jo mutters. It hurts to be snubbed, she thinks, and that is why we do it. We hope by erasing all presence of a person, we will make them a blank and then they will cease to be and disappear. The blood drains to her feet, down through the foundations of the grand house, down into the clay earth beneath Tulse Hill. Despite the sophisticated plum-coloured gown Jim bought her, they can all see that she is a scrubbed-up seventeen-year-old from Clerkenwell. She tugs at the lace cuffs. How would her school friends, girls like Milly Jones, cope with being catapulted into somewhere so posh? She had mentioned the modelling job to Milly when Jim asked her to stop going to Rathbone Place but Milly said she found the crowd stuffy and sitting for them as dull as dishwater. She would rather clear tables at the Crown. Jim said she would be too busy posing for him to work for Mr Hill any more and besides he would teach her more.

'And what am I meant to live on, Mister Master?' she asked him sternly.

'A fee. I will give you a daily fee, of course.' He had not given her a penny yet, but she thought it would be churlish to complain when he was buying her new dresses and gloves and meals whenever she was with him. But he had already taught her how to etch and she had completed a fine portrait of him one afternoon after a long breezy walk in Holland Park, his face relaxed, his mind calm. 'So that's how you see me, squinting.' He had laughed. 'I have puzzled eyes but my mouth is happy.'

Someone has come to sit beside her. Alexander Ionides is a remarkably striking man in his fifties, with lively deep brown eyes and smooth black hair. Jo guesses that he is sorry for her, and that he believes that if Jim is going to bring his mistress to a party where she knows almost no one, it is his duty to never leave her side. She already feels fond of him. Some of Jim's friends have refused to invite her into their homes.

'Jim tells me you're an excellent book-keeper. I've given him a commission to paint my sister. I'd like to talk with you, if I may, about handling the instalments.'

48

'Of course, Mr Ionides. Shall I come to your office later in the week?'

'Please have lunch with me on Thursday.'

'I'd be delighted to. And thank you.'

As he moves away, she catches the fresh lemon and black pepper drift of his cologne.

Jo crosses Bond Street. It is a late summer afternoon. The plane trees are dusty, their long pieces of fallen bark aground like canoes in the gutters. The freshly revealed patches of bark are a gorgeous buttery yellow. The lunch with Alexander went well. He took her to his club on Savile Row, flattered her without flirting. Her head is swimming from the glass of white wine. She slips a ring on to her wedding finger.

A bell rings above her head as she enters Broadbent and Sons, the first fine art dealers she sees. You're on stage, cries a voice in her head.

'Good afternoon, my name is Mrs Abbott. I have some etchings you may wish to consider.' Jo makes her voice Mayfair and opens the portfolio on the glass counter.

'Good afternoon, madam, Archibald Broadbent at your service.' The assistant slides his glasses down from his bald head to his nose and turns up the lamp.

'They are the work of Mr James Whistler, whom no doubt you are acquainted with. He showed at the RA last year and Mr Millais greatly admired his work.' Her rehearsed lines issue with ease. This acting is a lark.

'I see.' The assistant passes over a superb Wapping etching, says nothing and hesitates at another. Jo is impatient, disappointed. Was Jim's work as good as they believed it was? This was going to be harder than she thought. He could plainly see that she was a fraud from top to toe.

'Mr Millais said, in fact, that Whistler's picture was the finest piece of colour that had been put on the walls of the Academy in years.'

'Not a great consideration in etchings, I can assure you, madam.'

49

He pauses again on the small portrait Jo had done of Jim. It showed the sorrow around his eyes and the enthusiasm around his mouth. He sets it aside. She is uncertain whether he has chosen or rejected it.

'A fine self-portrait, drawn when he lived in Paris. But he's American, you know. And has lived in St Petersburg.' She is dizzy with effort, and noticing that her hands are quivering, she dips them out of sight. She is ashamed of herself, her part in this, her inability to understand the workings of the commercial world and his inability to see great genius. She has the urge to slink out. But they need some proper food, some fresh meat.

'I'll take these three at four guineas or these four at five.'

He has selected her portrait of Jim. She is elated. Her nervous system is giddy, her spine tingling with emotion. She has sold her second piece of work. She will keep her share in a separate purse and never part with it.

When she gets back to Wapping, she cannot contain herself. 'Look Jim,' she spills the money on to the table, barely glancing at him. 'He took four and one of my – '

Jim sways as he comes towards her. 'I feel very seedy, mon coquelicot. Not myself.' His face is covered in a blotchy rash, his hands are clammy and a fine sweat is beading his upper lip.

'You have a fever, my love. Sit down. Have you eaten?'

'Lord, no. *Pas question*! I have stomach cramps, then vomiting.'

She realises later that he never asked which etchings she sold. She decides not to tell him about the one the dealer took of hers. Would he be angry that she passed off her work as his? Or worried?

The doctor diagnoses rheumatic fever and prescribes rest and sea air. They begin to pack and buy tickets for the boat to France. Her father and Bridget see them off at Charing Cross station.

Jo leans out of the railway carriage door.

'Write often, Jo,' Bridget passes her a bundle of new notepaper and envelopes tied in a purple ribbon.

'I will. Have no fear. And take good care of Mam.'

Her father squeezes a coil of notes into her hand. 'I'd sorely love to be coming with you. See all you can, daughter. Learn the language, read the books.' His voice cracks and Bridget takes his arm. 'That's my girl. Go where life didn't take me.'

Jo is too troubled about leaving her mother and Jim's health to let herself be excited about the journey. Now that it is suddenly happening, she has had no time to prepare, to daydream the way ahead. She is terribly sick for almost all the trip and stays below deck, feeling green and trying not to inhale the stench from the passageways and lavatories. She and Jim play cards and she reads to him but he mostly sleeps and eats little. Finally, he persuades her to go out and see the French coast as the ferry draws near land. For a brief moment the coast looks so like the Dover coastline that she thinks they have gone full circle, then she notices the differences or imagines them, she cannot quite tell. Is it the light? Is it the air? The shape of the fields? It is new and she is new. A newcomer, at last.

Jo's pencil is shading in the outline of a granite menhir, an enormous rugged stone. She looks out to where the sea vanishes into the delicate blue sky, making a band of silvery air hover on the horizon. The high white breakers of the Atlantic gather far out, roll and build and collapse to pound and agitate the shore, leaving a wide, lacy swash. She is sitting with her back against another menhir, gazing into field upon field of standing stones. They look like an eerie procession petrified in time. Were they erected all at once or did each stone mark a year over centuries? The sense that something happened here is palpable: human or animal sacrifice – or both. She stares for hours, wondering how Stone Age people erected these megaliths without steam engines. Jim reckons that they rolled them on logs over land to a pre-dug hole into which they tipped them upright and then filled in the soil around the buried base. They stood as almost 7,000 years of resistance to the quarrel of the wind and rain. She leans back into the rock. Is the sea ever envious of the vastness of the sky that overarches both it and the land? Does

51

it welcome the light of the sun or could it live in endless dark, turning constantly on itself, unseen? Of course, it needs the pull of the moon.

She sketches clumps of heather around the foot of the menhir, and a white plant she fails to recognise sprouting from a crack in the rock. Once she focuses, the landscape looks like a green piece of tweed, that when you examine it more closely, you find flecked with strands of many colours. Now she can only discern the pinks and purples of the heather. Beyond lie the salt marshes that stretch up to the tilled fields of oats and barley and the thatched hamlets dotting the distance. She closes her eyes, inhales the sweet, salt air, can taste the salt on her lips and smell a sunny, sandy scent on the backs of her hands. The copy of Baudelaire's *Les Fleurs du Mal* and her English-French pocket dictionary lie unopened by her feet.

It is the first holiday she has ever had. Her parents would take Bridget and her to the narrow beaches of Ramsgate, to the pier at Brighton, for the day, where a line of boarding houses, hotels, arcades and cafés tried to frame the sea, contain it, the groynes and seawalls acting as though they could portion off its waves. There the odour of sausage and bacon fat and fried onions would overpower the briny breeze.

She watches swathes of colour in the sea move and change from greyish green to pewter blue. She tilts up her head. This is her first experience of such unbound openness and distance in every direction, a distance studded by these strange, imperturbable rock formations that comfort her, connect her to ancient history – ancestors who had the same compulsion to make a mark, to create an object that could outlive, outlast them. She feels at home.

Bridget has written to say that her mother is stable and even has some days when she gets out of bed and sits by the window watching the street. Jo smiles when she remembers introducing Jim to her family a few months before: her father propping up the mantelpiece in his weddings and funerals suit; her mother out of bed and dressed in green velvet, her eyes avid, her face brighter than it had looked for months; Bridget still in her apron, straightening things that were not crooked, checking on the honeyed roast pork; and Jim splendid in a yellow waistcoat and yellow necktie, thrusting forth a huge bunch of daffodils as if he had produced them himself. He hopped from one foot to the other and complimented them on the house, the furnishings and noticed the details of a sampler her mother had sewn as a girl, framed on the wall. They were all enchanted, mesmerised.

'I'll come next Saturday and cook you all breakfast, American-style. Buckwheat cakes – my grandmother's recipe – you've never tasted anything like it. A Canadian friend has just brought me a tin of maple syrup. Have you ever tried it, Mr Hiffernan?'

'No, Jim, but I'll try anything once. That's how I brought up these girls – if you're offered food from another country, give it a go. Look at tea, coffee – '

'Tomatoes even,' Bridget said. 'They were brought back by explorers from South America in the fifteenth century. And we consider them our own.'

They looked at Jim as if he carried all the adventure, promise and success of every American city they had ever heard of. They named Chicago, Illinois, Washington, D.C., Brooklyn, New York, places where relatives had arrived, malnourished and penniless; then named various brothers and sisters, the cousins, the uncles and aunts, hoping that Jim might have met them once or heard tell of them. They had never encountered anyone who had criss-crossed the atlas like he had and it was as if he had spun the globe and jumped off right into their sitting room. If he knew any of their people, they had silently decided, he could become their people too. Jo watched as they sought desperately to find a way to make him belong, be part of a particular and scattered genealogy, as if he could be the thread to the dozens with whom they had lost contact.

'Massachusetts, you say you're from? All right, so. Boston. We have people there. Billy and Peg Flanagan from Youghal. Is that right, Kitty?'

'And Jack and Johnny Russell from Bantry. They're in the railroad, I do believe.'

America was walking in their parlour, talking in their midst. They would grant him anything if only –

'Oh, there are Irish forebears on my father's side,' Jim said at last.

He had delivered the link they craved, the dependable, familiar blood that would cover and even explain all ills of penury, eccentricity and dandiness. Jo's father slapped him on the back and poured him a whiskey.

'He's short but that doesn't mean he's not driven.' Her father had hugged Jo after Jim had left.

'He has good manners and is certainly confident,' her mother added. 'I like him.'

Her father topped up his whiskey glass, raised it to the light and swilled it around the glass as if its gold augured well. Bridget said nothing. Jo sensed that she found Jim too full of himself, which made what she had to say more daunting.

'He's started a portrait of me. In oils. A big painting that will hang in the Royal Academy on Piccadilly when it's finished. I have to sit for long hours and with the cost of travelling there every day, it would be easier for Jim's work if I stayed in Wapping for a time.'

'In his house, daughter?' asked her father.

'Yes, where else, Da?' Jo regretted her tone at once. Her nerves made her misjudge things.

'Only if he has separate rooms. Has he a chambermaid?' her mother asked.

'Of course. I'd have my own sleeping quarters.'

'So, he won't marry you, is that it?' Her father thudded down his glass.

Jo could feel her life narrowing to an unlit house at the end of a cold, dark street, damp washing hung around her, four screaming infants, hands tugging at her skirts, fingers sticky in her hair. She wanted to tell them that she would never marry, never be bound to obey any man. She had made that promise once.

'We've discussed this before, Da. He asks me every day to marry him. I'm not ready.' What Jo did not say was that she knew Jim merely asked as a joke. They both knew the truth: that his family would cut him off if he married someone like her. For now, Jo preferred the freedom of being his mistress.

'This is more than I can understand, Patrick.' Her mother's eyes were wet.

Bridget passed her a handkerchief. 'You'll break Mammy's heart, Jo.'

Jo's temper stiffened her ribcage. Her father refilled his glass.

'I'll go down and see the lodgings tomorrow, Kitty,' he said.

And indeed he did. But Jim had headed him off at the pass, arranging to meet him at the Rose where he bought him a fine dinner and several pints of ale and they spent the afternoon telling each other stories. Jim heard all about the tugboat captain days, how well her father knew the river, the tides, the traffic and the smuggling. They never visited Jim's cramped room and by early evening, her father was addressing Jim as his son-in-law.

But Jo's mother was harder to persuade, was more concerned about the judgemental whispering, the neighbours' gossip. Jo could still hear the chill in her mother's voice that night when she spoke as though Jo was no longer in the room.

'Marriage would be the making of her.' Her mother twisted her handkerchief into a ball in her hands. 'Why can she not see that?'

'Ah sure, she's always been one to have her own mind,' her father said.

'These have been the happiest days of my life, with your father, as Mrs Patrick Hiffernan.'

Jo could not bear it any longer. She stood up and began to pace the small room, her skirts sweeping between the armchairs and the table, her mouth quavering. How much better it would be to live as a man, who could determine the shape of his own life and marry or not if he chooses, who he chooses. She remembered the secret childhood drawings of herself in breeches, with cropped, ragged hair, wearing a mischievous goatee. She once showed a drawing to her mother who had snatched it away, telling her it was not nice to show such things. Jo had drawn the breasts of a woman and her diamond sex as if they could be seen through her dress. She remembered being quite alarmed when her breasts began to develop, but then grew to love watching the small changes occur as if another being was coming through her into the world, leaving the slim-hipped, boyish child behind. When her mother helped her to lace up her first corset, she saw herself like a vase holding up a bunch of flowers to better show off their shape and colour. She had come to realise that she loved her female body but not what convention demanded of it.

Jo had knelt down in front of her mother, knowing full well that dramatic display had never got her what she wanted in the past. 'Mammy, forgive me. But if I do what's expected of me I shall never paint. Jim is teaching me so much I need to learn. Nothing makes me as happy as that: to make art, to talk about art, to go to a new city just to see the art in their museums. Jim makes me feel that I *am* art. No one has ever made me so complete, so content.'

She had never spoken to her mother so forcefully, so honestly before and she feared she would shatter her as lightning strikes and splits an oak.

'God put you on this earth to be a wife and mother. That is what is meant to be. Someone respectable. Who the dickens put these ideas into your head?'

Bridget came to stand at her mother's side and put her arm around her. Jo simmered with rage. Part of her needed to be the good daughter, the one that made sense of all their choices and their sacrifices. It came so naturally to Bridget. Jo glanced for help from her father. He ran his hand over his brow.

Then her sister spoke. 'She loves Jim with all her heart,' she began tremulously. 'But it's the kind of love that – that – 'Bridget reached for a way to persuade herself almost as much as her mother. 'But her heart needs an open door. It's not like your heart, Mammy, or mine. It's...it can't be caged.'

Jo kept her head bowed. She was fearful of looking at her mother's face and wanted to embrace her sister for attempting to express what must be so alien to her, for daring to support her. No one uttered a word. Jo could hear the ticking of the grandfather clock and its wheeze as if from dirty lungs before it chimed eleven o'clock. Would the sound never end? It seemed to Jo that it was closing a chapter of her life and opening the many pages of an utter void.

'*A robin redbreast in a cage, puts all heaven in a rage,*' her father said, as if in a daze. Jo felt a flourish of fondness for him. Her dear old Da had wanted to say something that could gather his women back under his wing.

'You used to recite poetry, Patrick.' Her mother clutched at Jo's hand as if one of them was drowning.

'I seem to have neglected it. Just when I need it most.'

'*The invisible worm... Does thy life destroy,*' her mother said in a firm, low voice.

Would she ever get those words and the image of her mother's sad, hurt face out of her head?

Jo can see Jim at the window of their boarding house at the edge of the small village of Carnac. She waves, knows he will appreciate the wildflowers she has threaded through her hair. He is wrapped in a blanket, the fire well built in the fireplace. The room is stifling after the cool fresh outdoors and Jo longs to open the window. She sets down the produce on the table: a Camembert, a baguette, a bottle of wine, a few pears and apples and a bag of walnuts. She has missed his touch. They must have had sex every day for four months before his illness. She does not know how she knew what he would like but she did. They made each other a better lover each time they touched in their desire to create more pleasure than the time before. She had been continually giddy and distracted, her face so relaxed with pleasure that men followed her in the street. She supposed lust had the effect of a drug and as with any drug, she told herself she was not really addicted and then she swam into its arms again with relief and welcome.

'I have to get to Paris, *ma puce*. I'm missing everything. I'll never paint again if I stay here.' His colour is good, his eyes strikingly clear.

She bends to kiss him. His bristle grazes her chin. He gives her a creaturely nuzzle.

He is a worse patient than she is a nurse. 'The doctor said not to rush. This morning you had a headache.'

'I need to finish a painting for the next Salon. Something in these white skies has got into me. It's a large vertical portrait. Full-length, something I've never attempted before, or at least, not resolved till now. It's of you, of course, *ma chérie*. With that look I love – that early morning look before you quite remember who you are in this waking world, and you very slightly resent being pulled from the amorphous world of dream.'

'Sleepy, confused, bleary-eyed, hair unbrushed. Will anyone wish to see that, Jim?' she teases.

'But, that's just it, Jo. *Ecoute.* They all do see it already: the men in their wives and daughters, the women in themselves. I want to give them these daily intimacies back – the ones we all know but society makes us hide and never speak of.'

'You're sounding well again.'

'Yes, yes. I'm in capital spirits!' He gets up, shakes off the blanket and comes towards her. 'Those flowers are perfect.' He gently strokes her hair. 'Let me make you sleepy, *mon coquelicot.*' He gives her that sneaky, sinful smile that always makes her excited.

She lowers her eyes. He has not had sex with her for almost three weeks. He takes her in his arms. He feels strong and his hardness presses against her.

'You've made me well and now I'll make you famous!'

'Mon âme, hélas! n'est pas assez hardie.' French is clumsy in her mouth, pebbles under her tongue. She is not sure he recognises the Baudelaire.

'You are the most magnificent woman I have ever met. I searched for years to find you. Two continents...' They begin to kiss. 'Or three, depending on who is drawing the map...' He

58

starts to undress her, unhooks her dress, her skirt and her stays, lets them fall to the floor. She unbuttons his trousers and his stiff cock is freed into her hand. Heat and energy plunge down to her sex. He gathers up her underclothes and touches her.

'I've never felt such wetness.'

'I've stored it up for you.' She smiles with some coquetry at first, but as desire courses through her, her body feels powerful, even majestic. A queen is not a coquette. She surveys her kingdom and likes what she sees. As she pushes against him, she is flowing out in every direction as if she can swim underwater then soar through the air. She is flying east over vast land masses, can hunt in dense, lush jungles of the south, navigate barren desert plains, vanquish the highest snow-capped peaks. She has lived in India and Africa, her body brown then deepest blue-black. She is dancing, with many hands touching her limbs, an ecstatic, wordless music roving inside and out in brightly coloured notes.

Then her mind and body focus with minute attention. She tries not to reach for it too soon or hold it off too long. Bit by bit it builds to the quick, assured rhythm of his fingers and yet it always seems to surprise her when it comes and she shudders and cries out in answer and then she guides him inside her.

'Well, well, Miss Volcano!' he raises his eyebrows with pride.

She leans back on to the table and he lies on top of her.

They lie still, breathing heavily. Lord, how she loves pleasure's self-forgetfulness. After a sweet lull, their surroundings slowly return and they realise where they are and giggle. Their clothes make a hurried trail across the floor. He brings his fingers to his nostrils and smiles.

'I've dipped in the ocean.'

'You're cured.'

'I won't wash this hand – ever.'

She laughs, delighted. He looks so resolute again.

'I didn't know a man could be so responsive, so able to show his happiness. I love you.'

'I have never loved anyone the way I love you.'

'It's terrifying, Jim.'

'To love or be loved?'

'Both. It's a precious glass vase we pass from one to the other.'

'A new kind of glass – unbreakable.'

'No, fragile, Jim,' Jo says in a clear and serious voice. 'And we must always treat it so.'

'When will you let me paint you like this, Jo? Soft and open, all of you?' His gaze travels over her body.

'I don't know.' She wants to pull the sheet up. The lover has gone. The painter is back. 'I don't ever want you looking at my flesh in that way of yours that sees the line and the colour and not the person. The living breathing person. It would deaden me, make me freeze. I fear it would deaden us. To make my body something other men can have.'

'Yes, and I'm not sure I want that either.' He laughs and takes her chin in his hand. 'You're mine.'

She will be sad to leave the simply furnished, whitewashed room. She has become accustomed to the peculiar pieces of driftwood, smoothed and bleached by the sea, hung on the walls. Some resemble entwined figures, others, mythological amphibians watching them through several dry eyes. Sometimes at night when she could hear the crash and roll of the waves, she imagined that the sea wanted them back. She had heard that early embryos have webbed hands and feet before they develop digits and she fancied that some people could not bear to live their lives within the sound of the call of the sea for fear of its pull in the dark.

They have decided to go to Paris and begin work on a new portrait. Once they are settled, Jo will go home and visit her mother and collect more of their belongings. On their last evening in Brittany, they sit at the window and watch the full moon. It is rose pink and low, an urchin of cloud hanging from it. There is the homely hoot of a passing owl. They drink wine from pewter mugs and watch as the moon glows bright and papery as it rises, sheds silver light along the floor and the walls of their room. They are both writing to their families by candlelight, ready to post the letters from Paris. Jim has been so concerned about his health, he has put off writing to his mother. Jo wonders if the skies over London will be clear enough for her mother to see the moon from her bed. She wishes she could give her this moon, its borrowed light.

'Is that why it brightens us,' she asks Jim, 'because it gives us sunlight in the darkest night?'

'Write that down, my poet,' he says.

She wants to paint it.

Jo adores Paris. People dress better, make eye contact more. The edges of the buildings look more rounded and the windows with their cream shutters are like sheltered eyes. Flocks and flocks of starlings. They have rented an apartment in a tall building in Boulevard de Batignolles in the 17th arrondissement which overlooks a wide, stylish street with two columns of plane trees running down its centre. It leads to the Place de Clichy at one end and over the railroad tracks heading out from Gare St-Lazare at the other. The *quartier* retains the atmosphere of a village that has been joined to the larger city in much the same way as Clerkenwell is attached to Holborn but has kept its own identity. The air is fresher than in the city centre and the drains' stench less noticeable. A park has just been opened near where they live and the Fromagerie des Moines sells excellent Norman cheese. Their building has a very large, arched wooden door from the street that leads on to a small courtyard, strung with washing lines, the windowsills dotted with geraniums. It smells so different from London – the distinctly earthy smell of dark, Turkish tobacco and the pungency of garlic frying – even the bread has a sweet strong fragrance – perhaps French flour is milled differently? She wonders if the French enjoy more small pleasures than the English, or if she simply notices them more because they are novel. But when she watched a family having a picnic in Jardin du Luxembourg last Saturday, she could hear them praising the baguette, the *saucisson,* the black olives and the Brie as if they were still new to them and always *'magnifiques'.* A cheese and ham sandwich in Hyde Park would not be the same experience at all. And even though most Parisian ladies and gentlemen did not acknowledge Jo's presence, she feels herself delight and expand in their society. Her own enthusiasm grows in parallel to Jim's, so enlivened to be back, *enfin.*

Almost as soon as they got off the train and deposited their luggage, Jim took her to his old haunt, the Café Guerbois, to see who was there. It seemed to Jo to be made utterly of glass and mirrors, so that when you walked towards what you had taken to be another room, you met yourself coming towards you. Fantin and Alphonse arrived to greet them. She could follow their French, although she was still slow to speak it. Jim had spoken only French to her for the last week of their stay in Brittany, so although her ear was accustomed, her mouth was not. She would have to purse her lips more to form the vowel sounds and learn to wave her hands to accompany the words. She had faced the mirror the day before and gesticulated and approximated a French lilt, rolling her eyes, making mocking sounds and laughing to herself. 'But, this Jo, here, what is she doing, eh? Tell me, what exactly she plans to do in Paris and who exactly she knows, because, even so, you know, you must know to know, the people...'

How she loved watching people pass the curved windows of the café and cross Avenue de Clichy. They walked with such an air of relaxed importance. And what fashions. Many of the younger women no longer wore crinolines, but a narrower skirt that lay flatter at the front and gathered into a bustle at the back. She wanted one. It looked so demure, so much more compact. The colours of the dyes – a deep cherry-red, a dark violet, a startling canary yellow – were richer and more vibrant than in London.

'Jim, I can't be seen another day in this old thing. They'll think I'm nothing but a country bumpkin.'

He laughed, squeezed her arm.

'You're the pet of the set. We'll make sure you're dressed to the nines. Look out, Paris!'

'You look beautiful, Jo – always – ' Fantin leant in towards her. 'But especially after your sojourn in the fresh salt air.'

'Thank you,' Jo said. 'We're both refreshed. Being in Carnac was like going back to the beginning of time. The world itself could have started between those lines of rocks.' Her tongue was struggling with the French and kept reverting to English in frustration.

'You'll find the air much cleaner here than in London,' Alphonse inhaled on his cigarette, blew the smoke dramatically upwards.

'Everything's cleaner since I was here, thanks to Haussmann. I'm not sure I like it,' Jim said.

'New immigrants need new, wider streets,' Fantin pulled thoughtfully at his beard. 'They say the population of Paris has trebled in this century, you know.'

'We've got a studio in Rue Vaugirard,' Alphonse said. 'The Latin Quarter is fairly unchanged. No one is shocked when you tell them you're an artist. I'd forgotten that.'

'*Au contraire,* they expect it!' Jim clapped his hands. 'It's the same with intellectuals. They've always been more accepted here than in London.'

Fantin swept his long ginger hair back off his freckled face. 'London chases all its best thinkers away.'

'Luckily it draws a fair few to it too. Those who need to think in another direction, I suppose.' Jo was aware of thinking aloud for the first time in front of Jim's friends. France had made her more confident. 'I think of London in a completely different way from this distance.'

'How so, Jo?' Alphonse tugged at the hem of his jacket as he spoke as Jo had seen him do before. It reminded her of struggling to take off a dress her mother had put on her that she did not like, the same tugging, as if in fear of being engulfed by someone else. But yet he seemed gentler, more at ease in his own country, his own body. Perhaps he had simply been

63

homesick all along. Jo could see that he spoke more animatedly in French, more forcefully, as if English had suppressed part of his personality.

'It's the first time I've visited the continent, so the buildings seem taller, the roads wider and the people more glamorous – being in Paris feels like I've travelled into London's future. Is this your home town, Alphonse?'

'No, Dijon. But we all three studied here at the drawing school – we called it the *Petite Ecole* – with Lecoq de Boisbaudran.'

'But listen, Jo, they look at paintings differently here.' Jim lit another cigarette and sipped his coffee. 'There is less concern about who a portrait is of, than how it is painted. Technique is all. There isn't the same ludicrous need for a story hanging on every picture.'

'Any interesting art is happening here, with Degas, Courbet and Manet,' Fantin said. 'And you should see the nudes!'

'And the bric-à-brac – she must see that,' Alphonse said. 'Let me show you the stalls run by *les pêcheurs de la lune.*'

'Fishermen of the moon?' Jo laughed. 'That's all of you chaps!'

Alphonse signalled to the waiter to bring the bill and Jo marvelled at their spruce black waistcoats and white aprons, their movements economical and graceful, as if they were trained dancers. As she finished the last concentrated silty sip of her hot chocolate, she was sure that Paris would be kinder to Jim and her than London had been.

All along the rue des Rosiers, stalls were laid out and people were jostling as they looked for curios among the wax flowers and feathers, ostrich eggs and statuettes. There were stalls of buttons and brooches, clocks and parts of clocks, clothes and boots, laces and threads. With its synagogues and kosher restaurants, and the sound of haggling, it reminded Jo of the warren of tumbledown streets off Brick Lane. Alphonse found her an exquisite ivory comb, its handle engraved with small monkeys, with their tails interlinking. Jim and Fantin called her over to another stall where Jim had chosen a gold-topped walking cane, which he paraded up and down the street until the stall-holder demanded his money. Then Jo spotted a pair of sad eyes gazing at her from behind another stall. She tugged at Jim's elbow. It was a huge bearskin, spread out on the wall.

'That's not for sale, mademoiselle,' the stallholder waved his hands flatly to and fro. 'No, absolutely no.'

'Oh Jim, we have to have him. Those eyes are begging. We'll need no more furniture if we have him. Please.'

'I have said already no. It was my father's from Brittany.'

'Brittany is the centre of the world! We would love this bear. We just arrived from Brittany. There is nowhere on earth like it, monsieur.' Jo flirted, flashing her smile and selling the man's region back to him. The man gave a helpless shrug.

Jim pulled a note from his pocket like a magician pulling a red silk handkerchief from behind his ears. 'Will this settle it, my good man?'

Jim carried the bearskin back to their apartment and up the four flights of narrow marble stairs. He unrolled it on the floor and laughed, gasping for breath.

Jo stood on it, threw off her bonnet and raised her arms, 'My first wild beast!'

'Surely not!' Jim pretended to be peeved.

'Prove it!' She began to back away and he chased her, dashing and darting around the room, until she let herself be caught. They began to kiss, an urgent, breathless kiss. Jo lowered herself on to the rug and pulled Jim down on top of her.

'We'll christen him Benjamin,' she laughed.

Jo opens the shutters on to the early morning. The boulevard is glistening with recent rain. The slate rooftops are only a shade darker than the overcast sky. Jim is still asleep. Jo has set up her easel by the window and has sketched the scene in pencil – the low cast-iron railings of balconies on the opposite windows; the schoolchildren in blue and white uniforms in a noisy cluster outside the school gates; the old ladies in black making their way to the church of Sainte-Marie further down the boulevard.

Why does life here seem so immediate, she wonders. She wants to show her father all the details, like the man cycling past with two baguettes in his pannier. Or is she more immediate? She would never get up and start to paint without getting dressed in London. Standing in her nightgown and silk slippers, absorbed in what she is doing, her chest light, she does not notice that she is humming, is barely aware of the rattle and hiss of the trains heading out of the station, or the whirring rhythm of the collared doves in the eaves. She is mixing yellow and white for the children's straw hats. There is already a brisk trade at the corner kiosk, selling cigarettes and newspapers. A man in a black beret is opening his paper to read it on the pavement. He is there every morning. And the one with the top hat, waiting at the corner, pretending he is not. The one who waits for her and follows her, while she pretends she has not noticed. The carriages and cabs are rattling over the cobblestones. She wants to get as much painted as she can before Jim gets up – if he sees it too soon, it might put her off. The last painting was one she started in Carnac of a small farmhouse situated between two lines of standing stones that stood guarding it like infantry. She had brought it back to show Jim since he was not yet strong enough to venture out.

'I'll make the house more solid,' she remembered explaining, her hands hovering in nervous circles over the canvas.

'No, you're right. The house is frail against these huge hulking rocks. I'd add more black to that grey,' he said. 'The stones are good. They have heft. Do you need all those details in the rock? It makes them too fussy, too human.'

'But I wanted that human quality. I thought – ' but she couldn't complete her sentence. She had lost the will to defend herself.

Then he pointed to the parts of the painting she was most proud of, felt were the most accomplished and said they showed too much work. 'Too heavy on the thatch of the house. Paint should not be applied thick, Jo. It should be like breath on the surface of a pane of glass... A picture is finished when all trace of the means used to bring about the end has disappeared.'

Jo convinced herself that she was too occupied looking after Jim – shopping, preparing food, cleaning, laying the fire, emptying the chamber-pot, washing clothes and dishes – to finish the canvas. But the truth was that she no longer had the heart. She was not up to the task of portraying the tension between the farmhouse and the stones, was not even sure what it meant any more.

Later when she was unpacking their things in Paris, looking for a place for the drawing board, the pastels and pens, the dentist's tools pushed into corks that Jim used as etching needles, the old book which held the copperplates and the paper, she came across her abandoned canvas. Jim had whitened it out with gesso and begun a landscape of the sea seen from the boarding-house window. She felt altogether winded as if she had been punched. Tears sprang to her eyes and she covered her mouth. Her stomach churned. In her indignation, she was ten years old again in Miss Trimble's gloomy, under-heated classroom. She had the highest marks for the three Rs, but the end-of-year prize had been awarded to Thomas Ackroyd, because as Miss Trimble informed the class, his conduct was better than Miss Hiffernan's. Jo had emptied her desk, picked up her satchel and stormed out of the room, ignoring the teacher's protest. She had kicked a broken cobblestone along the pavement with hard, aggressive kicks. 'Polite Master Ackroyd,' she mimicked Miss Trimble's clipped Belfast vowels. 'Well-behaved Master Ackroyd.' She spat out his name as she walked along Theobald's Road. Thomas Ackroyd who never asked a question, never uttered an opinion, had no character or personality – nothing ever came out of his mouth that was not put there by his parents. He was a puppet, a puppet from the 1840s. He would become a town mayor and attend functions and behave impeccably nicely. She walked a stiff, awkward puppet-walk with stiff, angular limbs till bystanders stared and she grimaced and jerked her puppet-head. She could not go home yet, so had hung around the entrance to Lincoln's Inn Fields, watching the barristers come and go. Some flapped hurriedly past in their robes and wigs, like royal ravens speaking their own tongue. The candle blossoms of horse chestnut trembled in the May breeze. How unjust that she was not rewarded for her work and her talent. How unjust that she could not become a lawyer and fight such injustice. She sat down on her satchel. Where there had been a torrent of rage, was now just a deadly quiet, a dry melancholy that reduced her to dust.

As Jo paints the scene in the street below, she can feel Jim's eyes on her painting, can hear his advice. She tries to use the thinnest stroke of blue for the pinafores, lifts her hand with an upward flick to capture the buoyancy of their movement. She can hear him getting dressed in the room next door. She turns the easel to the wall, tidies away the paints and brushes. She knows he will be cleaning under his nails with a small metal file. His hands are as well kept as hers.

'*Bonjour* sweetness,' he says. 'You're up early. Couldn't sleep?'

'I slept wonderfully. I've been painting the scene from the window. Paris is so busy!'

'Oh, let me see.'

'Later,' she says lightly. 'Oh and it's the housekeeper's day off. Can you clean out the grate, please, my darling boy, and I'll make coffee.'

He stands with his hands in his pockets. 'You look beautiful, Jo. Did I tell you that today? Young and not as certain as you pretend to be. Sometimes I forget how young you are.'

She has been standing barefoot in her cambric shift for four hours. Her head aches, her ankles are swollen and her knees about to buckle. Her toes curl into Benjamin's fur. She cannot believe that Jim wants her to pose in nothing but a plain shift. It will cause a scandal.

'Jim, I'm famished.'

'Me too, starving.' But he is not listening. She is holding a small bunch of flowers. She suddenly loses her grip and lets them fall.

'My hand's cramped.'

'I'm nearly there, please, Jo. Hold still.'

'I have to eat, Jim. The flowers look better there. Truer, somehow, to the white girl whose eyes are just this side of disappointment sinking in.'

'It's the texture of the white fabric against her white skin that's the most captivating. Five more minutes and I'll show you. And wait till you see the bear gloating!'

She begins to count back from one hundred. She would love a soak in a hot bathtub perfumed with rose salts. She dreams up the softness of her mother's face when she helps her to wash her hair and she realises that hers is the first face she gazed into, the first face she loved, with its silver-blue eyes, its mass of thick black hair against the lightly freckled skin. Will she have forgiven her yet? The question leaves a knot in her stomach. Her eyes close. She cannot close her eyes. Her own concentration matters. He can tell if her attention falters. The painting needs her alert, yet relaxed, as they enter in a kind of breathing together, a kind of mouth-to-mouth with eyes, the look-of-life, she calls it.

Yesterday Jim had spent three hours painting her hands and when she looked today, the work he had done had been completely repainted. She would watch as anxiety and pleasure fought with each other as he worked, as if they came from the same source and each sought dominance. His perfecting delight was followed swiftly by destructive doubt. There came a point each day when she had to make him stop, when he became so self-critical that nothing could match what he saw in his mind's eye.

But finally the intricate weave of the shift, white against the coarser white curtains, is looking splendid. She longs to understand how he can depict movement and stillness at once, conjure something warm to look at that you could sense would be cool to the touch. She remembers once when they went to the National Gallery to look at Stubbs' *Whistlejacket*. The immense suspended power of the horse, its poise and vitality always took her breath away. They had spent so long looking at *Venice: The Basin of San Marco on Ascension Day* by Canaletto that she was almost surprised when she looked back into the gallery and saw people move and talk and exist on a human scale again. She loved the vision of the Doge venturing out in the red-tented, ornate galley to seek the impossible – to marry his bride, the sea. When would she see Venice for herself, walk along the Molo, visit St Mark's Square and the Santa Maria della Salute with some of the best paintings ever painted? She had painted copies of Canaletto, Carlevarijs and Guardi for Mr Hill but Jim inhabited a painter's mind in a way Mr Hill never could. 'Canaletto could paint a white building against a white cloud,' Jim had said. 'That was enough to make any man great.' As well as studying how the paintings were made, she looked at how the models posed. She liked Goya best. His women with their bold eyes that looked so right, so ebullient and defiant, because they were slightly crooked and protruding.

She shifts on her feet. 'Please Jim, I'm going to drop.'

'Look Jo, come and look at your hair – what I've done. Have you seen how Rembrandt handles hair? I'll show you. Like this – with spring.' He hops back and admires his work and Jo lets her body slump.

'Rest, *ma chérie*. Thank you.' He removes his eyeglass. 'Where on earth would I be without you?'

'Down with some trollop in Wapping, I imagine.'

He laughs. 'Rest. I'll make a spot of lunch.'

'Or chasing after some cancan flibbertigibbet!'

'Who told you that?'

'Never you mind.'

She flops down onto Benjamin and bends up her knees to ease her lower back. Her shoulders crunch as she relaxes them. She is hoping that Jim will not return to the canvas with a cry of horror, announce it all a catastrophe – a clumsy, clotted, cake mixture which he will then erase or threaten to throw into the Seine. She needs air. Later, she will take a walk to the new park off the boulevard. The smell of the paints clings to her nostrils like gas fumes. She gets up dizzily and opens the long window onto the afternoon. The pigeons repeat their low rhythmical thirteen-note coo. She coos back.

70

Jim comes back into the room. 'There's nothing for lunch.'

'I know. Housekeeper's day off.'

'And worse, there is no money. I haven't a sou. We'll have to go out and see who we can bump into. Look spry, *mon coquelicot!*'

That afternoon, they happen to meet Edouard Manet, an old friend of Jim's, crossing the Place de Clichy, who invites them for lunch. He is a tall, elegantly dressed man with sparkly, alert eyes and a thick sandy beard. His manner is avuncular, courtly. Jim jokes with him about the time a few years ago when they took the train to Manchester to see an exhibition by Diego Velázquez. Jim tried to dodge the fare and Manet insisted on paying for him when the ticket inspector loomed at the end of the carriage.

Manet laughs and says, 'I still have not got the searing eyes of Pope Innocent X out of my head.'

'And I'm still haunted by the chin of King Philip of Spain. Or was that the inspector?'

Jo secretes some bread in her bag for later. She will try to persuade Madame Cléments to accept a small watercolour in exchange for groceries for their evening meal.

'You must come and see my new work, Manet. It's a vertical portrait of this fine girl. All in white.'

'Certainly, *mon ami*. We're neighbours, I believe. Did you see Ingres' *La Source* at the International Exhibition in London?'

'We did indeed,' Jo says. 'Jim couldn't sleep for a week afterwards.'

'They'll all say I copied him. But I started this long before. And there is no Athenian or Roman artifice in mine.'

'It's not a nude, either,' Jo says quietly.

'No, but I can assure you, she's exposed as if it were,' Jim adds with a touch of glee.

'I prefer the word "candid", Jim,' she says.

Manet gives her a half-smile.

71

Over the next week, Jim completes a series of etchings for an exhibition he hopes to organise in Paris. A letter from America brings disastrous news: Jim's mother has fallen ill and his brother Willie has joined the Civil War as a surgeon for the Confederates.

'But why isn't Willie fighting for the Yankees?' Jo asks.

'Oh, my family have a confused sense of what's theirs. They are not pro-slavery but they're pro-aristocracy and they think the Union will destroy that.'

'But doesn't the Southern aristocracy thrive on having slaves?'

'Exactly. It's a bloody mess. And if anything happens to Willie, it will kill my mother.'

'And it will not be so good for you, either,' Jo says quietly. The Civil War is stalking their apartment and Jim slouches on the sofa with a hounded look.

'It's already not so good. There's less money available now. Mother has begged me to come and if she gets worse, there's nothing for it – I shall have to leave at short notice.'

Jo does not speak. Perhaps if she stays silent, the threat will go away.

They have never been so hard up. Jim writes to his step-sister, Deborah, in London to ask her to wire some money. For a couple of days, he is distracted and restless and cannot settle to work.

One early evening at the Café Guerbois, Jim and Jo are playing backgammon when a lean, refined-looking man wearing a bright yellow cravat comes towards them.

'You must be James Whistler,' he says in fluent English. He has penetrating eyes and a slim, expressive mouth.

'Indeed, sir.' Whistler jumps to his feet. 'And you?'

'Charles Baudelaire.'

They shake hands.

Jo is stunned. He is not at all how she had imagined. His thin hair is receding and he looks older than forty-one, but his voice is kind. Jim tells her later that he has used laudanum and hashish for years and is fighting ill health.

'I've admired your etchings, Whistler – the Thames scenes and the self-portraits of course. Have you another exhibition planned in Paris?'

'Most certainly.'

'I hope to write a notice about it.'

'Marvellous. And may I present Miss Jo Hiffernan.'

Jo takes his hand. *'Enchantée*. Your work is tremendous,' she says. 'It's brought a new generation to poetry. It's powerful and beautiful.'

'Thank you. It's brought more lawyers than I'd have liked to poetry too,' he laughs and sways like a pine in a strong breeze.

'Can I buy you a drink, Monsieur?' Jim asks. Jo gives him a swift kick under the table. There will be no francs left for food.

'Allow me. As a welcome to the City of Lights.'

'Two pastis,' Jo says. 'Thank you.'

Jim adds a splash of water to their drinks and they watch them cloud. It reminds Jo of the colour of an old, sick eye. She is not sure she likes the taste. 'Liquorice is the taste of death,' Bridget used to say. Suddenly she misses her sister, her easy innocence, her lack of guile. Here she is sitting with one of the most notorious men in the whole of France and all she can think of is her virginal sister and how shocked she would be.

'I must express my gratitude for your review of my river etchings in the *Revue Anecdotique.*' Jim offers Baudelaire a cigar.

'You're more than welcome. The Thames has such a different personality from the Seine. It's industrial and constantly at work, like something mechanical. And you represented the profound and intricate poetry of that. My mother was born in England, by the way.'

'Ah, that's why your English is flawless,' Jo says.

They light their cigars. Jo inhales the thick friendly scent. She has always found it soothing – the smell of men relaxing and enjoying their wealth, or the pretence of it.

'Do you ever do woodblocks, Whistler?'

73

'Please, call me Jim. Mr Whistler is in his studio struggling with lead-white. Yes, I have done woodblocks, why?'

'I know a publisher who's seeking an illustrator for a book of poetry – *Passages from Modern Poets*. It could be dreary and the term "modern" will be elastic, to say the least, but the job is paid.'

'That is extremely kind of you. Can I offer you a drink? Calvados, is it, Baudelaire?' Jim leaps up and almost dances to the bar. He turns to wink at Jo.

'Now tell me, Miss Hiffernan, what shall you do in this illustrious metropolis of ours?'

'I shall sit and ponder it.'

'Much as I do then.'

'Yes, I have written some verse.' Jo blushes as soon as she has spoken. How idiotic to mention her drivel. She topples down into her ordinary self.

'You have a formidable school around you: Keats, Byron, Shelley...and you can still die young. Sadly I am too old to die young.'

'And I suspect you will always be too young to die old.'

He smiles at her curiously, leans towards her. She can smell his perfume.

'You are ravishing,' he says. It would sound better in French, Jo thinks.

Jim returns with the drinks and they talk about studio space and money and time, the three devils hounding any artist.

'Listen, I'm joining Courbet for a drink – why don't you two come along?' Baudelaire pulls on a pair of yellow gloves and stands up.

'We'd be delighted. Does he still frequent the Brasserie Andler?' Jim slips his coat over his shoulders.

'From five o'clock every afternoon for his *prix fixe,* unless he's in Ornans. He goes there to hunt, walk the hills and generally dry out.' He stretches his arms over his head and circles his shoulders. 'Oh, why do the things we need to create also drain us?'

74

'It's the old dilemma, isn't it? Multitude versus solitude,' Jim begins. 'We need one to inspire and the other to produce.'

'Yes, and it's something the modern world will only accentuate, I'm afraid,' Baudelaire says.

They come to the rue Hautefeuille and pass a strange turreted building on the corner. Baudelaire pauses and looks up.

'That's Courbet's studio. It was once an Augustine priory, you know. And I was born in this very street.'

'Really? Will it be safe from Haussmann, I wonder?' Jo asks.

'They say Boulevard Saint-Germain will plough through here eventually. Many a night I spent slung in a hammock up there.'

'Didn't Courbet once say he couldn't abide poetry?' Jim asks.

'Oh, he'll say anything for effect. He likes to think one should speak the voice of the people.'

'Poetry renews their voice, though, doesn't it?' Jo says.

'Well, it reaches their deepest emotions, which is the point. The ordinary voice rarely manages that.'

That's it, Jo thinks. She wants more than an ordinary voice. She wants to renew and enrich others. Somehow. With poetry, with painting. To make the invisible visible. The way Baudelaire includes her in his address enlivens her again, makes her feel smart and spoken to. She wonders why she has ceased to feel this with Jim and why she did not even notice until this moment.

They are hit by a strong smell of meat, spices and vinegar and a hot smoky blast of cigarettes and cigars. Brasserie Andler is a long narrow beerhall that is more like an Alsatian tavern than a Parisian café. Baudelaire tips his hat to a plump lady in a black dress and white lace collar, squeezed in behind a marble counter, where she is busy writing down orders in a black ledger.

'Not too keen on too many mistresses on her property, old Madame Andler,' Baudelaire whispers as they pass under huge hams and garlands of sausages of all shapes and sizes hanging from the ceiling. Waxed cheeses as big as millstones are stacked along one side of the room. They have to weave between benches packed full of people at two long wooden tables towards the back room where a group of men stand around a billiard table. Baudelaire leads them off to a room to the side where an attractive, dark-haired man with a thick black beard is holding court. Jo can tell that this establishment is not Jim's cup of tea and he keeps his hat and gloves on to signal that they will not be staying long. She recognises Courbet from the Nadar cartoons satirising him and his work. He acknowledges Baudelaire and makes room for him at the table but does not pause in the full flow of his anecdote.

'So each time I went to wretched confession – I was maybe thirteen – I would invent the most hair-raising escapades I'd had with women, with men, with sheep – involving all kinds of sexual positions and implements – good God, I could barely keep a straight face!' And here, he begins to tremble with laughter and stamp his feet. He gulps from a tankard of beer and wipes his mouth on the back of his hand before continuing in a gruff, rural accent that Jo has trouble deciphering. 'So they ran out of Hail Marys to give me and called in the Cardinal, some archbishop no less, to deal with me. "How long has it been since your last confession?" And by God, I let him have it – the foulest litany you've ever heard – two women and a buck shagging – it was Bacchanalian, I promise you!' He bangs the table with his fist. 'And then the canny old archbishop popped his head around the edge of the confessional and caught me reading from my notebook of sins. He just roared with laughter and made my rediscovered chastity the subject of his sermon. He's a character in my latest painting – wait till you see it! It will cause a scandal of immense proportions!' Again, he wheezes in another spasm of laughter that spreads around the table like wildfire catching tinder.

'And that was the best thing you wrote at the seminary, eh, my friend?' someone shouts.

'Absolutely, Proudhon! The only thing. Here, do you all know Pierre-Joseph Proudhon, from my home region? Another Franc-Comtois.' He scans the room with territorial possessiveness.

'You, sir.' His gaze lights on Jim. 'Proudhon, meet – no, do I know you?'

'James Whistler, monsieur. We met a few years ago with Fantin-Latour.'

'Of course we did. An Englishman, eh? Well, Proudhon wrote one of the smartest lines of thought of this century: "Property is theft" – and it is, except when a pretty married woman is involved!' The gentle-mannered Proudhon stands up and comes over and shakes Jim's hand. A man with full whiskers and spectacles, he looks less inebriated than anyone else in the party and somewhat embarrassed at being singled out.

Courbet goes on in a deep voice, 'We're going to collaborate on a book – art and ideas. He provides the ideas and I supply the art. More beer, Andler – on the tab, please. You and your lovely lady friend will join us.' Courbet shoots Jo a brief appraising glance and continues to regale the room.

Jim declines and making his excuses, he waves to Baudelaire, takes Jo's elbow and steers her past the rows of barrels of sauerkraut that line the bar and out into the brisk night air. Jo ties her velvet scarf more tightly at her neck. 'We could have had one drink to be polite,' she says.

'It was too hot in there. And anyway, you have to meet Courbet earlier in the day to get any sense out of him,' Jim says.

'He's like a lion who's swallowed the ringmaster and now runs the circus.'

Jim hoots with laughter and takes her hand.

'He can be a churlish bear, or bore, but he can paint. And fast.'

'And prolific. I read somewhere that he produces pictures in almost the same manner as a tree produces fruit. That image stayed with me.'

Among the people bustling through the streets, a family of stilt walkers in gaudy pantaloons strides home a storey above them and they overhear three prostitutes arguing about where to buy the cheapest bowl of soup.

'Let's follow them to the cheap soup,' Jim says.

They have finished the sitting for the day. 'Time...time, I need more time, Jo. To get this white girl ready to submit to the Academy this year, I'll need to work night and day.'

'We also need to rest and eat and make a living.'

'Murger said that artists need an audacious mathematics in order to survive.' Jim is seated at the table, carving wooden blocks for his commission. Jo is reading poetry, her feet curled under her thighs on the settee.

'Listen to this, Jim.' Jo begins to read Théophile Gautier's 'Symphony in White Major' aloud.

'It's perfect. Read the last stanza again, Jo.'

> *What magic of what far name*
> *Shall this pale soul ignite?*
> *Ah! who shall flush with rose's flame*
> *This cold, implacable white?*

'It has the sorrow and loneliness of your portrait, don't you think?'

There is a battering at the door. Jo goes to answer it. A red-faced, irate man waves a bill in her face, asking for Monsieur Whistler. 'He's working and can't be disturbed.'

'I'll disturb him all right.' The man tries to shove past her.

'Wait, I'll get him. What did you say your name was, monsieur?'

Jim is already beside her. 'Must we have this unseemly discussion about money, now, Monsieur Picot? I told you in my last letter that I would pay you next week.'

'What letter?' he snorts. 'I received no letter. On the other hand, monsieur, I've sent you three – three months I've waited for the payment on this furniture. I'll send my men to collect it this afternoon.'

'And what are we meant to sit on, may I ask? This is absurd!'

'No, what is absurd, monsieur, is that you and your wife make promises you have no intention of keeping – '

'How dare you insult me and my wife?'

Jo puts her hand on Jim's arm. He is spitting.

'Oh, it's fine for you in your fancy patent leather boots, when I have five children to feed.'

'Next week, monsieur, he needs time,' Jo says firmly.

'If she even is your wife,' the man adds as if Jo has not spoken. 'From what I hear – '

Jim's fist springs up and punches the tradesman on the jaw. He staggers back and clutches the banister. He cannot conceal his shock that a man smaller and thinner and allegedly more genteel has dared to take a swipe at him. He begins cursing and threatening to call the gendarmes at the top of his voice.

'Americans,' he says with contempt and turns and thumps down the staircase. 'I'll be back.'

'Boy's a dear, Jim, where did that come from?'

'Military academy. I learnt boxing at West Point.' He rubs his knuckles. 'Well, we simply won't be at home this afternoon when those duffers come to call.'

'They'll keep coming, love. They'll send the bailiffs next.'

'I haven't time for this stuff and nonsense.' He runs his hands through his hair and slumps on to the doorstep. 'One more week and I could finish this portrait and we could skedaddle back to London.'

'Perhaps he'll take a watercolour or some etchings. Shall I try?'

'Was his nose bleeding? I feel wretched. I am not a violent man. I wasn't even a good soldier, left West Point in disgrace. I should go round and apologise to the fellow at once.'

'*Scènes de la Vie de Bohème* was never quite as good fun as this.' Jo puts an arm around him. 'If only a Carlovingian coin would magically appear that we could sell and carry on a little longer.'

'Or a new commission.'

'I'll take some etchings to Picot this afternoon.'

'The only way one can possibly entertain being a Bohemian is by having a wealthy dead papa or a rich missus.'

'Poverty is more frightening if your family have known it.'

'Eat *la vache enragée* is how they put it. The enraged cow! Let's try Café Momus and see if we can scrounge something.'

The telegram reads, 'Mother dead. B.' Jo packs her possessions into a trunk and makes the journey back to London alone. Jim will empty their quarters and follow in a couple of days. She does not cry on the train, or as the ferry pulls out of Calais harbour. It is only when she sees the stark chalk cliffs of the English coast in January sunlight that she begins to weep. Later she can hear the cheers on deck, see people leaning over the railings to catch a glimpse of families and friends waving from the quayside. She wants to stay on the ship for ever, rocked on the waves, surrounded by the enormity of sky and sea, no destination in sight, perpetually about to arrive. She weeps for her father, imagining his pain and bewilderment upon finding his loved one dead. Was he with her when she died? She needs to know every detail of her mother's last moments and chastises herself for not being there to hold her hand, stroke her hair, do the last thing she requested – even if it was merely to raise a teaspoon of sugared tea to her lips.

Bridget is there waiting at the barrier at Charing Cross. Her face is much thinner and her clothes drabber than Jo remembered.

'You poor lamb,' Jo says as she embraces her. Bridget is stiff, pulls away first. They walk in silence towards the exit, a porter following with Jo's trunk.

'I barely recognised you in those clothes – that enormous bonnet. Please don't wear that to the funeral, Jo.'

Jo wants to spin on her heel and push her way back through the heaving crowd and back onto the train, any train. Bridget's respectability clings to her like the invisible strings of early morning cobwebs that Jo will wreck just by walking through. She must keep sight of her own world, she tells herself. She misses Jim with an instant and overwhelming thirst. This will be the longest time they will have spent apart since they met.

'I won't if you don't wish it,' she says. English feels peculiar on her tongue, like sand in a sandwich. 'How's Da?'

'I doubt that it's struck him with its full force yet.'

Jo is afraid to ask. 'And you?'

'Gerald has been a rock. We're to be married in the spring.'

'That's marvellous news, Bridge. Congratulations.'

'Mammy was helping me make the wedding dress. The pieces were all laid out on the floor the night she died. You'd have thought it was a shroud.'

Why will her sister not admit how she is feeling? How can she remain so dry-eyed and cold? Grief has made her hard. Or is it resentment?

'I'm sorry I wasn't here. To help. And when she died. You must be exhausted.'

Bridget's face softens.

'How long will you stay?'

'We're moving back. Jim's heard about a place to rent in Chelsea. He's coming as soon as he can.'

'Good. We've missed you.'

Jo suddenly senses the weight of the months of care and worry that she has missed. She pictures the way they used to be as young girls, giggly with telepathy, finishing each other's sentences, sharing everything. Bridget would creep to her bedside at night and gently prod her cheek with a single, icy fingertip till she gradually woke up and would pull her sister in under the covers and warm her feet between her calves. She remembered the sandy smell of her hair as she nestled into her arms and the sweet berry breath. Bridget would whisper that the snarling tigers had come back to get her again and Jo would sing her back to sleep.

81

'When did you stop wearing a crinoline?' Bridget asks as they climb into a hansom cab.

'Oh, months ago. No one wears them in Paris.'

'People are staring.'

'Ah, let them blooming well stare.'

As Jo looks at her sister's face caught in a permanent frown, she wonders if her breath is still as sweet. Then she becomes acutely aware of her sister's breathing as they sit side by side in the cab, their chests rising and falling in time and it strikes her that it is because their mother is no longer breathing: she will find her chest still. A cold wave of guilt engulfs her, then the colder grip of terror. She tries to distract herself by looking out of the window. The long, slow length of the Strand and the white crescent of the Aldwych seem dull and too familiar. People are heavily wrapped up against the north wind. A black man with his wife and two children try to cross the street towards the slums of Holborn, under-dressed for winter, with bulging red and orange-striped bundles tied to their backs and the mother balancing another bundle on her head.

The front door opens onto the Hiffernan family smell of food and clothes and bodies that still carries her mother's presence in it. Jo had never noticed it before and it makes the hallway seem overwhelmingly human.

Her father stumbles as he gets up to greet her and seeing that stumble breaks her. They sob openly in each other's arms.

'I'm finished, daughter dear. A dead duck.'

'I know, Da. I know. I'm sorry. It's life's hardest thing.'

She rubs his back, patting him as if he were a baby on her shoulder. He seems stooped. The tall tree is felled.

'There's nothing for me here. No point to it at all. Poor Kitty, my poor Kitty. Can she really be gone, Jo and that's it?' He weeps into a handkerchief.

'Hush, hush...' Jo whispers. He has an unwashed smell about his neck. She vows to never leave him for so long again. The drapes are pulled against the daylight.

'May the Lord forgive me but I see nothing only blackness and more black.'

'There, there...' She uses the words he used to soothe her as a child come to him with a hurt. 'Come and sit down, Da. Rest yourself.'

The furniture in the small sitting room has shrunk and as Jo sits him down she wonders how she will ever have the courage to stand up again, to walk away from this life. How could she ever have left?

'Tell me, daughter, is it wrong to pray when I'm not sure he's there to listen?'

'It's not wrong. I'll pray with you.' Jo begins, '"Hail Mary, full of grace..."' Together they say the prayer. He is calmer now but unlike Bridget, he has gained weight and his face seems swollen with grief. His eyes have a strange, stray look.

'Forty-four and still a slip of a girl to me.'

Bridget brings them a tray of tea. They sip and stare into the middle distance. None of them moves as if they are each holding a bowl full to the brim with precious liquid and to move would break the meniscus and spill it everywhere.

Bridget gets up finally and goes to the dresser. She gives Jo a package.

'Mam hoped to give you this herself.'

'Thank you.' Jo unwraps it to find a copy of *Mrs Beeton's Household Management*.

'It's sold thousands,' Bridget says in a low voice.

Jo runs her hand over the cover and the spine and knows what it must have taken for her mother to buy it for her.

The drapes are drawn and there are lit candles and bunches of purple and yellow crocuses around the room. Fresh snowdrops and a rosary have been laid in her mother's hands. Jo walks slowly as if against a strong undertow in a wide, dark river towards the coffin that rests on makeshift trestles in the centre of the room. Her mother's face is so blue-white that for a moment Jo can distinguish none of her features. Her heart leaps and twists like something freed from a cage. She believes for an instant that there has been a mistake. Closer, she can see it is her. Her hair lies lankly on either side of her face. She would have hated that. Jo fetches her hairbrush and hairpins from the dressing table, and begins to brush out her mother's hair and murmur to her. She fixes it up into the style she loved, pinning it at the temples. Voices travel through her head: Is my hair all right, Jo? I look a sight. It's fine, Mammy. I always feel like a million dollars when I have had my hair done. A hundred strokes, she would say and would stand Jo in front of her by the fire and brush her hair, until the rats' tails were loosened and the static crackled in her ears. Jo would love the drowsiness of being petted melting down her body.

Then she notices an envelope marked with her name on the bedside table. Her hands shake as she opens it.

> My dearest Jo,
>
> I have wanted you to have this letter as a final gift as I know that we parted with some rancour between us. I never wanted to hold you back, but you being so forward did make me fear for you. But that fear does not diminish the love and admiration I shall always keep for you in my heart. I remember watching your curiosity for all things grow and how long you would hold your stare as if you were trying to gaze right inside something. Do you remember how I used to snap my fingers in front of your eyes? Then I would see what you saw in your drawing. It is your gift and do not let it go to waste.
>
> I also want to tell you that I know about the baby you lost. I suppose that silent grief built a wall between us that perhaps I could have found some way to dismantle. The Lord's disapproval and shame prevented me from speaking, when I should have comforted you. Anthony wronged you and so did I. I ask for your forgiveness now and make the wish that

you know that the day you were born was the day that I felt most blessed.

Your ever-loving
Mother

Jo folds the letter as if it could break in her hands and watches her fingers folding a piece of paper as though from a planet away, an inhospitable planet with no oxygen, no water, no sunlight. The room spins and there is a wild howling spinning in it, filling it up, rocking her back and forth, pushing away the four walls, struggling against the ceiling. She is a craven she-wolf and the supernatural howl rising up through her body is hers.

The next morning before anyone else is awake Jo hunts out the small leather trunk from under the bed where she kept her childhood drawings. She searches for the drawing she made of her mother that afternoon when she was sleeping. She wants to see the live face, superimpose it over the gaunt mask that haunts her. There she is, the mouth relaxed and half smiling, the lines around her eyes soft, her little determined chin, her thick lustrous head of hair. Words come and she begins to write a poem, a lullaby, a goodbye. For a miraculous few minutes there is respite from the grief and the settling warmth of her mother watching is all around her.

III
The Princess of the Land of Porcelain, 1863-4

Jim pampers Jo for weeks after the loss of her mother. Every morning he comes back from the High Street with a fresh cream pastry or a fruit tart to serve her breakfast in bed and the newspaper. The mornings are the hardest, she tells him, as they lie watching the April sun move an oblong of windowed light westwards over the bedroom walls. Now it is her mother who is the one who is lost in the fog and Jo calling out her name. The thread attaching them is fraying, thinning out, and Jo fights to keep it tangible and firm.

'I wake up each time I turn over in the night and death is there like something impossibly heavy lying along my body that I can never shift.'

'It will shift. Some people say it takes seven seasons for the body to get used to a death,' Jim says softly. 'It will shift.'

He leaves cartoon drawings of them for her to find around the house, with the jokes they share, their pet names. They form a comic diary of their life together and cheer her up.

'You'd make someone a great mother,' she teases when he brings her a chicken broth he has made. Each evening he prepares a pot of camomile and valerian tea and reads her Alfred de Musset until she settles, loses her fear of insomnia, and drifts into sleep. Then she wakes before dawn and tries so hard to sleep that she presses her head into the pillow with the effort of something setting in cement and her body pleading to be let go.

Jo spends less and less time drawing or painting. To draw the world she must look out on it and she only wants to look in. She can only manage to write poetry and sometimes she thinks that each poem has a painting hidden within it.

Jim's spirits are good. While he was still in Paris, Gustave Courbet and John Everett Millais both came to the studio at Batignolles. Jim tells her that he was so nervous he spoke too

87

much, made lewd jokes and spilt Marsala wine on Courbet's sleeve. But Courbet was impressed. 'Oh, Jo, you should have seen it!'

Jim got up and imitated the older artist prowling around the room, his brooding eyes scanning *The White Girl* from different angles and at varied distances until he declared in a thick provincial accent, '"It's a fresh sensation. It's superb,"' he said. '"Your best work. Look at it, man, why do you behave as though you have no talent? You've arrived!"'

Jim had been elated. He had leapt up and embraced Courbet, stepping on his toes in clumsy over-excitement. 'Courbet loved your expression. The sadness of your eyes and the laughing eyes of the bear! Of course he wants to meet you. But I'm more than happy that there is the Channel between you.'

'He did meet me once, that evening in Brasserie Andler.'

'Yes, that was before. He didn't even stand up. He'll regret that now.'

John was easier to deal with, he told her. 'He won a place at the RA at the age of eleven, for Christ's sake! And his wife has just had their fifth child, so how he finds peace to work, I've no idea. But he was nodding and quiet. He stood perfectly still in front of the portrait and seemed to drink it in. That's how he can work – that mental discipline. Ultimate focus. The one-pointed mind. Then he went right up to it and peered at the edges where the white stripes of the sleeve of your shift stand out against the folds of the white drapes. I knew I had him.' Jim acted out Millais' response for her, making her laugh with his buffoonish mimicry. 'Then he simply said, "Splendid! Ready for the R.A. Excellent work."'

Later when Jo asked Jim how he managed to furnish their new house, he was sheepish. She had to coax it out of him.

'I sold everything in Paris.'

'Everything of Monsieur Picot's?'

'I'm afraid so. He did insult you.'

'True, but we owed him money. How can we possibly go back to Paris now?' Suddenly Jim's life is a sham – the apartments, the porcelain, the fancy clothes, the expensive wines are all built on a surface as thin as canvas. 'I'm afraid to open my own front door. I can go back to work, you know.'

'Listen, how do you think Baudelaire survives? He went to Amsterdam because he was up to his neck in debt. Then he moves back to another *quartier* and starts again. Without the hand-outs from Manet, he'd be in debtor's prison.'

'I will handle Mr Ionides' instalments.'

'You do and you shall. Do you think I cherish these financial skirmishes? I can assure you that I don't relish living like this.'

When Jo is clearing the plates from their supper that evening, the words 'fresh sensation' play in her head. The painting had pleased Monsieur Courbet. She had pleased him, one of the greatest painters in France.

Jim's commission from Alex Ionides is finally under way and going well. Every afternoon he sits for Fantin, who is painting an enormous canvas in homage to Eugène Delacroix, who had died a few months before. He had been greatly mourned by everyone they knew and Fantin wanted to show ten different artists and writers surrounding his central portrait of Delacroix, including Alphonse, Edouard Manet and Charles Baudelaire. Jim is flattered that Fantin has placed him centrally in the group and tries repeatedly to be patient as a sitter. He is also pleased that the way he has been positioned beside the others does not reveal his short stature. In fact Fantin has made him look as tall as Manet, who is gazing in his direction with remarkable admiration. Jo knows that Jim would not have agreed to the time required to sit if Fantin had not in some respects made the painting also a *Hommage à Whistler*.

'God, Jo, I don't know how you do it. This interminable sitting. I keep fidgeting and itching.'

'It's good for you to be introduced to this fine art. It has its own discipline: active yet passive.'

'Fantin is a statesman of a painter. Solid, dependable and enduring. He'll marry rich, mark my words,' Jim says.

'And that makes you what? A courtier?'

'A very headstrong courtier who is having a liaison with the Queen.'

'You'll always be more unpredictable than Fantin or Alphonse.'

'I'm unpredictable even to myself, *ma puce.*'

It is late summer before a trunk finally arrives from Paris. Jim opens it, enthralled. He lifts out a tissue-wrapped parcel and presents it to Jo. It is a black bear muff, glossy and gorgeous.

'I had to sell Benjamin but think of this as Baby Ben.'

Jo holds it up to her thighs and saunters saucily around their drawing room. They fall into a fit of laughter.

'But this is what I've been waiting for.' His eyes are gleaming. *'Vraiment trop belle!'* He unfolds two sumptuous red and gold kimonos and spreads them across the couch. Jo caresses the silk.

'It's like smooth running water. I've never touched anything like it.' She slips one over her shoulders and takes tiny, demure steps along the length of the floor rug, then bows and kneels in front of Jim. He laughs and leans over to kiss her.

'Aren't they divine, my geisha?'

He dives into the trunk, unpacks and holds up a beautiful print.

'They're called *Ukiyo-e* prints. Fabulous, no? It means "floating world" – time spent just watching the slipping world slip by in theatres and teahouses. They're from the Edo period when Japan was virtually cut off from the rest of the world.'

Jo takes the picture. 'The colours are so delicate and clear. Their skin seems translucent.'

'They're actors and lovers and courtesans. It was the first time images of ordinary people were made. I can't wait to show you *La Porte Chinoise*, a new shop in the Rivoli arcades. And the darling Madame de Soye, who's lived in Japan – can you imagine? – brought these back with her.'

He unwraps several blue and white porcelain bowls and tilts them towards the light.

'We saw porcelain like this at the Japanese exhibition last year,' Jo says. 'But my, to be able to touch it! How do they get such sharp white and deep blue?'

'Most of the techniques are secret. Some regions have white-stoned clay – that's all Madame de Soye would explain.'

'Everything in this room should be blue and white.'

'Yes and all our guests must come in oriental costume. And we'll get two sleek and supercilious Siamese cats.'

'And call them Lapsang and Souchong!'

'And you, my dearest one, will be Princess of the Land of Porcelain.'

The way Jim is staring at her with an oddly paradoxical intensity and remoteness, she can tell he either wants to paint her or go to bed with her. His expression is solemn, appraising and curiously distant as if he is removed from the everyday way of looking and is peering instead into her deepest self with all its wants and needs. It is such a penetrating form of attention that Jo wants to stay right where she is, enjoying the building desire and the delay of touch. He looks as though he is memorising her and she recalls once when they came back from the Wilton Music Hall in the East End that Jim immediately began to draw the interior from memory. There was the massive chandelier, the balcony, the heavy velvet drapes, the cast iron pillars and several of the performers in minute detail. He told her it was a method he learned from Boisbaudran at his school in Paris: how to retain the exact outlines and shades of dark and light for when you could put the image to paper.

He disappears to the studio upstairs and she can hear him beginning to prepare the easel and canvas and lay out the paints and brushes. Her trust in him has developed her trust in herself. As she observes his progress, she is more and more part of the process. When he asks her opinion about his work, he considers it carefully, and she surprises herself with her own forthrightness and growing instinct for art. Still, right now, she would rather go to bed with him than sit for him. She hears him calling her name.

One evening in early autumn Jim and Jo are invited to Tudor House, the home of the painter and poet Dante Gabriel Rossetti, who saw Jim moving in to the same Chelsea street and introduced himself. Jim persuades Jo to wear the kimono and carry a fan. When they arrive, a boy dressed in a medieval page costume approaches them with a tray of goblets, encrusted with coloured glass beads and filled with red wine. It is the most bizarre place she has ever visited. On the terrace, a young poet is reciting an extraordinarily perverse poem while beating his thigh with a riding crop. He is dressed in plum-coloured breeches and his mauve shirt lies open at the neck. He has a soft girlish mouth and long wavy hair. A small furry animal darts between his short legs. 'What was that?' Jo asks.

'I've no idea,' Jim says. 'An incontinent racoon? A gregarious badger?'

They walk out into a garden festooned with orange and red lanterns. Some kind of ox with a big dewlap stands tied to a stake. 'That's the Bull of Bashan,' a passing stranger remarks.

'What is it?' Jo asks. The hump-backed, large-eared bull watches them with large somnolent eyes.

'A zebu,' he explains but she thinks he must have invented the name. A couple of monkeys swing from the sycamore branches overhead. 'Look, Jim! Only a live monkey could replace Benjamin in my heart.'

'Who's Benjamin?' A young woman with enormous, blackened eyes is standing next to her.

'A bear we bought in Paris. Unfortunately only his skin – '

'We couldn't afford his body,' Jim says before being guided away by another acquaintance towards the further end of the garden where Jo has spotted a kangaroo.

'I'm Fanny Cornforth,' says the young woman, putting out her hand.

Jo introduces herself and admires Fanny's loose-fitting, brocaded gown. Her long blonde hair is held simply in a brocade headband.

'Say I can touch your kimono,' Fanny says.

92

'Please.' Jo extends a sleeve, but Fanny runs her hand down the embroidery over Jo's chest. Jo is so thrilled and surprised she almost laughs out loud but bites her lip and pretends nonchalance. For a moment, she cannot think of anything to say.

'Gabriel loves the oriental too.' Fanny is watching her closely. 'I'm part of his collection of the exotic and all. He done me as a Roman goddess in the latest portrait. Venus, my eye!'

Jo laughs. Fanny is more down-to-earth than she looks. Jo relaxes at once around her. She wants to wear a red ribbon at her throat too.

'"Not as she is, but as she fills his dream". Was his sister Christina right?'

'Well, his dreams are prettier than mine and people buy them. And here he is. Gabriel, this is Jo Hiffernan. She came with Jimmy Whistler. Our new neighbours, I hear tell.'

'Good to meet you, Jo.' Gabriel is all tall bone like a serving spoon, with fine light hair flopping over his quick eyes. He is wearing pearls and a silk scarf. He seems proud and warm and tender and not afraid to show any of it. Jim has told her that as no one understands his paintings, he is writing poetry.

'Look, Fanny,' he goes on, 'the thing is that Admiral Nelson has just eaten a number of cigars and seems to be expiring on my Persian rug.'

'Oh, Lord above. Ask Penfold to remove him.'

Gabriel dashes back into the house.

'It's the pet wombat. We've had him for years. He killed his mate trying to copulate. Poor Guinevere – he hounded her. Their mating is not gentle. More like rape, I'd say. Perhaps you saw him – he looks like a magnified hamster with a face on him like a koala bear.' Fanny sounds weary of the animal kingdom.

'Gabriel looks upset,' Jo says.

'Oh don't fret, he always looks like that. Mad large eyes that look constantly provoked – he can't help the hair.' Fanny mimes stroking a goatee and wild tufts of hair sticking out above her ears. 'Let's go inside, duck. Madame Rose is going to lead a séance.'

'Who's she?'

'Moi.' Fanny takes Jo's arm. 'We had a visit once from Gabriel's ex-missus. I could swear she haunts this house and all. Have you anyone you'd like to call forth?'

Jo hesitates. 'Yes. I – 'Her eyes sting. 'My mother died earlier this year.'

'Oh, I'm sorry, love. I didn't mean – '

'It's only when I say it out loud, it catches me unawares. She'd been ill for a long time.'

A gentleman with a carnation in his lapel passes them and whispers 'Orea,' appreciatively to Jo.

'Who's he when he's at home?'

'Frederick Sandys. Always spouts Greek. Another artist.'

Frederick pauses behind them and Jo can hear him ask another gentleman, 'Who's that stunner?'

'And what about your family?' Jo goes on.

'I don't have parents. Brought up in the foundling hospital. Then I got a job here in service. I'm telling you before everyone else does. Gabriel adores me, even though he says I'd talk the hind legs off a donkey.'

'And may I ask if you love him?'

'How did you know that's one of my favourite questions. It's hard to measure, to tell you God's honest truth. Never had much to compare it to, me. We had a bad marriage each and this works better. In fact, I've had two. It's a game, isn't it? A sort of pageant where you both play roles until it's boring, and there's no fresh exchange any more. Then you begin to count each mean thing he withholds, resent each extra thing you deliver. Then bingo, it's bad trade and time to depart.'

Jo is agog. She has never heard a woman talk like this.

'And how's your trading partner?'

'Highly profitable.' Jo laughs and then regrets what she has said. It has been so long since she confided in someone that she does not know how to express her feelings. She suddenly needs to be very sincere. 'I do love him. Very much.'

'I could see that. Everyone can.'

94

'Not everyone wants to, however. His stepsister and her husband refuse to let me past the front door.'

'Oh pooh! And they're not at the best party in the whole of London, are they? I'll see you shortly.' As she turns to go, Jo can see that her top lip protrudes slightly over the bottom one. It is the most sensual mouth she has ever seen.

When Fanny next appears in the drawing room, she is wearing a black and red lacy shawl over her head and is laden with gold rings and bracelets. She has a red rose in her décolletage. She takes her seat with five others at the table. The oil lamps are dimmed and the candlelight is absorbed by the tapestry-covered walls. Three peacock feathers flutter in a vase as people take their seats in a wider circle around the table. Something brushes Jo's ankle and she gives a small yelp. Gabriel lifts the tablecloth and calls, 'Lancelot, come out of there!' and a grumpy-looking armadillo trundles out and is shooed from the room.

The guests are whispering and giggling, until a voice, misjudging the fall of silence, blurts out, 'I have severe wind.' Everyone laughs, happy to release the building trepidation.

'Good evening, ladies and gentlemen. I am Madame Rose.' Fanny's voice sounds older and deeper and somewhat Eastern European. 'Tonight we are gathered to convene with spirits. We request that good spirits visit us and tell us the wonders of their world and the unknown secrets of our own.'

Two years ago the Queen had consulted an American medium after Albert's death but it remained a mystery whether or not she had managed to contact him. Heat prickles under Jo's arms and the centre of each cheek tighten with tension. She imagines what her skull would look like without flesh – the dark hollows of the eye sockets, the ruinous nose cavity and the everlasting, grim stumps of teeth. Then she thinks of her mother's skull, the slow action of dehydration and decay and the insects gradually burrowing their way through the wood, the clothes, the stringy flesh. She feels faint. The room is stifling and the air thick with sandalwood incense. She wants to leave desperately but is scared to disturb the séance and to draw attention to herself. Then something Fanny said reverberates and troubles its way up to the surface of her mind like a thorn working its way out of flesh. Foundling. She tries to take a deep breath. Her lost baby. Her chest is a ton weight. Would it speak to her or cry for her through the crowded room? She is sweating profusely now. She remembers dabbing and concealing the milk from her distended breasts and the veins like dark, untaken roads stretched across them. She searches for Jim's eyes in the dim light, finds them. He nods, quizzically raises his eyebrows and blows her a kiss. She can inhale again and she tries to focus on the calm space between her thoughts. She circles her thumb in her palm, mouthing a nursery rhyme her mother used to say: 'Round about there, went a little hare...' She is able to settle. The six people seated around the table lay their fingers on its rim.

'Who is there?' Madame Rose's voice sends a quiver down Jo's spine.

Each of the six begins to recite the alphabet and nothing happens. There is absolute silence. They begin at 'A' again and the table seems to tilt as a lady in a cerise velvet dress utters the letter 'E'. The slim gentleman to her right starts the alphabet again and the table turns and tilts when another gentleman with an outlandish moustache speaks the letter 'U'. It spells out the name Eugène. Jo thinks of Delacroix and looks at Jim. He looks shaken, his gaze fixed. She spies Fantin making a surreptitious sign of the cross. The lady at the table holds a handkerchief to her mouth. Her companion lays his hand on her shoulder.

'What would you like to tell us this evening?' Madame Rose asks.

Everyone in the room hushes again. They can hear the amplified ticking of the clock and the strange high cry of a peacock from the garden. Someone clears their throat. The alphabet is intoned again and the letters spell out 'BUTCHER'. The lady in cerise gasps. 'My brother! He was a master butcher in Farringdon. Is he happy? Is he with mother?'

The alphabet is started again and the table tips at 'N' and 'O'. Someone snorts and suppresses a snigger. Jo feels both intrigued and foolish. What if her mother were to come to tell her that her pain has not ceased and that it is most lonely and pitiful where she is? Jo could not bear it. But yet to know that her mother continues to exist in some form somewhere, comforts her and wins her over with an inexorable force. Jo is intensely aware of her feet all of a sudden. Her shoes pinch. She remembers her intense need to see her mother's feet one last time before she was buried. She had got up in the middle of the night and crept to the room where she was laid out. But she found that she was unable to disturb the body and instead she stood and cried at side of the coffin for no longer being able to picture the shape and the size of her mother's feet.

Later when she told Jim, he listened and then said, 'If that was a dream I'd say that you were frightened of stepping into your mother's shoes.' He was right. At first, she went round to see her father and Bridget once a week for Sunday lunch, but could not wait to leave. She felt as though if she stayed for more than two hours, she would never have the strength to leave again. Her father's need made her feel guilty. And under the guilt lay disappointment and loss that she could not bear to examine. Sometimes she would catch his eye across the table and he would look away.

'I hate for you to see me like this,' he once confided as she stood at the door to go.

There was not a joke, or a song or a drawing that could make it any better.

'It takes time, Da, only time.' She was ashamed of her own platitude but it was the only truth she could muster.

In April Bridget had married Gerald and moved into a new house in Islington. Her father employed a live-in maid called Mary and was managing more. He often came to dinner with her and Jim and she would cook his favourites of her mother's dishes. The familiar smells brought the memory of her mother waltzing into her kitchen and comforted them both. She might not be able to cure his grief but she could nourish him. She had also tried out Mrs Beeton's recipes. The best were her stewed breast of veal and peas and boiled calf's feet with parsley and butter, with rich sweetmeat gingerbread nuts or seed cake with baked apple custard to follow.

After the séance, Jo wanders into the breakfast room where Gabriel is showing off his collection of Nankin blue-and-white. Some sort of pale stoat or ferret is balancing on top of the dresser and Jo fears for the priceless platters and bowls on the racks below.

'I bought them at auction in Farmer and Rogers.'

'Is that on Regent Street?' Jim is enthralled as Gabriel's porcelain collection precedes and exceeds his. He holds an almost translucent bowl up to the light. 'I'm surprised this appeals to you, Gabriel. The line is so clean and your taste in design is often, well, how can I put it, slightly more florid.'

'Intricate, yes, not necessarily florid,' Gabriel says. 'I like utmost simplicity and clarity.'

To Jo the house and garden with its rare menagerie are anything but simple and clear. She admires a wallpaper design of green and gold fruits.

'That's by William Morris,' Gabriel tells her. 'He's an exceptional artist and pioneer.'

The next moment Fanny tugs at her elbow and whispers, 'He has an exceptional wife and all who Rhino can't keep his paws off.' She picks up a walnut from a bowl and cracks it open with her teeth. She hands Jo one half.

'Some medieval artists used the floral to offset the plainer elements,' John Millais interjects. He has a long, kind face. Jo had been introduced to his wife, Effie, earlier in the evening and had found her charming. She warmed to them both.

'I'd be interested in the Raphaelite Brotherhood, myself,' Jim says. It is evident he has had too much to drink. 'Raphael was one of the greatest artists there ever was. Have you seen his cartoons at Hampton Court?'

Fanny comes to whisper something in Gabriel's ear. He clasps her waist and looks at her tenderly.

98

'My Rhino here believes that women's bodies should be free-flowing. How natural is it to be entrapped in a whalebone vice?'

'I can't imagine how I wore a crinoline for so long, but I can't imagine going anywhere but here without a corset,' Jo says. 'This kimono makes me feel as if I'm wearing a waterfall.'

'Bravo! Rules and realism are wretched.' Gabriel raises his wine goblet.

'That's why artists will always be drawn back to the mythical and the allegorical,' John says.

'Quite,' Jim says. 'But there's the danger of slipping into the classical notion of the mythological. *Psyche at her Toilette* and such like. Then we're back to square one. I like the Brotherhood's emphasis on the symbolic. It's closer to my own ideas of art for art's sake. My next portrait of Jo will be about the power of Japanese art – its insistence on beauty over narrative.'

'Aren't all artists drawn to the sublime?' Jo asks. It was something Mr Hill used to say. 'And every new generation has to find a new way to grasp it.'

'As long as I have you, I can touch it,' Jim says with a tender smile. 'You're real, but myth can lean towards Romantic idealism too much for me.'

'And someone like Courbet has leant too far the other way, certainly,' Gabriel laughs.

'Vulgarity can be mistaken for realism, I'm afraid.' John gets up and pats Gabriel on the back.

'And aestheticism can be mistaken for anti-intellectualism,' the young poet says. He has just entered the room with a cigar in one hand and a dormouse in the other.

'Yes, exactly!' Jim stands up in excitement. 'Why is one assumed to have no intellectual purpose if one chooses to elevate the senses?'

'It's middle-class puritanism, pure and simple,' the poet continues.

'And what do you think of those riverscapes of Turner's?' Jim asks. 'To my mind, Aelbert Cuyp, who he imitated, is by far the better artist.'

99

'You're right, his glazes are magnificent,' John says.

'My God, Turner's oils are greasy and bombastic. But I urge you to see his watercolours. His watercolours can make you weep, I assure you,' says the poet. 'They are frighteningly tentative and ragged.'

Jo leans over and asks, 'What was that incredible poem you were reciting earlier?'

'It is called *Leaves of Grass* by Walt Whitman. He is immense, is he not? A friend sent it to me from Boston. It made me tremble for days. It is the most naked anyone has ever been in verse.'

'It sounded like what I imagine the mouth of Manhattan would say if it could speak.'

He laughs, sweeps his carroty hair off his face. 'And pray, madam, what would you voice?'

Jo thinks for a moment. 'The Crystal Palace. Three of my favourite words.'

'Yes, I agree that "the" is rather overlooked! I should be Ascot racecourse then: constantly trampled upon.' He grins wickedly and blows cigar smoke from the side of his mouth.

'And pray tell, what is your name, you russet figment of curves and glass?'

'Jo Hiffernan.'

'Ah, Jim's infamous "White Girl". I can see why. I'm Algernon Swinburne by the way.'

Jo is standing in a loose grey dress, tied with a thick sash of red silk, a pale coral pink kimono falling off her shoulders. Jim has erased and reworked how the kimono folds into light and shade for several days. He has tied a long brush to a stolen billiard cue to help him continue to work as he views the painting from a distance. Jo holds a fan and is posed in front of an oriental screen depicting birds and flowers in soft washes of red and gold. She is a beautifully wrapped present that Jim is no longer as interested in opening.

'Hmmm...' he mutters to himself, his brush hovering over the palette. 'Alizarin crimson? Rose madder? Yesterday, I was loudly certain which was right. Today, it looks quietly wrong.'

She has stood like this every day for the past fortnight so Jim could work intensely on the new canvas. He is happy to be back in a rhythm of work after the social whirl of Christmas and New Year soirees which he loved and then bitterly resented.

At first, the new project was engrossing for them both. For Jim it marked the transition of beginning to use oriental influences in his work and for Jo, it represented the new version of herself: the girl who had left home and become a woman; had lived as a man's wife; had travelled in Europe and learnt to speak French; and had lost her mother. Her English, like Jim's, had become coloured by smatterings of French. They communicated in a mix of languages, less as an affectation but more as a linguistic joke. Paris was closer if they spoke in French. The Salon would accept *The White Girl* and Jim's career would happen today, *enfin*. They also often used French to speak to each other privately in public as many English people seemed incapable, as Jim put it, 'of using their mouths to explore another tongue. That instinct stopped with Drake.'

Then one morning the letter from the Royal Academy arrives. He recognises the envelope and hollers for Jo to come. He is dancing with the envelope above his head. She watches as he reads the letter, his face collapsing. *The White Girl* has been rejected. She cannot believe it.

'I'm so sorry, Jim.' She goes towards him but he veers away.

He sits heavily, holds his head in his hands, his body deflated. He looks pale and sick. The physicality of his disappointment frightens her. Suddenly she has been rejected by the Academy too and somehow by Jim, as if she was not a good enough model.

She sits next to him but he does not notice. It is as though the painting is a dead body lying between them. She is surprised that she feels partly to blame.

101

'There's simply no point in going on,' he says. 'My work is worthless. Why do I bother? It's too hard.' She reaches for his hand but he will not look at her. He talks to the floor. 'They don't just reject my work, they reject my mind – everything I've ever thought, my heart, my soul.'

'They're not ready for it yet. Someone else will see it and understand, I know it, Jim. It's a terrific picture. Remember that it takes only one yes and the soul is mended.'

He asks Jo to re-read the letter as he cannot be sure of the truth of it. The confirmation makes him furious. He snatches the page back and paces the room shaking it as if it is on fire and will burn him up.

'Those old duffers know nothing! All they want to show are hideously pink paintings of ball gowns and bald babies. I'm beating my head against a brick wall.'

'Great men have always done that. The not so great ones give up. It's perseverance now, my sweet boy.'

'But you're only ever as good as your next painting. The last one is gone and with it my self-belief.' He rips the letter up into tiny pieces and tosses them over his shoulder. *'Merde* and double *merde!'*

'So keep with the new one, Jim. That's all there is for it. It's fresh – it will be stunning.' She tries to buoy his mood, keep him from a sulk which could paralyse him for days.

'It's infernally backward here – I can't stand these Islanders a minute longer. We're going back to Paris. *The White Girl* is going to the Salon, if it kills me.'

'That'll wipe the smile off their faces.'

'I'll set up my own show in London like I did in Paris.'

'Call it "Rejected by the Academy" – people like us will flock to it.'

'Isn't that the way to fight 'em!' He punches the air. 'Brilliant idea, *mon coquelicot!* I'll speak to Tom Mathison about his gallery in Berners Street. He's shown interest in the etchings. Let's go into town, right away.'

'Not this afternoon. I've invited Fanny and Algernon for high tea. We're planning another table-turning event. Maybe

102

my mother will visit the next time. And I'm baking a Madeira cake. Bridget gave me the recipe.'

'I'm too fidgety. Can you entertain them?' He pats his pockets. 'Oh God, I seem to have no spondulicks. I swear these trousers have holes.'

'Don't they all, my love?' Jo gives him some of the housekeeping money she has set aside and forbids him to bring home another piece of oriental crockery.

'I'll call in and visit Patrick on the way home. Shall I bring him for supper?'

'Only if he can bring it. Fish and chips? We have to give it a try. There's a new shop opened just around the corner. They say it's an experience.'

He grabs his hat and walking cane and brandishes it over his head as he marches up the street.

Jo opens all the windows and leans out of the sash window at the back to get a lungful of fresh air. It reeks of sewage and the clotted river weeds at low tide. Jim is anxious that a draught will bring on a recurrence of rheumatic fever, so insists on keeping the windows shut and the fires stoked up even on the mildest of days. The acrid paraffin stink of oil paint clings to her hair and her clothes. The fumes have given her a headache and a bad taste at the back of her throat.

She watches sailing vessels navigating the tide, people crossing Battersea Bridge, holding on to their hats in the wind. It reminds her of a Japanese print by Hiroshige of people moving across a bridge in a sudden shower, their bodies bent by sharp diagonals of rain. In places, the surface of the Thames is green and looks almost solid, like a gooseberry jelly, while in other patches, the wind wrinkles it into a thin, greyish skin. A barge named *Regain* sails upriver. The old blackened factories on the other bank belch smoke into the overhanging cloud. Down in the garden, the poppy seeds she sowed have burst out in red and yellow. The forsythia is dripping with deep golden blossom and the purple columbine buds are about to flower. Her gaze follows the river eastwards and she imagines

Wapping docks further downstream and the young woman she was when she met Jim. So much has happened in the past two years it feels as if a decade has passed. She decides to lie down for a while. Neither Jim nor she has been sleeping well. She thinks of her bold, brisk, seventeen-year-old self, the one who knew everything, could still want everything and believe that wanting made having. She seemed older then than she is now. Now she knows less but has opinions on everything. And as Plato said, knowledge is certain, opinions are uncertain. She is less certain and yet more secure. She looks at the backs of her hands, her bare fingers. Is she the woman she hoped to become? Or is she growing inward rather than out, like a toenail that tries to embed itself deeper in flesh? Perhaps this is growing up – a slow hardening, a lessening of feeling, a narrowing of dreams. Is she happy? Happier, yes. Sometimes she has to imagine herself alone again to see where and how her edges meet the world around her. She has been so impatient for her own life to begin and now that it has, some part of her is still waiting and there is nothing worse than waiting.

She has just started her period. It was four days late. She was relieved to see the first dash of blood, but the pain with a late period was more severe and the pain when it coincided with a full moon was the worst. They had been lucky so far and Jim always withdrew when she was at her most fertile. She kept careful track of her dates each month in a small red notebook. She picks up a collection of stories by Edgar Allan Poe and soon the aching throb in her lower back makes her drowsy and she begins to doze, half listening to the linnets and blackbirds trilling in the garden.

She has not really painted since the death of her mother. She had done a good sketch of Fanny one afternoon as they sat in deckchairs in St James's Park. It was the first warm weekend of the year and they been shopping for unusual fabrics in Whiteley's, the new drapery shop in Westbourne Grove. Fanny designed and made most of her own clothes and offered to show Jo how to use her new Singer sewing machine. It worked like a dream and Jo longed for one of her own. She could make dresses and mantles for Bridget, bring her wardrobe more up to date. Fanny had insisted that they take the Metropolitan Railway from King's Cross to Paddington for the thrill of riding in the world's first underground train. It was so fast, Jo still could not believe it, and something about the exhilaration of the speed, the darkness of the tunnels and the closeness of other bodies seemed to make everyone cast more stealthy looks at each other, measure each other up. But to Jo it was a form of Hades, was as spooky as Dante's underworld and she much preferred to be above ground in the spring daylight.

The trees were daubed with pink cherry blossoms and Jo was stirred by catching their honey scent on the breeze. They had sat in St James's Park under the shade of an arching willow, watching children trundling iron hoops along the paths and hearing adults scolding and tut-tutting about the new menace. The sunlight on Fanny's hair was diffused and glinted on the yellow strands. Jo was at ease and expansive in her company. She had forgotten how wonderful it was to make a new friend. Fanny's frank directness made her laugh and made her funnier in response. She seemed alert to how Jo thought in a way that reinforced and drew out her wit at its best. Jo liked herself more because Fanny saw who she was and liked it, wanted to be near it, not be it – no, Jo realised, there was not a rivalry there, that would spoil it, but there was an equality based on respect, a tiny bit of mutual awe and a great understanding. They had already developed a knowing shorthand, each becoming more exposed to the other. Jo found that she could not lie to Fanny or lie to herself if her friend was there to listen. Sometimes she felt absolutely compelled to talk to Fanny to be able to make sense of the mess of her own emotions.

Fanny's main theme was love. She read Gabriel's books about Eros, dreamt about it, invented theories. While Jo was sketching her as she relaxed in the park, she turned to her and asked, 'So, tell me, why do you love Jim?'

'Because...'

'Because why?'

'He's kind, funny, handsome – '

'Many men have those qualities.'

'Look straight ahead, please, Fanny. I love him because when I'm alone with him I can be most myself. There's no pretence. Women act like women around their men; I don't need to.'

'But isn't being a woman an act? The way we walk, talk, eat, sit, look, think even.'

'Yes, in public. In private, I am whatever I fancy. I hold up my breasts when I take off my stays because I like the feel of my body, released, not for him watching. I do it when I'm on my own too.'

Fanny had turned to face her again.

'And when we are with other people I get so excited by him I don't want to leave his side lest I miss something he says or does that will never occur again.' Jo went on with increasing clarity. 'It may sound ridiculous, but when I leave the room I feel an urgency – almost suspense – to see him again.'

'You see, duck, you don't really know why you love him.'

'No, you're right. It's like a great painting, the best part is the part that can't be spoken about.'

'Critics will always find the words. And demolish it.'

'Oh good God, I know. They crush Jim every time. He may get five superb notices and one poor one, and it's the poor one that will burrow inside him like a tapeworm. "Smudgy and uncouth", one chap wrote in the *Telegraph* once. Jim will never forgive him.'

'And Gabriel told me he wrote to the *Athenaeum* when they said that *The White Girl* looked nothing like the heroine in *The Woman in White*. He's got gumption.'

'He hadn't even read Wilkie's book! That incensed him – the idea that a painting can only illustrate.'

'And does he take you for granted, knowing how tied fast you are to him?'

'No. I know certain men around us who make him nervous.'

'A little tussle with attachment strengthens it, keeps them on their toes.' Fanny smiled and raised her eyebrows.

'No, I wouldn't torment him. When we lived in Paris, a gentleman in a top hat would stand and wait outside our door every morning and would follow me to the patisserie. He would never speak but he had that look that seems to undress you. And, for some bizarre reason, I nearly undressed for him right there in the middle of the boulevard. When Jim discovered it, there was an almighty row in the street and Jim threatened him with a duel. Lucky for us, the man ran off.'

'Yes, that look has nothing to do with how beautiful you are, how well-dressed you are, the shape of your figure. It's an animal scent.'

'You're telling me! It's so primitive and raw it makes me want to match it, lose all restraint.'

'Gloriously base! Don't I know?'

Jo laughed but did not blush. She tried to concentrate on her drawing. She had never spoken like this to anyone. Fanny was staring at her again with an odd look on her face. It reminded her of someone else who had given her that look of, what was it? – pleasant shock. It was Charles Baudelaire that evening in the Café Guerbois.

'Could you see the horn in his trousers?' Fanny asked.

Jo did blush then.

'Look ahead. You're spoiling the drawing.'

'Am I spoiling you, Miss Hiffernan?' Fanny said in her direct and deep Madame Rose voice.

Jo could not answer. Her whole body was flustered and hot. She had a shortness of breath and her corset pressed uncomfortably on her ribcage. Her desire was like an avid bee hovering over several perfumed flowers, wondering where it was going to land. She watched two young men tap a football back and forth, their movements light as dancers'. 'Give it a love tap,' her father would say when he meant a light touch. Jo could see a bee striking the cymbal of a spread white flower and making its way towards its dark centre. As the men called to each other in Italian, Jo willed one of them to look over, notice her and give her something stable and known to respond to. Neither of them did. When she looked at Fanny again, she had

107

tilted her head back and a wry smile widened across her face. Jo was severely tempted to trace her fingers down the length of Fanny's white throat.

Jo finished the drawing and was closing her sketchpad when Fanny asked to see it.

'But this is no *ordinary* drawing!' she said with a note of unalloyed astonishment. 'It is superb, I'm telling you. The draughtsmanship, Jo. This is as good as any I've seen of me by Gabriel or Frederick. Any of them.'

'Have it.' Jo tore it out and handed it to her. 'Please.'

'You can't give away your best work.'

'I'll do more of you, I promise.'

'But you haven't even signed it, my girl!'

For months Jim works on two paintings at once: the Ionides' commission and *The Princess* portrait of Jo. On the day *The Princess* is finished, he collapses on the floor of the studio, shaking all over with a form of fit. Jo runs out to get the nearest doctor. Doctor Linden is a very small Scot with a humped back and a built-up boot on his right foot. Jim explains how they have both been suffering from insomnia, headaches and cramps. As the doctor begins to examine him, Jim says that they suspected it was influenza at first or something imagined that they passed from one to the other, when Jim did not feel like looking at the portrait or Jo was tired of standing for it.

'Portrait, you say, sir?'

'Yes, I'm a painter.'

'You should have said so, sir. You have painter's colic. I very first saw it in white lead factory workers: convulsions, frothing at the mouth, a blue line on the gums, hallucinations.' He checks Jim's mouth. 'And I had better check you too, young lassie.' He signals Jo to come forward and open her mouth. His clothes give off the musty whiff of moth balls but his breath is minty. 'Yes, I am afraid it is as I surmised: you are both suffering from white lead poisoning and need to halt any exposure to these compounds at once.' The doctor catches Jim rolling his eyes as he snaps his leather bag shut.

'But it's like me asking you to give up your best scalpel, doctor. We use it for its opacity.'

Doctor Linden continues more sternly, his accent thickening, 'I mean *at once*. The stuff should be banned, I tell you. I know some painters who do not care one iota about what their behaviour does to their bodies as long as they can focus and hold up a paintbrush. But this can cause madness, I am warning you. The damage will be irreparable: it is called death.'

Jo is more concerned than Jim about the doctor's visit. As they lie together in bed that night, she insists that they leave London and take a proper rest from paint fumes. She is desperate to return to the wild, wide sea of Carnac, but Jim persuades her that they should travel down to Spain as far as Madrid and visit the Prado, which neither of them has seen. Jo would love to see the Velázquez and the Goya more than anything but she is worried that they are not strong enough for such a long journey and that it would be best to be in a country where they both spoke the language if they were to be taken ill. Besides, she argues, they can hardly afford a hotel in Spain.

A few weeks later, Edouard Manet writes to say that he has a small cabin on the coast near Biarritz and offers them the use of it to recuperate in. Jim arranges for *The White Girl* to be collected from the Royal Academy and shipped to Paris for submission to the Salon. Alphonse decides to rent their home in Lindsey Row while they are away and they pack their trunks again and head south.

The first two weeks at the Bay of Biscay are cloudy and sultry with thunder breaking over the sea and great forks of lightning shattering the night sky. Jo has never seen such torrential rain. A flash flood floats a carriage all the way down the main street of the village of Guéthary and leaves a deluge of sandy mud ghosting the pavements. Despite the overcast weather, their headaches are clearing each day and both of them are sleeping better despite the hard high bolsters.

Jo had loved seeing the French countryside again from the train and sat on the edge of her seat peering out at the lines of Lombardy poplars skirting the lanes and the fields, and the meadows opening out onto the roads and canals without hedgerows, the hundreds of red poppies nodding along the borders of the tracks. It looked as though you could walk for miles, unhindered. Jim had given her a beautiful collection by Tu Fu, an 8th-century Chinese poet, with the most exquisite woodblock illustrations. She read it aloud to him, his head resting on her shoulder. They were distinct in their own world and yet in public: their intimacy passing between them with small glances and clandestine touch. She watched the lines on his face softening as he fell asleep, wishing she could see the shapes and colours of his dreams. Maybe one day, she fantasised, they'll be able to visualise dreams in pictures, allowing everyone to see inside someone else's imagination. If they could see how differently the world appeared to each person, would that make them more alien to each other or closer? Once last spring, she was admiring the seedpods on the mimosa tree in the garden of Tudor House. To her, they were a mild amber colour, yet Jim said he saw them as rusty pink. When they saw them again a few weeks later, they were just the colour he had described as if his eyes could detect the imminent colour beneath the visible one.

She noticed a windmill on the top of a hill in the distance. It was not moving. Then, as she watched through the carriage window, it seemed that no wind was blowing, as if the entire earth was holding its breath. All the branches on the trees and the cornstalks in the fields they passed were motionless. There was nobody in sight. The sky was streaked with fine mare's tails. Something was going to happen – this was a dangerous stillness – and her body shuddered as she pulled her lapels tighter around her throat. Another train rattled past towards Paris and when she looked out of the window again, the trees, the flowering weeds, the grasses on the railway embankment were all moving again: the pause was over, Jim was still asleep, safe in her arms.

Finally the sun appears and they can leave the *gîte* and their nit-picking, bad-weather tempers and go down to the beach to paint. It is a scorching noon, the kind of bright, still heat that hits you like a blast from a hot oven when you step out of the shade. 'The sun is splitting the stones,' Jo echoes her mother, as they walk. The sharp medicinal smell from the pine forest makes them inhale deeply and swing their arms. 'Clear out the lungs,' Jo says. 'Blow away those city cobwebs and shake off the colic.' They pass through thickets of broom, its lemon yellow flower giving off a musky, dry scent. She notices that she does not smell oil paint when she breathes in any more. Here and there are patches of charred ground faintly redolent of woody smoke. Jim explains that broom grows even better after a forest fire. The stem of the plant may be destroyed but the fire encourages new growth from the roots and germinates the seeds stored in the ground.

Jo is wearing a loose cotton dress, red espadrilles and a straw hat that she haggled for in a market in Biarritz when they got off the train. She could be ten years old again, her skin freckling, her blue eyes clear, the whites the blue-white of inside a mussel shell. She clasps a stiff twig of rosemary and then sniffs the sweet earthy freshness on her fingers. Jim often teases her that if she ever lost her sight, she could survive by her sense of smell alone.

The path is edged with patches of red and white clover and nearer the beach are buoyant tufts of sea pinks. She is coming out of a dark cave and enjoying the light and sunshine and her body and mind again. They set up their easels in the shade with a view of the beach. Jo copies Jim, as if painting is an everyday occurrence for her. 'Start small and easy,' he urges. 'A watercolour. Beach, sea, sky. Three colours.' She is too hot, thirsty. Perhaps she should walk to the village instead. She is vague, dazed by the white light bouncing off the sand, the sparkle on the water and the immense dome of bright blue sky. She takes off her espadrilles and walks down to the shoreline, lifts her dress and paddles in the clear shallows that magnify the soft sandy ridges. She begins to kick the water up into a silver fountain that splashes down her front and cools her off.

As she walks back to her easel, she imagines being able to swim and a sense of floating and remembers what Jim had said about 'the floating world'. She watches the sea and attempts to inhale and exhale with the rolling waves to let the rhythm of the beach become her rhythm. If only she could be still and full of each individual moment, let the present world slip inside her. She listens to the scratchy whirring of the grasshoppers in the dunes and the squabble of seagulls. Two are fighting over a morsel that one drops into the waves. The other swoops down to snatch it and soars higher and faster until it becomes a speck and then nothing against the blue distance. She dips her brush in the jar of water and mixes white into blue. She does not remember how to start. She makes a blue mark, remembers a sketch by Turner of the Margate sky. She wishes there were clouds. This unbroken blue has no depth. The sea is a metal sheet arguing with the sun.

She has painted a band of blue, a band of silver and a band of pale sandy gold. Now she is running watery white between them for the shifting borders of the shoreline and the horizon. Strangely, the shore seems horizontal and the horizon vertical. They appear on the same plane but, she decides, for the painting, they are not.

'Don't you ever want to stop, Jim?' she asks after a while.

'No. You have to want art more than anything, to lead a life of art.'

'Maybe I'm happy to lead a life of love.'

'Art is love, for me. They're not exclusive.'

'I know. But art comes first. Love is art enough, for me, perhaps.'

She is not sure that Jim understands her. She reconsiders what she has just said – 'Love is art enough' – and wonders if this is the beginning of her giving in to being merely a muse and why is a muse always a merely? She will always be the sea, her edges indistinct, adapting to the land, reflecting the colour of the sky, whereas Jim will always be the sky, over-arching, determining her mood, never able to quite touch her. He can hold up the sun and moon, but she can merely shine them back. And who is the land? Perhaps Fanny reaches her more deeply than Jim. He has become so driven by his work that it has made him irritable and impatient. It is as if the magic she provided is wearing thin, like a song that once moved you to tears and on frequent hearing has become maudlin, or spins around in your head and will not let you go, so you can never hear it like you first did.

Jim is painting the breakers in full flourish, lost in airy concentration. He does not need her. This feels new, she thinks, and some part of her feels it as a rebuke. Petulance curdles her belly. The brush is stiff and unresponsive in her hand.

'Will you teach me how to swim later? They say salt water is excellent for Painter's Palsy, you know. This can be our own spa.'

'Yes, yes, not now. Later. This is marvellous. So free of people! I'll just paint landscapes from now on. Sitters are too temperamental and they drain me. This gives me energy. Don't you think?'

Jo says nothing.

'Jo?'

'I don't know.'

'What's the matter?' His tone of voice does not alter. He does not look at her.

'Onions.' She could say anything. 'A strong offshore wind will advance later, bringing rain,' she mutters.

'What's that?'

'I said "onions".'

'Hmmmm.'

'You destroyed my painting,' she says tersely. Suddenly she knows where the grievance stems from. It has inflamed her out of nowhere, burning through her with its own heat and speed like a forest fire in an arid land.

'Your painting, *chérie?* I have barely glanced at it. What's wrong? Let me see.'

113

'No.' She moves defensively in front of what she has done. 'Keep away! It's private.'

'Did I say something?' He looks baffled, but a half smile still plays on his lips as if her temper amuses him.

How can he say that about his sitters? She is his main sitter. He means that she drains him. She is shouting. 'It's nothing. *Nulle. Nulle. Nulle.* Take it, I'm sure you'll do something better with it. Like my painting of Carnac you erased.'

He looks at her anxiously. She will not meet his eye.

'Jo...' He comes towards her with a paintbrush in one hand and a cigarette in the other. 'Look at me.'

'Leave me alone,' she says. She wants to leave but wants to protect her work. She wants to know how to paint again and cannot fully accept her failure of application, or is it talent?

'But you had abandoned it. I didn't know you wanted that painting. I needed the canvas. I – '

She turns to walk away, shoving the easel so that it falls on the carpet of pine needles. She strides down to the sea. He comes after her. She wants him to follow her, but she is too far inside her own fury for anyone to reach her. She hates him, she tells herself, hates his voice, his art, his endless discussions about art, his disappointments, his manias, his extravagances, his perfectionism.

He takes her arm. She swings out of his grip.

'Tell me what I've done, *ma puce*. Please. You've no idea how much I adore you. You are the perfect woman, you know that. Have I – '

'Well, I'm perfect when I stand stock still for you for hours, but when I want to move, do something you haven't imagined, you stop seeing me. Listen, Jim, it's hard being perfect. Sometimes I'm not. I'm not able for it – it's a burden.'

The spate of rage pulls away towards the horizon like a huge ocean liner leaving a coracle tumbling in its wake. She pushes it and its frail and whining voice back down. He tries again to hold her, takes her shoulders and twists her towards him.

'What do you want? We'll do whatever you want today.'

114

'It's not about today, Jim.' She is quiet, almost hopeless, drifting like a life-belt on the open sea, with no one to rescue, only herself. The sea is flat and dull, the sky heavy with stupid sunshine. She will never be an artist.

'This is hopeless.' Her anger has transferred into him, become his. Sweat pimples his brow and upper lip.

'Go and work.'

'I'll be damned if I'll be told what to do.' He starts to take off all his clothes and turns and sprints into the bay, then dives into a breaking wave and swims out in fast, even strokes.

She is enraged again, the quarrel stolen from under her and she stomps in the water, dragging the hem of her dress through it.

She decides to walk to the village to buy bread, ham and cheese and passes back through the thickets of broom. If she is scorched and charred, will she grow back stronger? When Jim looks at the flowering broom does he see the withered shreds of tobacco brown beneath the yellow intensity? Can he see what will become of them when he has painted his fill of her?

She takes a flagon to the water pump and refills it. She eats her lunch, listlessly, watching the sea, not looking for a sighting of Jim, looking but pretending not to, and then scanning everywhere on land and sea for a small dark spot of human movement. Nothing. A sailing boat skims along like a white butterfly parallel to the shore. A boy throws a stick for a scruffy mongrel further along the beach. Two girls collect cowrie and razor shells in a basket. Somewhere in the three bands of colour is Jim. They no longer have any benign beauty, are not a spreading glory for the eyes. They have become malicious waves, indifferent sand and callous sky. She remembers the strange stillness in the train and hopes it is not a premonition.

She goes back to the *gîte,* carrying the remains of the food and an easel on each shoulder. Jim's clothes are lying on the path. She looks back at their crumpled form and wants to weep. The blaming chant of the grasshoppers escalates. She goes back and folds each item into a neat pile. What if his sweet warm body never fills them again? His shirt collar is threadbare. She

115

should have mended it. She returns to the *gîte,* frantic now. She paces the small cabin and then tidies up and sweeps the floor. She marches back between the pine trees to the sea and scans its expanse. She detests its open blankness and her puny, desperate human need that feels so enormous but is utterly insignificant to the blasted water. She will sit and wait by his clothes on the beach. If she puts them on her lap, will her body's power channel Jim back to her through his belongings as she has seen people do in séances? She closes her eyes and sees the bright whiteness of the sun against her eyelids. The afternoon is endless. Her life has ended.

Something moves through the wavering heat haze. It is a woman in a white frock or shawl at the far end of the beach. The figure seems to be part of a curve of sand, moving out of it. Then she can make out that it is a man with a long white cloth around his shoulders. She gets up and runs towards him, tears springing from her eyes. He is wrapped in sailcloth. He looks like a disciple, weary with faith. He takes a while to see her, squinting ahead.

'Jim! Jim!' she waves as she runs.

He is crying.

'Oh, Jo, Jo, Jo... Forgive me. Forgive all I've said or done. Don't ever leave me.'

His face is sunburnt, his lips cracked and shrivelled with salt. They hold one another tight. 'No, my darling boy. I promise.'

They kiss each other's faces, saying 'I love you' over and over, weeping, out of breath, then laughing. Jim begins to explain how he had been caught in a riptide, dragged out westwards past the headland. He had swum against it until he was exhausted and was trying to keep afloat when a fisherman picked him up and brought him back to the village. 'The hardest thing was not to panic, not to thrash away my reserves.'

'My poor lamb.' Jo strokes his face and looks into his dark eyes. 'I thought I'd lost you. That you wanted to be lost.'

'Oh yes, I thought of it. Swimming to Biarritz and taking on a new identity.' He pauses. His teeth are chattering, his hands trembling.

'As what?'

'That's just it. James Whistler is my life and I am his. And when I realised that I wanted to swim back to the life I have and couldn't, I – God, how I cherished you. Cherished it. I could see it fading like a dream.'

'There is no other dream.'

'I know, my love, I know. I will put you first from now on.'

'No, Jim, your art will come first, as it must.'

'But you never mentioned that painting. That was months ago. Jo? Were you very hurt?'

'I didn't want you to know how much it mattered. I felt ashamed. I did abandon it. You're right. I abandoned myself. I don't know how to...' she can barely say it. Why is saying what she needs so arduous?

'What, my sweetness?'

'Put myself first,' she wants to say but she cannot trust it enough to voice it. 'Keep painting,' she says.

He kisses her and pulls her closer. 'I will help you. I'll sell some work. We'll get a maid.'

She smiles and kisses him back as if she believes him.

They walk in step and hand in hand back to the gîte. She lights a log fire to heat water for the bathtub.

She feels a pang of love when she watches his naked body – the narrow hips; the two dimples at the base of his back where traces of pale down grow; the crisp line of his collarbone; the dip between his clavicle and neck; the crescent-shaped scar on his sunburnt left shoulder; the dark V of hair on his chest; his long fingers; his penis timid as a young boy's.

'I don't think I'll ever paint the ocean in the same way again,' Jim says as he lowers himself into the steam.

They decide to leave for Paris the next day.

They move into a small apartment Fantin is renting on the rue Laromiguière in the fourth arrondissement. It is closer to the centre of Paris and away from the bailiffs and creditors of the Boulevard des Batignolles and untouched by the modernising schemes of Baron Haussmann. Fantin and Jim go out in search of a separate studio for Jim. Nearby is the rue Mouffetard, a narrow, pretty, cobblestoned street that bustles with fruit and vegetable stalls every morning and in the evening comes alive with pimps, prostitutes and pickpockets. People say that there are thousands of artists and artists' apprentices living within this tiny quarter. Jo leaves it until the last moment to shop so she can pick up slightly damaged produce cheaply or for nothing. Oxtail, trotters and tongue are tasty for stew and the local butcher has taken a shine to her. She is freer in Paris. She even welcomes the stink of the drains. The weight of mourning her mother's death rolled off her as the harbour wall at Calais gave the ferry its deep welcoming thud. The recurring nightmare has not found her yet. For months she had dreamt that a pair of white plaster feet cut off at the ankle was coming under the door. The feet would walk through air and head towards her face. They were marked with small pencil Xs like the marks sculptors use to prepare plaster for a bronze casting. If they can fly without wings, she thought in the dream, they can bite her without teeth. She covered her face with her hands. The scream that would waken her never seemed to be hers – she was startled as though disturbed by an outside noise. Then slowly, thickly, Jim's voice was there as if calling from a valley, a long way off, 'I'm here, I'm here,' and the stranger's scream was there too and she recognised neither Jim nor herself. He had to shake her and then hold her tight, hauling her from the pitch-black pit, her heart pounding so hard that she feared it was something external beating to get back in.

One bright morning at the beginning of May they meet Manet to go to the Académie des Beaux-Arts and find out which works the Salon committee has selected. Their faces are relaxed and confident but as they chat and joke, they move skittishly from one subject to another, barely listening to each other. Jo knows their reputations and future commissions rest on their work being accepted. There is already a small crowd clustered around the columns of the grand entrance. Jo can spot Fantin and a bedraggled, bleary Alphonse, who has just arrived from

London, still carrying a suitcase and portfolio. Fantin waves and comes sprinting up to them.

'We've all been rejected!'

'What, all?' Jim raises his walking cane. *'Ce n'est pas possible.'*

'Mais oui, Whistler, all of us!' Fantin twists his hair off his brow where it stands in a stunned tangle.

Manet shrugs in dismay. 'How can they be so fatuous? What can we do, *mon ami?'*

'Well, I'm not taking it lying down. I want to see for myself,' Jim says.

There are several hundred disgruntled artists milling along the corridors and pushing through to the glass-covered noticeboard. Infuriated shouts and remonstrations pass up and down the flagstoned hallways, under the grand paintings lining the walls and the crystal chandeliers scintillating overhead. When Jim scans the list for his name, it is true, it is not there. He raises his fist and smashes the glass. The crowd lets out an enormous cheer as Jim raises his bloodied knuckles.

'Café de Bade! *Allez-y la résistance!'* someone shouts and the crowd seems to heave and swarm and suck them in and they advance out of the building as one wave. Jo grips the sleeve of Jim's jacket as they are pulled, pushed and pummelled along the narrow streets to the café where other artists have already spilled on to the pavement. Inside, Fantin has commandeered the top of a table, shouting, 'This is a disgrace! Almost 4,000 painters rejected – many of whom I can assure you are geniuses that the Salon should be honoured to exhibit. Gustave Courbet and Edouard Manet for example, – ' there is wild applause, ' – Edouard Manet – they are too intimidated, too scandalised…'

'Too bourgeois!' someone adds from the crowd.

'Exactement!' yells another protester.

'They are too scandalised to show a modern woman seated nude beside two clothed men when their walls are plastered in the female nude. Manet's magnificent *Le Bain,* gentlemen, and ladies, must be seen and must be seen now!'

119

Everyone begins to chant, 'Be seen now! Be seen now!' their voices getting louder and stronger as the repetition grows.

Jo is shocked at how quickly the reporters arrive and snake their way to the front, notebooks in hand. They begin interviewing several of the artists. Jugs of beer are passed out by the patron. Many of the artists have paid their tab with the paintings or sketches that decorate the walls of his café. He looks invigorated with pride as he sends out a waiter to buy more bread and cheese. Jo takes a piece of charcoal from the fireplace and starts to write on a tablecloth. She and Jim hold it up: 'Salon des Refusés'. A great whoop and whistles rise into the air. Jim and Jo, followed by Alphonse, Manet and Fantin begin to march into the road, stopping the traffic of horses and Tilbury carriages and cabs. The crowd follows pell-mell with all their solitude, their toil, their frustrated ideals and their penury boiling up and over. Two young lads have scaled a lamppost to urge them on.

They march back to the Académie and set up camp outside the huge wooden doors. Jo has not seen Jim this exhilarated for months. When she loses her footing on the kerb and stumbles, Manet takes her arm, helps her to navigate the swell of the throng. She can sense his wish to hold back from the rabble. She has never experienced this collective mood of exultation before and wants to get closer. If only Gabriel and Fanny were here to see Jim in his element – the feisty little captain of the rejected punching the air. He has climbed up on to the base of one of the columns and begins to speak.

'How are we meant to live if we can't show our work? There's a whole generation of new artists – a first-class generation – a new movement that they wish to ignore. I tell you now, we will not grant that wish: we will not be ignored!' The crowd echo his words in a chant. Jo joins in, shouting until her throat grows hoarse.

'They want history and they want the Bible and myth and allegory, but history is now,' Jim continues. 'Gustave Courbet is now. We refuse to be stuck in the past. We refuse to depict medieval scenes in colours that match their latest interior decor, with titles from a Charles Dickens novel. We refuse and refuse again!'

They stay drinking wine, tearing open baguettes and wheels of cheese, arguing and smoking until dawn breaks red over the rooftops and creeps up in a fine mist along the Seine. Jim and Jo go home to change but are too fired up to rest. At noon Fantin comes to tell them that Emperor Napoleon has demanded to visit the Académie to see the rejected works for himself. The gendarmes have cleared the entrance. A few artists refused to move and have been carried off, others scuffled and then escaped into the crowd. It is rumoured that five artists have been beaten by the police and another two collapsed in the cells. The Académie has been cordoned off.

Jo and Jim return to the Café de Bade to rally support and hear the latest news. Fantin and Alphonse go to join the protest outside the local gendarmerie. The air is tense with anticipation and the exhilaration of imminent battle. Later that day, Manet arrives with the news that Napoleon has ordered the opening of another annexe next to the Salon in the Palais des Champs-Elysées to show the rejected work.

'The avant-garde has arrived!' Jim shouts as he embraces Manet. 'The work will be seen!'

'All the critics will be there,' Manet says in quiet triumph. 'Our Salon will get far more attention than the traditional one and the public will discover a new way to look at painting.'

The mood in the café soars and tips over into a party, strangers embracing, dancing and singing. They all enjoy the unfamiliar, juicy taste of victory.

Artists have been given two weeks to withdraw their work if they wish. Within a couple of days, no one can quite believe that 7,000 tickets have been sold for the alternative exhibition. It is already an almighty success and the Latin Quarter is buzzing with artists designing, making and borrowing their outfits for the grand opening.

As Jo, Jim, Fantin, Alphonse and Manet arrive at the Palais, dressed to the nines, for the opening, they soon see that the show itself is a chaotic jumble. Paintings are crammed on every inch of every wall, under-lit and full of horrors which the public love.

'Most of these deserve a fate worse than rejection,' Jim whispers as they pass through the galleries. They notice a cluster of people ahead laughing and pointing at a painting and when they get closer they see it is Jim's *The White Girl*.

They overhear one young man ask, 'But is she a spirit perhaps?'

'Clearly a medium in a trance,' asserts another.

'Why is she not properly dressed? Who is this painter?'

'Whistler. Never heard of him.'

'Is it any wonder?'

They keep walking as if they have not seen it, but Jo is aware of the broken quality in Jim's expression. She swallows a singeing at the back of her throat and pulls her bonnet closer to hide her burning face. The others say nothing. Fantin pats Jim's back and Jim walks as if he is sleep-walking, his fighting energy evaporated.

In the next gallery, there is an even more raucous crowd hemmed around another work, screaming and howling with laughter. Consternated middle-aged men are tearing their wives away from the throng as if the painting could bite. Jo can make out over people's heads that it is Manet's *Le Bain*.

'Who's for lunch?' one of the mob quips.

'A rum picnic!' says another, turning away. 'What's Paris coming to, I ask you?'

'Lord God,' Jim says. 'This is barbaric.'

'It's the worst kind of zoo,' Jo takes his arm. 'I've never seen any art treated like this in my life.'

'You'd think they'd never seen a nude before,' Manet says.

'Or visited a gallery.' Jo links Manet with her other arm.

'Maybe they haven't,' Fantin says. 'But this context isn't helping our cause. There is avant-garde and there is atrocious – '

'And no distinction betwixt or between.' Jim's voice is shaking. 'I want to tell them a thing or two.'

'Let's leave. It's too sickening.' Manet brings up his handkerchief to partially mask his face.

As they jostle their way through the mob towards the exit, Jo sees a handsome couple giving serious consideration to one of the paintings. When she gets nearer, she realises that the two figures with linked arms are both women. One is dressed in trousers, a topcoat and top hat. Other people are turning to stare and snigger behind their hands. Jo guesses that the woman wearing male attire is the painter Rosa Bonheur, notorious for fighting for special dispensation from the police to forego skirts so that she could paint out of doors. People say that the couple rarely come into Paris and Jo slows her pace to watch them for a moment longer. Is Bonheur's work somewhere in these vast halls or has her work been accepted by the Salon itself again this year? Few women have achieved that renown and honour. Jo remembers seeing *The Horse Fair,* one of her paintings, and being amazed that a woman could have such command over a crowded scene of highly strung horses. Suddenly the couple turn and Bonheur's eyes meet Jo's for a second. Jo wishes she could transmit her desire to paint, imagines that Bonheur can read it written in her glance. As Jim steers her towards the exit she is emboldened, resolved to become steadier in the pursuit of her own work.

When they emerge into the street, a small agitated man approaches Manet. 'Have you heard about Courbet? His painting *Le Retour de la Conférence* has been rejected even by the Salon des Refusés.'

Manet, Jim, Fantin and Alphonse rally round him. 'What are you saying?' Jim asks, his tone laced with irritation.

'Yes, I assure you,' the fellow continues, 'his band of drunken priests cavorting along a country road had been censored for its "offence to clerical decency".'

Fantin winks at Jo and pipes up, 'But everyone knows that provincial priests have the best cellars in any district.'

Manet and Alphonse smile but Jim is muted, expressionless. He leans over and whispers to Jo, 'The old fox has managed to trump us all: rejected by the rejected.'

Jo searches the sea of faces for Courbet but he is nowhere to be seen.

The next day, the gazettes come out with the reviews. They congregate at the Café de Bade as usual and read them aloud to each other, sitting in an anxious knot around one table, drinking too much coffee and moving on to brandy as the day progresses.

La Fille en Blanche disquiets the critics. Jim reads from the paper in a mocking voice, '"Who is the white girl?" they ask, "what has befallen her, why is she wearing merely a shift?"' He thumps the table. 'All they want is story, story. What about the style, the achievement of the paint?'

'Here, listen, this is better,' Alphonse shakes open another paper and begins to read. '"Whistler has tried to invoke a sense of white upon white that creates an almost musical layered harmony. I dub it *Symphonie en Blanc.*" That's marvellous, no? He got it.'

'Really? Let me see,' Jim is thrilled. 'At last, one intelligent response.'

'That could be the painting's new title,' Jo suggests.

'*Symphony in White?* Yes, it's perfect, Jo.'

As for Manet's masterpiece, it is a common affront, say the newspapers. When Fantin reads out a quote from a critic who calls it 'immensely vulgar', they boo and hiss. Manet remains subdued and then looks utterly demeaned when he sees the cartoons satirising it in the newspapers. Jo opens up *La Vie Parisienne,* the new magazine for the upper classes, and leafing through it, discovers caricatures of both Manet and Jim's paintings. The first shows a clothed gent bending over a plump, ugly, naked woman and the second depicts a waif-like, rather drippy maid in an apron, holding a weed. The attack stings. She holds up the page.

'Look, this is meant to be me! They missed the point entirely. They have to belittle her because this white girl isn't chaste and refined.'

'Don't worry, Jo, that picture has such immense integrity. We all can see it,' Manet says softly.

But Jo is worried. The paintings will not sell and Jim and she will return to London a penniless laughing stock. She thinks of all the hours they both spent on that picture. For what? So she could be known as the used servant girl who did not merit a portrait? The shame she experienced when the Royal Academy rejected the painting intensifies. Jim will not ask her to pose again.

'They feel entitled to the portrait of some landed lady who has paid an unholy sum to be preserved in paint,' says Fantin.

'And they get glory for recognising,' Jim adds.

'But this is real life, *quoi*. The future of painting, Jo. Trust me.' Fantin's kind dark eyes hold hers for a second. Then he grabs Jo and Manet's hands and raises them up. *'La Société de Cinque*. The avant-garde must be small enough to sneak through the enemy lines. Travel light and never falter.'

'Abominable banality. I didn't think Paris could produce it,' Jim shakes his head and swallows down his brandy. Jo leaves her glass untouched. If this is what can happen to Jim and Manet, talented male painters with secure incomes, how could she ever hope to achieve any recognition as an artist? She runs the pads of her thumbs over her nails and the noise of the café disappears.

Fantin leans over to her. 'Can I get you a tea, Jo? Something to eat?'

'Thank you, Fantin. I'm a bit queasy.'

'Don't be sad, Jo. This is a new beginning for all of us. You too. This is the time to start painting. Everything is open.' He squeezes her hand.

She smiles. 'I know. I can feel it. I sense the energy, the urgency – ' she shrugs.

'I would love to see what you would do.'

'I've still so much to learn.'

125

'Learn by doing. It's the best way.'

The next day the crowd around their tables at the café has grown, with younger artists drinking in the drama and the debates. Someone tells them that a guard has had to be hired to keep the outraged public from attacking *Le Bain*, but mostly they are turning up in droves to laugh uproariously at it. 'Unartistic', the critics continue. The handling of the paint is too flat, they argue, built from blocks of colour with no tonal transitions.

'What you're doing with light is a revolution, Manet! Don't listen to them,' Jim jumps up and slaps his thigh. 'You've changed the way people will paint shadow for ever. Why the devil should shadows only ever be black or brown, I ask you? Why not blue and green?'

However, Manet is inconsolably hurt. He has begun to hunch and shrink inside his large frame. 'I'm not a rebel, Whistler. It's just what I choose to paint and how I choose to paint it. It's not the kind of attention I'm seeking.'

Fantin puts his arm around Manet's shoulders. 'But Baudelaire can see it. He called you the painter of modern life, which is the greatest accolade. It's achieved everything he says a great painting must: elements of the modern and the eternal. It's the classical revisited and it's superb, without question.'

'Don't take it to heart,' Jo places her hand on Manet's. 'You're the undisputed king.'

'Of a kingdom of five, I'm afraid.'

'Can't they see Giorgione's *Fête Champêtre* in it? I used to sell copies I'd done of that painting up and down the Left Bank...you remember, Fantin?' Jim lights a new cigarette from the one in his mouth and orders more coffee.

'He's right,' Fantin says. 'You see, it's fine if you want to depict nymphs and goddesses, but an ordinary modern woman with a candid stare and nothing on – *ah non, ça, ce n'est pas propre!'*

'If they just took a look at Raimondi's Judgement of Paris after Raphael, in the Louvre under their very noses, all would be calm. Two rivergods and a nymph can be found in just this composition.' Manet is trying to sound calm himself, but failing. He looks pale and darts his eyes towards the door each time it opens.

'But wait, listen to this,' Jim cries, holding up *Le Figaro.* 'It's a letter from an artist. Listen! This is a hoot! The correspondent complains that his painting is being neglected in a corner of the official Salon show, while crowds flock to the "rejected" exhibition. "Could you tell me whom I should approach in order to obtain my transfer," he writes, "from the hell of those admitted to the heaven of those excluded?" Isn't that a scream?'

Later they are just finishing off a large dish of bouillabaisse when the rumour goes round that Courbet is showing *Le Retour de la Conférence* in his own studio on the rue Hautefeuille. Fantin suggests they set off to acclaim it and shouts, 'Sally the light cavalry!' Jo can see that Jim is reluctant to join the merry band, his steps lagging. But when they arrive at the turreted building, the place is so full of critics, journalists, dealers, collectors and onlookers swarming around and spilling down the staircase that they cannot gain any access at all. Then through the crowd, another painter in a red beret recognises Jim and calls to him, waving a newspaper above his head, 'Hey, Whistler, have a look at this! It's just out! Here, Willem Bürger has reviewed your picture.'

Jim scans the notice hurriedly and looks up, his face beaming.

'Well, what does he say? Tell us!' Jo tries to read over his shoulder.

'"...a rare image, conceived and painted like a vision that would appear in a dream, not to everybody, but to a poet. What's the good of art if it doesn't show things you can't see?" *All right!'*

'Bravo, poet!' Fantin shouts.

'Enfin, my love,' Jo's eyes well up as she kisses his cheek.

'Bürger's the pseudonym for Théophile Thoré, you know, Whistler,' Manet adds. 'He's a celebrated critic. The tide is turning, *mon ami.'*

'You'll be next, Manet,' Jo says.

Whistler whoops, links arms with Jo on one side, Fantin on the other and they begin to cancan down the middle of the cobbled street. Manet and Alphonse run to join in and Whistler starts to sing one of his bawdy Negro songs at the top of his lungs. Jo is filled with the burning joy of success, as if she had painted the portrait herself.

IV
Symphony in White no 2: The Little White Girl, 1864

It is autumn when Jo and Jim return to their house in Lindsey Row. The plane trees on the streets of Chelsea have yellowed and rustle dryly in the cool wind. Fallen leaves and litter have blown into a heap on the doorstep. Although Alphonse has warned them that he is a hapless housekeeper, they are still shocked when they open the door to the mouldy stench, the piles of unwashed clothes and empty wine bottles on the floor and cigarettes bent into saucers on every surface. The house also smells of damp. There is a menacing stack of court summonses and a letter waiting from Jim's mother. The drudgery of London life engulfs her. They have agreed to keep Alphonse as a lodger to help pay the rent, but as Jo opens the windows and begins to sweep the floors, she resents the compromise and the intrusion. Mrs Abbott is back and will have to take herself down to Broadbent and Sons with a collection of Paris etchings in the morning. She scrubs down the pantry and the kitchen, telling herself that Alphonse's stay will be temporary and that Jim will sell his latest portrait, the one he started in Paris, and will gain a new commission. She is unsettled and knows it is more than simply leaving France. The small opening for something to begin for herself has closed. She is like a fruit that looks ready but never ripens.

Jim comes into the kitchen in a whirl of agitation. She can tell by the way he is smoking – the fast inhalations and the snorting out of the smoke – that it is bad news. He is running his hand through his hair as if to untangle the latest problem. He shifts his weight from one foot to the other. She assumes it is another troublesome creditor but eventually he tells her that his mother is seriously ill. As Willie is still fighting in the Civil War, his mother has asked if he can come to America at once.

'What will you say?' Jo knows the answer before she asks. She knows how much Anna Whistler, who has lost three boys and her husband, adores her son, and how often her recent letters have pleaded with her Jemie to come home. Jim does not respond.

'So when will you go, Jim?'

'Listen, Jo, I have no intention of going back to America. My work is here. It would be the end of my career. No, it would be better if she came to London.'

'Can you ask Deborah and Seymour if they'll take her in?' Jo's voice sounds weak. 'They have a larger property.'

'And a larger family.'

Jo grimaces. The 'relations' she has not been permitted to meet. The last time Jim visited them, Seymour had taken him up four flights of stairs to his study to try to convince him, over a gentlemanly cigar and glass of reserve port, that he should give up Jo, that his reputation at the Burlington Fine Arts Club was suffering. Jim had said that was utter balderdash and added that if they denounced every artist with a mistress, they would lose over half their members and would never have countenanced Turner. 'No, Seymour,' Jim had gone on, 'who suffers is you. Your reputation. You want to paint clean modest paintings of a clean modest life and I dirty it up. You see the woman I love as dirt. You won't even tolerate having her over your own threshold. I won't stand for it.' With that, he told her, he had clattered down the stairs and out the front door without another word to his stepsister.

'But the truth is I don't think I'm welcome there, Jo. And besides mother would want to be here.'

'No, the truth is that you're too proud to eat humble pie or ask Seymour for anything.'

'I'll never speak to him again, if I can help it. He's trying to control my life and make it conform to his. He's a dullard Sunday painter with dullard Sunday attitudes.'

'I know what this means.'

'Don't jump the gun, Jo.'

'You know how devout she is.' Jo folds her arms and feels her jaw tighten. 'You'll employ a maid, I suppose.'

'Sit down, Jo. I don't want you to leave. That's the last thing on earth I want. It may not come to that. Not for some time.'

'It was fine to expect my parents to tolerate my living with you but you refuse to contemplate asking your mother to do the same.'

He does not reply, looks down, is overcome with an expression of bashfulness, or is it shame, she does not recognise.

'So, you'll choose your mother over me, is that it?' Jo shouts and flings the broom down to the floor with a loud crack.

'I didn't say that, Jo. She's a widow and – '

'You wouldn't even entertain marrying me, not because you are so bohemian after all, but because I am not good enough for your blessed holy mother. Well, I'll move me out and you can find someone who fits the Abbott McNeill Whistler dynasty.'

She leaves the room. She had tried to call his bluff, embarrass him into defending her, putting her first, at least with an attempt at some sweet, empty words, but he had given her nothing. His career. He said nothing about her, about them.

She goes upstairs and sits on their bed. Their unmade bed with Alphonse's soiled sheets. Their unpacked trunks stand beneath the window. A wreath of starlings blackens the sky and shifts and loops over the rooftops. How she wants to escape back to Paris where family and propriety do not smother her, even back to their cramped quarters with Fantin when sharing was fun and heady and they spent their time in the cafés or on the streets. She starts to unbutton her dress and unlace her corset. She lies back on the bed and thinks of the word dirty. Filthy. Tainted. Stained. Sullied. Twice she has been made soiled and punished for being the wrong class of woman or a woman of the wrong class.

Later Jim comes up soundlessly with fresh sheets and they remake the bed in a silent, jokeless pantomime. She bathes and washes her hair as if she can rinse the word sordid out of her mind. As night falls, the fireworks from Cremorne Pleasure Gardens nearby pop and whistle above the river. Jim has lit the fire and she sits beside it, her hair fanned out along the back of the chair to help it dry. They do not speak. She falls

131

asleep watching the flames unfurl and flicker with their blue hearts, their dark caves of coal. When she opens her eyes, Jim is sketching her on a copperplate resting on a drawing board balanced on the arms of the chair.

'You could ask.'

'Don't be unreasonable. You were asleep.'

'I have reason to be unreasonable.'

She gets up and stretches and tilts her head from side to side. He reaches for her hand but misses as she moves past him.

'Oh Jo, wait, you looked so beautiful in the firelight – '

'Ah give over, Jim. I'm weary and I need to relieve myself.'

That night as she lies in bed unable to sleep, Jo realises that she had felt spied on when she woke and found Jim drawing her. Not until their equilibrium is disturbed does she notice how much her generosity depends on it. She can hear a horse and carriage slowly passing the house and a dog barking further down the street. It sounds like a big, under-exercised dog. Its bark would probably suit several of the restless, solitary humans hearing it. Jim's hand rests on her hipbone. She listens to the even pattern of his sleeping breath. She thinks of how she usually loves to pose for him, revels in the concentrated remoteness with its flashes of tenderness that seem to encompass them both. This evening was different – she was in her own world and he in his. It reminded her of being in the studio in Rathbone Place. It felt like a job. Their floating world of intense awareness of the precious moment has capsized. The night feels vast and friendless. Anxiety leadens her stomach as she tosses and turns. She is lonely and sinking.

With Alphonse living with them, it is as if she is the mother of two sons. Jim regresses to the brotherly pranks he played on Willie, and Alphonse looks at her guiltily when she bends to pick up some item he has dropped on the floor. He has reverted to the moody scowl of his London persona and Jo spends her afternoons with Fanny, happy to be back in her vivacious company. They take the tuppenny pleasure boat up the Thames or ride the horse tram along Victoria Street with Jo entertaining her with tales of Paris.

They are window-shopping in Chelsea when Fanny tells her that Gabriel is so melancholy about the lack of critical attention his work has received that he cannot sleep and Doctor Linden has prescribed chloral. Now, she says, he sleeps like a rock but still wakens with crushing melancholia.

'Sometimes he's so still I think he's dead and I prod him to hear a human sound from my pet rock. Oh it was fascinating at first – a kind of study: how does he think and see the world from a rock's viewpoint and how can I enthuse or distract an igneous specimen? But day after day, it loses its intrigue, I promise you. I want to ruddy shake him.'

'Perhaps it's hypochondria. Give him a spare diet and cold water baths.'

'The English Malady, they used to call it, it was so common.'

'The Male Malady, more like. We ladies are meant to be gay and exist to bring joy to men. We have no time for hypochondria, we get hysteria instead.'

Fanny smiles and takes Jo's arm as they walk down Kensington High Street. 'Well, London looks more charming and less hysterical when you're in it, me old flower.'

Jo laughs and loosens her velvet mantle to let in the cool breeze.

'And no word from Jim's mother yet?' Fanny asks.

'No, and let's pray she's found a new quack or a new cure and will cancel.'

In mid-October, Fanny and Gabriel come to dinner at Lindsey Row. Fantin has arrived unexpectedly from Paris. Jo and Jim have saved some French olives and pâté and cook chestnut-stuffed pork, with charlotte potatoes and creamed spinach and a chocolate and rum tart for dessert. Jim paints a huge peacock on the white tablecloth and writes everyone's place names on it. Mister Glowering comes down from his room with paint on his hands and stained clothes and barely speaks. Jo wants to ignore him but finds herself trying to include him and coax him to talk

133

about his latest painting. Fantin has met a new woman and is smitten. He is wearing a smart thrush-egg-blue waistcoat and necktie that she must have bought for him. Love and her money have made him flush and boyish and giggling. He produces a bottle of champagne. Jim is in exuberant form. He pours them all a glass and invites them to his studio where he has spread red rose petals over the floor to set off the canvas. It is another rich and colourful painting using the oriental theme, with Jo posing in a kimono and looking through watercolour prints of far-off landscapes.

'It's delightful! There is weight and form in the black and dancing lightness in the gold. Marvellous,' Gabriel says.

'Thank you.'

'A caprice.'

'How do you mean, Gabriel?' Jim's tone is wary.

'From *capriccio* meaning whim. It's bright and airy and yet her desire is sad. She's stranded between here and elsewhere – it's such a perfect metaphor for us.'

'*Caprice in Silver and Gold,*' Fantin says grandly.

'I like that,' Jo says.

Alphonse stays at the door. 'She's surrounded herself with objects from a world that is not her own and she is lost to both.' Jo notices that he is staring at her and not the canvas.

'It's a sanctuary and a prison,' Gabriel adds.

Jo has never looked at it this way and the words ring in her ears.

'Looks like a pretty prison to me.' Fanny laughs. 'You ever been down to Wandsworth?'

'Not at all, chaps. She's simply a beautiful woman surrendering to beauty,' Jim says.

'Is she surrendering though?' asks Alphonse. 'Sometimes the muse gets in the way of the necessary triangle of artist, painting and spectator.'

Jo tenses. 'With Jim, I always feel as if I were the painting already.'

'And the muse is also the spectator, the first spectator after all,' Jim says.

'Come on, Jim, you know we never paint for our muses, we paint for ourselves.'

Alphonse blocks the doorway as Jo tries to pass to go downstairs.

'Excuse me, Alphonse.'

'Oh, excuse *me*,' he says, moving slowly and deliberately.

Gabriel seems shaky and withdrawn when they first take their seats at the table, but as the evening progresses, he relaxes and becomes more voluble. The dark rings under his eyes emphasise their wide intensity. He says he is ravenous and explains that he became so absorbed in work that he forgot to eat again. Jo serves him a large portion. Jim asks what he is working on, but Gabriel explains that if he discusses it at all, its magic spell will dissipate, vanish as fleetingly as it came.

'Oh, he's become much more superstitious,' Fanny tells them.

'When I can't paint, there is sheer emptiness,' Gabriel continues. 'Then I say to myself, "It's over, so what have I got to lose? I'm not a painter." And then slowly I start something new.'

Jo notices that Gabriel's thin broad hands have a slight tremor. How can someone so accomplished still have such doubts?

'I hope and pray he'll be less mopey, now,' Fanny says.

'I'm always a curmudgeon when I'm not painting. Then it arrives and I enter a kind of a trance and it's almost effortless. I'm Janus himself – the two-faced god.'

'But why doesn't starting to paint get easier?' Jo asks.

'Each time it's the same blank canvas. There's nothing harder than the first mark.' Jim fills up each of their wine glasses.

'It requires persistence,' Alphonse says. 'I'm against the notion of magic.' He rubs at the paint stains on his index finger. 'It's hard grind.'

'Of course,' Gabriel says. 'Sometimes I take years to finish a painting.'

'And how do you know when it's complete, Gabriel?' Jo asks.

'When I look at it and see someone else's work looking back at me as if from another dimension.'

Jo considers the drawings she was happy with and all the others she discarded or simply gave away. How could she learn not only to trust the process but to value the end product?

'I know it's finished when I look at it and can't stand the sight of the blessed thing a moment longer.' Alphonse answers her as if she has addressed him. He holds her gaze. She looks away and when she looks back, he empties his champagne glass and lights a cigarette. His foot is tapping with nervous energy.

The men help to clear the table and then go out into the garden.

'Why don't you have a maid?' Fanny asks as they wash and dry the dishes.

'Money is tight and we need to rent the room.'

Jo likes this time they have alone, likes the rhythm of their hands as each piece of crockery passes between them. She can smell the white rose musk of Fanny's perfume.

'And how is it with Alphonse staying here?' Fanny slides a plate onto the stack in the tallboy.

'Jim likes the company. They're both up painting half the night. They compete with each other to see who can endure the longest.'

'And not just about painting.' Fanny gives her one of her shrewd looks.

'What do you mean?'

'Isn't it as clear as day? Alphonse is jealous.'

'Of Jim's work?'

'Of Jim's lover.'

'You're having me on. He's an old friend.'

'Why the hangdog expression?'

'He's always like that. Mister Glowering, I call him.'

Fanny laughs and murmurs, 'Of course, I could be jealous of Jim too.'

136

Jo pretends she does not hear her and starts to prepare a tray of glasses and Calvados to take outside. She is aware of Fanny's eyes appraising her body as she walks ahead and a sweet tension builds at her nape that a simple touch could ease away.

It is a dank, chilly November morning. Jo goes out to buy groceries and watches the sun rise and filter through the fog, making it look solid, like heavy white muslin. The last yellowed leaves shine on the dark branches overhead. The pavements are stencilled with fallen plane leaves, their leathery faces flattened along the gutters. It is still easy to breathe. Children exhale their steamy breath into the cold air and wave invisible cigarettes at passers-by. They kick through the leaf litter as the coal smoke begins to grey the fog into old boiled bone soup – greasy, heavy and murder to inhale.

Jim is still waiting for a letter from his mother announcing her arrival date and Jo hates the limbo and hates pretending that it does not exist. Jim pretends too, involved with his work with renewed vigour as if his time is running out.

Jo rattles out the ashes and shovels more coal into the range. She finds the jar of barley in the pantry and begins to prepare vegetable broth for lunch. Alphonse comes in and stands at the sink and then, to her surprise, offers to help. She hands him the peeler and a bunch of carrots. Since Fanny's comment, she has been self-conscious around him, catching him looking away, his cave eyes troubled, his hands fidgety. He has not paid his rent in weeks and Jo assumed that his nervousness was caused by his dire financial straits. Perhaps he is willing to lend a hand now because he knows Jim is supporting him. She slices open an onion and peels off the papery skin. Her eyes smart.

'You'd better have a word with Jim,' she says.

He gives her a suspicious look and then softens.

'Are you crying, Jo?' His voice is the gentlest she has ever heard it.

She wipes her eyes on her apron.

'It's the onions.'

'Jim told me that his mother is coming and that you'll be moving out. Where will you go?'

'To my father in Calthorpe Street.' She does not want to talk about it. She has barely discussed it with Jim.

'I could find us somewhere – '

Jo can tell that he is trying to sound offhand. A terrible vision of being homeless, scrabbling on the streets, looms up with a sharp wave of fear.

He opens his palm towards her and takes a step closer.

It occurs to her that there is an emptiness like no other when you cannot return someone's affection. Her throat is arid. How dare Mister Glowering betray his best friend and imagine she would betray him. She lays both palms flat on the counter and looks at him directly.

'We need this month's rent. It's difficult enough as it is and we can't afford to keep you.'

Alphonse winces briefly, runs his hand down his beard. He gives the hem of his waistcoat a habitual tug as if his clothes restrained his body, and his emotions overwhelmed him. His voice is cold when he manages to speak.

'I've spoken to Jim. Someone has offered me a job teaching drawing classes at the South Kensington School. It starts next week.'

'Great news.' She brushes one hand off the other and goes back to making the stock. He leaves quietly but his presence still stalks the room.

Jo is sitting at the kitchen table sorting out the bank statements and the bills, working out which creditors she can hold off for a while longer with another letter. The heat from the range is making her drowsy.

Jim bursts into the room shouting, 'He's nothing but a liar and a thief!' He can't stand still.

'Who, Barabbas?'

'Alphonse! He refuses to talk or open the door. I've asked Gabriel to mediate and he's refused. I'm at my wits' end. He's got work and still not a bean.'

138

'Go and see Alexander Ionides. He'll suggest something – a payment plan.'

'He simply must move out. I've told him but he's like a confounded limpet in that room. Tomorrow, he says.'

'And has been saying for two weeks.'

'He's an utter scoundrel and I can't wait to see the back of him, rent or no rent.'

'I'll speak to him.'

Jo opens the door without knocking. Alphonse is still in bed and the air is thick with the smell of sleep, stale smoke and paint fumes. There is an unfinished portrait of William Rossetti, Gabriel's brother, on the easel. He too is dangerously glowering.

'Listen, Alphonse, Jim and I need the room. I'm sorry but we have to ask you to settle up and leave.'

'Fine, Mrs Housekeeper,' he shrugs and turns away from her. 'Your food is lousy anyway.'

'You're leaving today, mister. You're packing up and you're out by noon.' She has her hands planted on her hips. 'No more excuses. Do you hear me?'

There is no answer from beneath the bedding.

'If you're not gone, I'll tell Jim how you propositioned me.'

He sits up slowly and his eyes narrow. 'I'll tell him you accepted.'

'Get out!' She screams and begins to grab his piles of clothes and throw them towards his trunk. 'You cad! Get out of our house!'

'"Our house"? You may act like the lady of the house but you're not and never will be. Jim's said he's as good as done with you.'

Jo cannot stop herself. She flies at him and slaps him about the face. Alphonse grabs her wrists and tries to pull her to him. She juts her knee into his groin and he lets go.

'You callow little shit,' she says as she leaves the room.

It takes Jo a while to restore the balance with Jim after Alphonse leaves. She watches for signs that it is over between them. The

139

upset and the impending arrival of Jim's mother at the beginning of December have caused a restlessness to coil through the house. Her life is filled with closing doors, stranding her on the outside. She comes to realise that part of her fury with Alphonse was diverted from its true target: Mrs Anna Whistler.

Jim redecorates Alphonse's room for his mother, choosing a pale lavender-white, the colour of phlox. He buys a dressing table they cannot afford and paints a frieze of fleur-de-lys along each wall. He continues to wreck her prudent budgeting. He throws out stale bread she had saved to make bread and butter pudding and leaves candles and lamps burning when he has left the room. He appears with boatmen he has met down on the river and offers them the most expensive wine. As if to keep up with Gabriel, he keeps acquiring Japanese porcelain, until she wonders if there is comfort in collecting things to create an illusion of plenty around him. Perhaps it makes him feel that his home is a museum and therefore he too becomes collectible, of worth. They bicker and argue and she shows him the books to no avail. It reminds her of Dante's Circle IV of *The Inferno* where the hoarders and the wasters are attached to huge boulder-like weights and charge at each other, flinging the weights. Then they separate and drag the weights back, only to begin all over again. One group keeps shouting, 'Why do you waste?' while the other cries, 'Why do you hoard?' Once it struck her that they were quarrelling to make it simpler for her to leave, as if it was a decision based on their own relationship. But knowing this does not make it any easier.

By the time of Mrs Whistler's arrival, the whole house has been spring-cleaned and Jo's nerves are frayed. Jim orders a cab to take Jo and her trunks back to Clerkenwell. She looks out on the back garden as if for the last time. It has died back, with only a few wan leaves hanging on to the branches of the sycamore and frost-damaged geraniums that she should have brought indoors. In his guilt and defensiveness Jim tries to press some of his favourite porcelain on her. She refuses to take it.

'It's just a bribe to keep me sweet.'

'Nothing is changed between us – just the domestic arrangements.' His hands flap like trapped birds.

'Oh Jim, you're so naive. I'll have to make an appointment to see you and only when your mother isn't here.'

'Nonsense. Let her settle in and come for tea and meet her the day after tomorrow.'

'You see,' Jo sighs. 'You've already decided what would be best.'

'Look Jo, I've no idea how poorly she is. And she's been on that wretched transatlantic ship for days.' His voice starts to crack and his brow is knitted in a permanent frown. 'I'm trying my darnedest to accommodate both of you.'

'It's not something you're particularly practised in.'

'Thank you.'

'For nothing.'

She picks up a duster that is lying on the windowsill and absent-mindedly dusts it. Then she catches herself and flings it to the floor and begins to cry.

'Alphonse was right.'

'About what?'

'He said you're as good as done with me.'

'He's wrong. Jo, look at me. I'm done with him, for certain. He blames you.'

'We're not just figures in a canvas that you can move around as it suits you. Oh, I'll just shunt that one offside under a layer of misty backdrop.'

He takes her in his arms and mutters, 'I'm sorry, *ma puce*, truly sorry. I hate to see you this distressed. We'll resolve it somehow. I love you.'

'Love has never been the problem. It's all the things you put before it.'

The hallway smells of over-brewed tea and bitter marmalade. Patrick Hiffernan welcomes Jim with his usual bonhomie and invites him to come in for a nip of whiskey. He asks after Jim's mother and tells him they are both more than welcome to call at any time but Jo can see that he is quietly seething. He makes too big a show of lifting Jo's trunks out of the way and then rubs his hands together and cannot stand still. Jo has the odd sensation of time reversing as they sit and sip their drinks in the parlour. Her father tells an old joke they have all heard before. Jim laughs awkwardly, keeps covering his mouth, shifting his sleeves up his arms and pulling them down again. This time Jim is asking her father to take her back. When he leaves, loneliness writhes and tightens into nausea in her belly.

She goes upstairs. The room she used to share with Bridget is dark, cluttered with knick-knacks she can no longer stand, and doilies spread on the surfaces of the cheap veneered furniture covered in chipped lacquer. Mary, the maid, comes to ask if she needs help to unpack. Jo thanks her with an ironic smile. Mary is a plump girl with a red face and black short hair. She has a thick Dublin accent and keeps wiping the corners of her mouth with her finger and thumb. When she admires a silk scarf, Jo offers it to her.

'Thank you so much, ma'am...I mean, miss.' Her eyes light up, a smile transforming her whole face, and then she tucks the scarf into her apron as though it would be best forgotten.

'Don't mention it.' Jo passes her a pale pink dress Jim bought her in Paris. 'Wearing this is like being next to the skin of a newborn baby.'

'It's beautiful.'

'Does my father treat you well, Mary?'

'Oh yes, miss.'

'Good. He's used to women who stand up for themselves so don't be afraid to.'

'I wouldn't dream of being rude to Mr Hiffernan.'

'I'm sure that you won't have cause to be.'

'God willing.'

'"D.V." as my mother used to say. *Deo volente.*'

As she leaves, Mary says, *'Carpe diem* is Latin for time is running out. Me da would say that every night before he took himself down the pub.'

142

Jo sits at the window and watches the sky darken. Dusk has already fallen at half past three in the afternoon. *Amo, amas, amat...* The rote rackets through her brain. *I love, you love, he, she, it loves...* The rain begins to fall, darkening the road, the pavements and spotting the hats and clothes of the people hurrying home, their heads bent. It falls in large isolated drops at first, more like a summer rain, and then in a persistent grey blurring sheet. Jo begins to dream-walk through the house at Lindsey Row, through the narrow hallway to the front room and then to the kitchen, up the staircase, across the landing into the bedrooms. She dreams each room, each doorway, every window and every painting like some kind of ghost that is not ready to leave its earthly habitat.

There is a faint knock at the door. She calls, 'Come in', and her father comes and stands behind her, placing his hands on her shoulders. He sighs and whispers, 'Ah now, you must feel caught between two ditches, Jo, but you'll be all right, my girl. If anyone will be all right, it's you.' Her body starts to relax under his touch. 'Do you know there is a certain plant that thrives in the fissures you find in rocks? Saxifrage, it's called. You'd not believe the variety of colours it can draw from the most inhospitable places.' He strokes her hair and then rests his hand on the crown of her head. 'One day I'll take you to the Burren in County Clare where in amongst the big slabs of limestone grow wildflowers you'll find nowhere else. Someone should draw them, document them.'

She knows what he is hinting at. 'Thank you.'

'And you'd love the way the rock pavements blacken when it rains. Then they dry off and turn almost white again.' He takes a breath and says on the exhale, 'Ah, daughter, it's a sight to be seen.'

She is quiet.

'Why don't we take a charabanc up to Hampstead tomorrow and enjoy a Sunday stroll on the heath? London's spread out and up a lot since you've been up there atop Parliament Hill.'

'Early. Let's go first thing – "when all that mighty heart is lying still".'

143

'After Mass.'

'What? You're back at Mass?'

'Since your mother died. I know I always said I'd had a bellyful of the priests but I can talk to her there. The sounds and scents give me comfort. Ah, sure the sea and the smell of turf would do just as well, but failing that – the organ music and the incense do rightly.'

'Why did you and Mam never go back to Ireland?'

'Too much emptiness, Jo. Who are you when the people who knew your name and your father's name are no more? I've never been one for visiting ruins. Mind you, there's one old friend, Molly's her name, who I would care to see again.'

'Let's go, you and me.'

He speaks on his in-breath, 'Yes. One day, we might. I wonder if she's still on the go. Molly Walsh.'

The furniture has been rearranged at Lindsey Row. The settee has been pushed closer to the fireplace and the two armchairs repositioned to face a wall instead of the windows. Mrs Whistler is ensconced in one of the armchairs, happed up in a tartan rug. She has a thin, oval face and greying hair pulled back into a severe knot, made more severe by her black wool shawl and black dress ringed with a white lace collar. Jo immediately regrets having chosen a silver and pink striped dress; she is over-lit, gaudy even.

'Mother, this is Joanna Hiffernan, my model and inspiration.'

'Very pleased to meet you, ma'am.' Jo reaches to take her hand, but Mrs Whistler does not extend hers. Jo is unsure whether it is an affront, a different custom or she is merely petrified of germs.

'Oh yes, that's a good likeness, Jemie.' She points to the Wapping painting on the wall above the mantelpiece. 'It looks like some sort of nefarious doings with those fellows. Why is she so sullen?'

Jo studies her hands, thankful that Jim had finally decided to paint over her exceptionally low décolletage in the portrait.

'I'm still recovering from being tossed on the endless swell.'

'I don't believe she has found her land-legs yet.' Jim tries to apologise for the slight.

'I never lost them, Jemie. That's why I suffered so.'

'Shall I prepare the tea, Jim?' Jo asks.

'Oh, the maid's preparing tea. Louisa!' she hollers towards the kitchen and a young girl appears. She is pretty, with strawberry blond hair, a fair complexion and playful, alert blue eyes.

'Yes, ma'am?' Her voice is slightly cheeky and her lips twitch as if she is suppressing a giggle.

'We ordered tea and scones and cake for three.' Mrs Whistler's head jerks when she speaks and her voice seems to strut about the room. She reminds Jo of a Trafalgar Square pigeon.

'Can I help?' Jo starts to get up.

'Absolutely not, Joanna. You don't know where anything is and besides it's the girl's job. She claims she's fifteen and has worked before – where was it?'

'The Old Brompton Road,' Jim says.

'Jemie tells me it's a highly reputable address.'

Jo is still smarting from the maid's invasion of her territory and refuses to look at Jim. Her jaw tightens as heat spreads up her neck.

'How do you find London, Mrs Whistler?' she says with forced enthusiasm.

'Jemie's been wonderful. He's got this place fixed up so nice and he has delightful friends. The Rossettis visited this morning. They're so elegant and well spoken. Gabriel's a published poet.'

'Jo writes poetry,' Jim says after a pause.

'Published?' Jim's mother addresses him.

'Not yet,' Jim says. 'I keep urging her to send them out.'

'It's so competitive these days,' Jo says.

'Life is competitive. I thought I'd be crushed underfoot getting off that infernal boat. I had to fight for air.' Mrs Whistler fans herself with a black lace fan.

'They say it's the cruel part of evolution, isn't it?' Jo says.

'Oh my dear, I do hope you have not been taken in by that nincompoop Darwin.' Mrs Whistler brings out a handkerchief and blows her nose. 'He will retract everything, I suspect, on his death bed. Most of them do.'

Jo thinks if the atmosphere grew any more chilly there would be frost forming on the inside of the windowpanes and a hoar creeping across the floor. She thinks of a Li Po poem she read the day before where the moonlight falls like frost on his bed and makes him homesick.

She looks at Jim. He has been taken over by a meek, subdued boy with his tiny black boots caught in his mother's web.

Louisa brings in a well-laid tray, her movements exaggerated and self-conscious as if she is auditioning for a part. Jim serves his mother with a solicitude verging on the obsequious. He even stirs the sugar lump in her teacup.

'Thank you, my darling. You are too good to me,' she drawls.

Jo stiffens. She is unaccustomed to experiencing jealousy around Jim – yes, he flirts with handsome women, but his attention has always returned to her.

'Mother saw Doctor Linden yesterday and was quite impressed,' Jim begins. 'He has prescribed a change of diet to help with the chronic intestinal disorder and more exercise to ease the high blood pressure.'

'Jemie, can I request that you refrain from discussing my ailments with all and sundry. You are like Uncle Wesley. It is a family matter.'

Jo sips her tea and is not hungry but takes a slice of Victoria sponge. She can barely contain herself in her effort to look dainty and a crumb gets caught in her windpipe. She begins to cough and splutter and then choke, her chest convulsing. Jim comes to slap her on the back and it releases. Her eyes are wet and she draws a handkerchief from her purse to dab them. Jim looks at her with alarm. He is signalling something with his eyes that she cannot grasp. His mother has protectively covered her mouth and a look of disdain pinches her face as she notices the handkerchief: embroidered on the corner in bright blue

146

thread is the butterfly monogram of Jim's initials. Jo fumbles it out of sight.

Louisa comes in to light the lamps and Jo watches Jim's eyes follow her around the room. He will not meet her gaze. She is cut adrift, hovering outside the group in the room, watching from afar, growing smaller and further away.

A strange greenish purple glow fills the sky as Jo leaves Lindsey Row. Who said that there is never green in the sky? The air is biting and metallic. It is hardly four o'clock and the afternoon is already slipping towards dusk. She draws her muff closer to her body. She stands for a moment on the pavement and decides that she needs to talk to Fanny. She wants to find a way to laugh about the situation, reduce it to something light and pliable, instead of this heavy, intractable burden. Lamps in the windows throw out a tender, yellow light and something in watching their glow from the outside makes her recall a dream that she had the night before. She was sleeping rough on a couple of chairs out in the street, her belongings packed in boxes around her. She wondered why nothing was being stolen and she was cold. Suddenly Jim's name came to her like a light, a bit of warmth and it occurred to her that she could go to him, she could go home. *Jim! Of course.* She felt unbelievable joy and relief. How could she have forgotten him, her home? What on earth was she doing sleeping outside? As she stood up to go back to him, she awoke and a dull surge of despair passed over her. Back in her single bed, her girl's bed, she had never felt so evicted and alone.

As she walks to Tudor Lodge, a flurry of snow begins to flutter around her. She quickens her step. Already she can imagine Fanny's warm, perfumed embrace, her laughter at Jim's dependency on mammy's approval and her mimicking of Mrs Whistler's nasal east coast twang. *'The Lord God above has guided me to my Jemie's side...'* She rings the doorbell and Agnes, the maid, answers. Both Mr Rossetti and Miss Cornforth are not at home. Would ma'am care to wait? Jo does not. She watches the snowflakes sink into her wool coat as she queues for the omnibus. Some flakes land on her cheek. She misses Jim's touch.

He has promised to come and see her between two and four the following afternoon when his mother takes her nap. It is as she feared. He is late and she is waiting. It is intolerable. The snow did not lie and overnight rain has washed away all but a trace of dirty sludge in the gutters. She has started weighing out the ingredients for an apple tart when he arrives, out of breath, apologetic. She wipes the flour from her hands, removes her pinafore and they go upstairs to her bedroom. He laughs that it is like wooing that sweet seventeen-year-old all over again. She fails to laugh. They are shy with each other. She sits on the bed, he on the stool of the dressing table with its cheap satin cover. She notices that the floor rug is threadbare at the spot under his feet, worn by two sisters brushing their hair, comparing their faces, their complexions, putting on face cream and dreaming of dazzlingly handsome swells. She clasps her hands in her lap. It feels like an interview but neither of them is sure who is the interviewer and what is the job. He has read her mind.

'So Miss Hiffernan, tell me about yourself.'

'Oh, I'm an ordinary girl in extraordinary times.'

'Or the reverse perhaps.' He throws her a quizzical, flirtatious look. 'Haven't we met before?'

'Not that I recall.'

'But I recall, I assure you.'

Jo pretends to study her fingernails, the pale crescents above the cuticles. 'Of course, I have so many gentlemen callers – '

'Oh don't say that, Jo. It kills me.'

'It's a game!'

'I hate to be apart from you.'

'And pray, may I ask what are you going to do about it?'

'I can rent you a room nearer to me.'

'I see.'

'Can I kiss you? Your mouth has never looked so gorgeous.'

'Why, sir, aren't you a tad hasty?' she says but she leans back on her elbows onto the eiderdown and lowers her face, still holding his gaze. 'But then again,' she teases. 'I must say that my lips are rather bored with each other.'

He laughs and comes to her. They roll back together and he pulls her deeper into a kiss. She has to hush him. She has heard her father come in downstairs. They have sex with their clothes on, rocking timidly on the single bed.

As she lies in his arms, she whispers, 'An ancient poet once said, "Let the beauty we love be what we do." I needed that, Jim.' She is reconnected and relaxed as if all the disparate parts have become whole again.

But once he leaves, she realises that they did not talk and sadness jolts through her. It will not do to meet for an adolescent thrill whenever it suits him, here or in some rented room in Fulham. For the first time since they met she senses the awful encumbrance of being a mistress. She feels kept.

She can hear carol singers in the street below. *'Deck the halls with boughs of holly, fa la la la la, la la la la...'* It is an ugly, frilly sound. What will she do for Christmas? One thing is for sure, she thinks, she will not be among the guests invited to Lindsey Row.

With January comes heavy snow. Jim is full of talk of the frozen gardens of the Pavloski and skating along the Nevsky as a boy. He boasts that at ten years old, he was by far the youngest pupil at the Imperial Academy and came first in a class of forty. He sounds cross that there has not been a proper ice storm that would freeze the Thames itself and then they could visit the Frost Fair and skate all the way to Greenwich on a curving white road. After her sitting, they go out for lunch to the Ship and Turtle tavern on Leadenhall Street, famous for its cellar swimming with live turtles. They find seats by the fire and unwrap their woollen layers, their faces shining pinkly from the cold. Jim rubs his hands together. They order turtle and hot punch. These days, Jim is only happy when he is out of the house. Since his mother arrived he has become morose and fed up about his work, has begun to doubt the direction his last two portraits have taken – it seems that too few people care

149

for the oriental theme or his endeavour to create an immediate sensation of colour rather than a 'story'. His attempts to make painting as close as possible to music are not understood. Critics have merely mocked his use of words like 'symphony' and 'harmony' as pretentious and muddled.

But for Jo, there is a story. She has been posing every morning for the second *Little White Girl,* which she sees as a different kind of sequel. The white shift has been replaced by a full white gown with elaborately laced sleeves. Jo decided to rest her arm on the mantelpiece to draw attention to a visible wedding ring and stare away from the room into a mirror on the wall and a future the young woman does not want. She holds an oriental fan listlessly in one hand as if the luxurious furnishings and ornaments cannot fulfil her. Her face has a look of forlorn resignation and Jim has painted it and re-painted it again as if to fathom what lies beneath Jo's expression. She cannot believe how much older she looks, even though the first *White Girl* was painted only two years ago.

There had been several days when she was snowed into the house in Clerkenwell and few vehicles could navigate the streets. When she returned to Jim's studio, she was tidying up his table and came across three sketches of Louisa's face, hidden under a pile of etchings done in Paris. A shot of indignant jealousy fired through her. She said nothing but later watched the maid carefully as she served lunch. Louisa had made cream of cauliflower soup and as she ladled it into Jim's bowl, the soup slopped over the rim. Louisa was apologetic and embarrassed and Jim murmured it was nothing and touched her arm with a quick reassuring gesture. Nothing in the air changed. Jim caught Jo's eye. Jo moved a strand of hair away from her face. Is this the way love is lost, she wondered, with the smallest gesture, almost unseen? Jim seemed distracted, as though he was still working out some problem on the canvas, his gaze inner and blank.

A bluebottle was buzzing in the room, pinging against the windows. It seemed to carry and amplify the discomfiting silence that lay between them, each of them trying not to slurp their soup. Finally, Mrs Whistler rustled and rearranged her grey moiré skirt with a brisk tug and then rolled up *The Times* and asked Louisa to swat the fly. The poor girl spent the next ten minutes flitting about the room whacking at it with immense and breathy effort and absolutely no success. Each time the paper landed, Mrs Whistler put her hands over her ears and jumped as though she herself had been struck. Then Jim shouted, 'Enough!' He marched over and took the newspaper firmly from her hand. Louisa barely glanced at him, looked lost for a moment and then went back into the kitchen. Was her briefest of glances appropriate or restrained? Jo could not tell. Her behaviour towards Jo seemed unaltered but she no longer showed the plucky defiance of a beginner. Something in her had been quelled.

Jo hardly spoke during these lunches and let Jim and his mother exchange their particular combination of remarks that had accrued over the years and she did not know how to decode. Jim would occasionally translate a family reference for her, but often that seemed too intimate and so he withdrew from trying to include her. Jo could see his struggle with loyalties, with his mother's excessive formality and Puritanism, and also how in the end he seemed to capitulate rather than challenge her. As she vanished from view, Jo began to see a different Jim from the man she loved and felt a streak of sad reckoning: how right she had been to never marry. Was this current portrait the last he would paint of her?

Jo goes on sitting for *The White Girl, No. 2* through the spring and persuades Algernon to write a poem inspired by it. He composes 'Before the Mirror: Verses Written Under a Picture', on gold leaf which Jim can paste on to the frame of the painting. Everyone loves it.

'"She sees by formless gleams" is my favourite line,' Jo says, kissing Algernon's cheek.

'Thank you, my darling. You're my favourite line. There would be no painting without you. And no poem.'

151

'If only they'd see,' Jim says, pouring Algernon a Scotch, 'that the other arts need painting just as much as painting needs them.'

'That's what I've been writing about till I'm blue in the face. Music, poetry, painting – they're all interconnected in a new aestheticism. Why must art always be tethered to a moral purpose?'

'Art for art's sake! And we're at the forefront of it, my dear boy,' Jim says.

'Cheers!' They all clink glasses.

Finally, the *Wapping* painting gets accepted by the Academy for the summer show. Jim's confidence soars. Mrs Whistler reads them *The Times*' critic's review as though she wrote it herself: 'Listen, Jemie, "If Velasquez had painted our river, he would have painted it something in this style". God has answered my prayers by leading me here.'

'I thought you found it nefarious and sullen?' Jo wants to say.

Jim takes on a commission to paint a portrait of the Greek Consul-General's daughter through their friend and patron Alex Ionides. Christine Spartali comes armed with her sister as chaperone and faints twice during the lengthy sessions. Jim tells Jo that his mother keeps rushing in with specially imported American canned apricots and fresh cream to revive her.

Their high spirits are marred later in July when Jim comes back with the newspaper one morning and reads out the headline: 'Great slaughter: rebels' retreat cut off'. There has been a massive battle at Gettysburg in Pennsylvania, with the largest losses yet in the Civil War. He cannot settle to work. He sits down to write to his brother at once. His mother is beside herself and takes to her bed. The headlines get worse and the information is unreliable. Finally the news comes that battle has lasted for three days with over 51,000 casualties. Is Willie still alive? Only one of his letters had ever got through the Northern blockade. Soon it becomes clear that Gettysburg is the turning point in the war with a decisive victory for the Union. Jim goes in vain to the

American Embassy to demand more information and comes to visit Jo in Calthorpe Street in a stinking temper. His mother is convinced that Willie is dead and keeps urging Jim to go home and find his body. He is restless and angry and will not relax enough to come to bed with her. The portrait remains unfinished.

It is a glorious summer's day. Jo has arranged to meet Fanny and visit the nearby Cremorne Gardens for the afternoon. It is one shilling admission to the pleasure garden and they rendezvous under the huge, pagoda-shaped bandstand. They stroll around the Venus fountain and toss in a ha'penny and make a wish – Jo, to return to Paris, and Fanny, to lose a stone so that she can fit into last summer's dresses. A couple of older, well-heeled men eye them up and down and follow them for a while. They ignore them studiously from behind their parasols and manage to lose them in the crowd that has gathered to watch the launch of a hot air balloon. Four people are clinging to the edges of the wicker basket. As the mooring ropes are untied, a great whoosh of air sends the balloon up above them. Everyone lets out a cheer and men toss their hats up after it.

'If only we could fly up and away and land somewhere else, like Constantinople,' Jo says, her head tilting back to follow the balloon's ascent.

'And take a stroll around the jewellery souks and spice medinas and come back tomorrow.'

'Or never come back. I'd like to paint the Levantine women.'

'Why? They're just like us under all that toggery.'

'Oh, I hope not. I want to become more like them. Mysterious.'

They watch as several boats dock at the pier and a party of glamorously dressed swells disembark. They include a young girl who has been crying and has covered her ears with her hands. She has long, dark, curly hair and large, unhappy, hazel eyes rimmed in red. She is dragging her feet and refuses to remove her hands, even though her mother tugs severely at her wrists.

'Why can't the girl block out the world for a while?' Jo wonders aloud. 'She looks like a child in a Goya painting with her big swollen eyes.'

'Yes, they already hold a lifetime of stories. Eerie, if you ask me. You can see the wisdom in some children's eyes as if they've been here before.'

'Then they lose it.'

Jo regrets that she has not brought her sketchbook and realises that she could run back to Jim's studio and find one. She tells Fanny she will meet her in less than ten minutes at the marionette theatre.

'And don't speak to any strange men,' Jo winks and calls over her shoulder as she leaves.

The house is quiet. As Jo thought, Jim's mother is in her bedroom or what Jim calls her 'withdrawing room', having an afternoon nap. She tiptoes upstairs to Jim's studio. She opens the door to find Jim in front of his easel and Louisa, standing beside a washstand, in the middle of the room, stark naked. The girl gives an astonished shriek and reaches for her apron to cover herself. Jim raises his arms in a gesture of surrender and steps back. His face reflects the alarm in Jo's.

'Wait now, Jo... I... we...' He puts down his palette and paintbrush and moves towards her.

'What in God's name is going on here?' she shouts.

She looks from Jim to the painting. She can see at a glance that it is more than one afternoon's work. The girl's slender body looks like a child's. She can feel herself blanch as a chill of light-headedness travels through her.

'Don't waken mother, Jo, please. This is nothing. I just...'

'Don't waken mother! I'll waken the whole of bloody Chelsea. How dare you, Jim! I don't know how you dare.'

Louisa has bundled up her clothes and is edging towards the door, her face and neck crimson. Jo marches over to Jim's desk and snatches up a large etching of the Ile de la Cité and rips it in two. She scatters others to the floor, stamps her feet on them.

Her body is on fire, her head thumping. Jim comes and tries to restrain her.

'Stop, Jo.'

As she swings out of his grasp, her limbs start to shake. Louisa has vanished. Jo tries to get at the painting, but Jim blocks her. She aims a punch beyond him and hits the canvas. She pushes against him and they wrestle, advance and turn, fastened, getting nowhere.

'You know what you've done. It's not nothing, Jim. You bastard. It's everything.' She is yelling at the top of her lungs. 'She's a child. Barely fifteen. You've touched her, haven't you?'

Jim releases her and goes to shut the door. His face is ashen. 'Jo, stop it, please, let's talk about this quietly. When you've calmed down. I'm sorry, darling, listen – '

'Don't damn hush me. The one thing I wouldn't give you, you've taken from someone else.' She does not know where to turn. Her fists are flexing. She wants to beat on his chest, get at his heart. His weak little heart.

'Answer me, Jim.'

'It means nothing, Jo. *Rien du tout.*'

'To you.'

'It's for the painting. You have to understand. I needed – '

'Oh you got you a maid all right. And what did I get? So much for that promise.'

She makes a lunge for the fattest paintbrush and before he can prevent her, she dashes it across the palette and swipes a mix of colour down the length of the portrait.

'There. That improves it.'

The door opens and Jim's mother appears wearing her pink bed-jacket, her face flushed with sleep.

'What's all this commotion, dear?'

'It's all right, mother. Go back to bed.'

'Don't expect me back here. It's finished.'

'Jemie?'

'Enjoy his portrait of the staff,' Jo says as she surges past her. She lifts up her skirts and rushes down the stairs and out of the house.

155

Jo wipes the flashing tears from her face as she strides back to the gardens and through the elegant ironwork gateway. Her body is transparent, a cracked window that is about to shatter, but cannot yet. She digs her fingernails into her palms. She tries to rub away the smear of flesh-coloured paint across her knuckles. She hurries past the amusement stalls and the booths of fortune tellers, seeking out Fanny's royal blue coat and feather-trimmed hat. Everything seems garish, hideous and makeshift now in the late afternoon light. The paintwork is peeling on the stalls and the booth's façades are flimsy. Two children pelt out of the maze screeching and crash headlong into her. She stumbles and almost falls. At last she sees Fanny and waves.

Fanny can see at once how distraught she is. 'My poor darling. Is it Jim?'

Jo nods and lets herself be led back towards the gates. She cannot speak until they are back in Fanny's sitting room in Tudor Lodge. Fanny asks Agnes to bring up some tea. Gabriel has gone out to visit his sister. Once armoured by cushions on Fanny's settee, Jo can let herself sob more openly.

'I'm – I don't know – I'm not even angry with her – it's all Jim's doing. He's a leech.'

Fanny holds her in her arms until she settles. As Fanny pours the tea, Jo goes on, 'I was always willing to pose as long as I was not nude. Of course Jim has made private sketches of me naked but I wanted to keep something back, something personal. I didn't want to be hawked down on Holywell Street. And he agreed.'

'I'm sorry, my sweet flower. The idiot. I know it hurts.'

Jo bites the edge of her index finger. 'If she is his new muse, he won't even look back. I will cease to exist. First his damn mother and now this.'

'This is an infatuation, Jo. It will pass. I'm sure of it, duck.'

'I still love him, I just can't reach him.' Jo warms her hands around the china cup. 'The worst of it is that he's more flawed than I ever thought.'

'He's just more human, I'd say.'

As she studies the small map of tea leaves drawn up the insides of her cup, Jo wonders if her disillusion will pass and if love needs illusion to remain intact. She remembers Jim taking her in his arms only the week before and whispering 'You're spoken for'. Was she spoken for? Did it really mean that he spoke instead of her and her own voice was dwindling to an inaudible hush? Was any recent affection only spurred by his guilt?

'If you ask me, Jim doesn't know what he's doing,' Fanny says. 'He'll have convinced himself that it's all for his art – '

'But that can't excuse everything.'

'It's certainly not a licence to betray others.'

'I've always thought of him as principled. He certainly demands it of everyone else.'

'He's quick to judge all right and also, you know, those kind of people judge themselves the most harshly.'

'But, Fanny, he didn't even look tormented. His main concern was disturbing his blessed mama's nap.'

A fast swell of anger makes Jo feel stronger and more stable. She has to stand up, suddenly, prowl restlessly around the room. 'I can't believe it. Right under his mother's self-righteous, stuck-up nose. I've been an utter dunce. I should never have agreed to move out or cut it off as soon as I did.'

'Love makes us stupid, my dear Jo. I've seen wealthy, successful businessmen throw away marriage, career, family and friends, everything they've built and cherished, for a passing fancy. Don't think you're the first or the most foolish.'

'Oh Fanny, I do adore you.' Jo sits down again and takes Fanny's hand.

'I've been through it all with Gabriel, you know. He goes through phases when he says that he simply has to see Jane Morris. You know, William's wife, Jane. I can tease him now, now I know that he won't leave me. But, I can tell you, I was enraged at first. Consumed by it. Like a ravaging disease, jealousy is. You look for things that aren't there. Every tiny thing becomes evidence of their mark, their influence and your wane. I call her Her Royal Highness but I know exactly where she's come from. Jane's like me, as common as muck.'

Jo laughs and leans in and Fanny kisses her cheek. She realises that she is still too indignant and incredulous to suffer deep jealousy. No doubt, it will come with its corrosive stealth to haunt her at midnight when she finds that she cannot sleep, picturing them together. She looks at her hands and moves her thumbs back and forth over one another. The painting, the nude painting of Louisa. The hours she stood for him. Was she bashful at first? Did he have sex with her and then paint her, or the other way around? The look on Jim's face. The caught boy. The brief expression of shame and then utter entitlement. Whenever she next sees his face, that look will be there.

'Come here, my pet.' Fanny puts her arm around her and Jo relaxes against her. She can feel Fanny's heartbeat through their dresses, hear her breath sharpen. A bright square of sunlight lights up the parquet floor. Jo can smell Fanny's perfume and the warm familiar smell of her hair, her skin. The atmosphere in the room tenses and then seems to soften. Fanny turns to her and kisses her on the lips. Jo lets herself be kissed, her anger riding the edge of excitement, confusing and thrilling at the same time. Then she responds, Fanny's tongue finding hers, the tension in her jaw relaxing, the muddle in her mind vanishing before this lovely, unforeseen focus.

'Only a kiss,' Jo says, the words are as thick as honey.

'Only a kiss,' Fanny answers but they turn their bodies towards each other so that their breasts press together.

Even though Jo closes her eyes, it as though she is looking into a mirror and falling into a world beyond it. Fanny's fingers begin to undo the top buttons of Jo's dress and bodice and she gently touches her breasts.

'Only the breasts,' Fanny whispers.

'Only the breasts,' Jo replies. Her voice rises out of a delicious dream she cannot allow to end just yet.

Fanny. The name is the first thing Jo hears in her head and senses in her body when she wakes up. She plays over what

158

happened the day before, the soft, full lift of Fanny's breasts in her palms and the loud shuddering glory of the cry she gave when Fanny touched her. She stretches down the bed and luxuriates in the heavy pull of want around her groin. They were embarrassed all right. She cannot help smiling when she thinks of their bashful giggling and the secret pride that they had gone further than either of them thought she dared. In full daylight. In Gabriel's house.

'You've a smirk on your face,' Fanny had said.

'I've a smirk on my whole body,' Jo replied.

The name and the image of the girl and the pleasure cannot be divided. She has the sight of Fanny's dark nipples against her pale ones. She was happy and she has no regrets. She gives her breasts a good friendly squeeze. No wonder men want us, she thinks. Is this how a man feels about women? An opening of the hard shell, a streaming of colour, like flags or ribbons from the chest, like pennants from a fortified castle on a mountaintop, and an impossible softness that you realise was there all along and feels like coming home. How she wanted to draw Fanny's body, the expression on her face. She had never wanted to capture something as acutely before and she realised that in trying to capture Fanny's joy she was trying to contain and keep her own alive. She knew deeply and sharply for the first time just what she meant to Jim as a model: that her beauty was also his; her enjoyment his way of saving his own too; that the paintings were his safeguard, the love lived. She had the vague and creeping sense that this knowledge could save her. It had to.

Then she thinks 'Jim'. And with Jim comes Louisa, the image of that girl, the painting of that girl and the flash of rage, all in one overwhelming sensation. She gets a shiver of disgust. Her skinny pale thighs. The blonde, wispy pubic hair. How could she be supplanted by someone so...so insubstantial? It shook everything she thought about herself as a woman, as a good-looking woman. As a prize. She will not be back in Lindsey Row if she can help it. He can darn well forget it. Get lost. Be gone. In a puff of smoke. A whiff of turps. She will sit for Gabriel Rossetti – see how he likes that. Or John

159

Millais. She'll go the whole hog now, why shouldn't she? Do a nude. That'll show him. Frederick Sandys wants to paint her and more. If Jim needs a taste of his own tarnishing medicine, she will give it to him. She will tell her father not to let him over the door if he calls. Let him stew.

Jim does indeed call two days later and Patrick Hiffernan does not invite him in. He goes off with him instead, down to The Crown for a stout and a jar of whelks. She can imagine them having a man-to-man, a tête-à-tête about girls and gripes and peccadilloes where Peter Piper has pecked a pick of pickled pepper when he shouldn't. Jo pictures them, headstrong in commiseration and comfort. Her father tries to coax her round, all sheepish on Jim's behalf but she refuses to answer him. She pounds the kitchen floor irately. She has been belittled and deserted by both of them. But as she seems to stamp out one fire, another erupts and every ache of missing Jim returns.

She wishes she could talk to Fantin. He knew Jim. Would know if this meant the end for her. And if it was? She could not bear to imagine it. But nor could she share him, if that was what he asked.

She waits for a letter that fails to come. Where are the fresh flowers, the violet-scented chocolates, the lyrical entreaties? She remembers Fanny once telling her that we do not know why love comes or why it goes. When does the end start, she wonders. What gesture or remark triggers it and is then parcelled up and ignored until it joins another small insignificant slight and another until there is a chain of unlucky significances strung together: the erased painting from Carnac, the quarrel in Guéthary, the inept way he dealt with his mother's arrival...and now Louisa. Was Fanny right – that it all amounts to checks and balances? Would he cut her out of his life as he had done with so many friends he had fallen foul of? As the anger and hurt abate, she has a hollow dragging sense of impotence, feels like some garment left dangling over a banister. She remembers the lines Algernon wrote on the painting for Jim. The flowers have taken flight in the hard east wind. She has become 'The White Girl' after all.

Then late one evening stones come flying at her windowpane. A whole week later it takes him. She pulls on her dressing gown and swings open the front door. He looks like a dog's dinner, full as a Lord and steadying himself on the doorframe. He skulks and pretends to defend himself from her imaginary blows with his walking cane. She has almost forgotten how short he is. His hat is tilted far back on his head and his tie undone. The lost puppy look that used to melt her heart does nothing but vex her. He begs her to let him in, slurs that there has been a disaster.

He slumps into the sofa and she stands firm with her arms folded.

'I've had a letter from Paris. It's Fantin.'

'What? He's hurt?'

'No, no,' he swallows and looks at her aghast. 'He's been accepted by the Salon.'

'Oh for heaven's sake, Jim! You scared the living daylights out of me. That's wonderful news. He deserves it.'

'It's a masterpiece – *Hommage à Delacroix*. I thought we were both in the lead, spurring each other on. Like in the Derby. Two true thoroughbreds. But he's pulled ahead. I'm through, Jo, finished.' He pushes his hand through his hair and refocuses his eyes. 'I'm on the wrong track.'

'Your pride is wounded – that's all. He got in there first. You will. You're good. You're just a bit slower.'

'I'll never be a painter if I can't bear rejection.'

'You'll never be anything if you can't bear it.'

'Oh Jo, I love you. You're my best girl. Nothing can harm me when you're near.'

'Don't try to peddle your charm, Jim.' Her hand is throbbing from the burn of a baking tray earlier that day.

'I'm begging you, Jo. Please come back. Can't you see I'm nothing without you?'

'You mean your painting is nothing without me. Pull yourself together. You sound like bad Vaudeville lyrics.' She

161

goes to the dresser and pours herself a whiskey and him a tumbler of water. 'You've soiled your own doorstep and you've got to clean it up, Jim.'

She asks herself suddenly if her faithfulness is a failure of will, or grace, or guts? Why should she stay? He reminds her of a rag-and-bone man, heaped with damaged and shoddy words.

'Louisa's gone. She left the next day.' He pulls at his moustache and speaks through his fingers.

'Oh, another unfinished portrait. Let me see... *Symphony in Flesh, number 1: The Servant Girl.*'

'How droll.'

'I'm waiting. I have a right to my self-respect.'

'Not when it becomes hubris.'

The word hits like a slap. 'Don't use words you know I won't understand.'

'Listen Jo, it was wrong. A blind spot.' He spreads out his hands, rubs his thumb around his palm. 'I made love to her once.'

She is a windowpane blown open in the howling windy night. 'In our bed?'

'Why does that matter?'

'If *I* matter, answer me.'

'In the kitchen.'

'Oh, rough up against the sink or over the table?' Like we once did, she wants to add, but she is worried that her voice might crack. Her eyes wander around the room. It is too intense to look at him. There is a patch of damp browning the plaster above the dresser. It is bubbled like overweight buttocks. Did he prefer Louisa's young girl's body, her boy hips, her bud breasts? Was she a virgin? She has a sudden, violent need to hide from him, never show herself to him again.

'I made a mistake. It wasn't what I wanted from her. I can see that now.' He sounds punctured.

'But it was a way to get it. The nude. How did you imagine you were going to show it?'

'Come on, Jo. *S'il te plaît.* Forgive me. I miss you, for crying out loud. I've lost my bearings. Being around mother makes me crazy. I'm a numbskull who wants all the trouble he can get. I want to fight someone, let fly at everyone. Beat their brains out. It's my only infidelity, Jo, I swear on my father's grave. You're all I want, all I ever wanted. Don't you know how much I want you?'

She sits down, rests her chin in her hands. She is quiet and calm. Her voice when it comes hardly resembles her own.

'Hour after hour, day after day, I've stood for you, sat for you, waited for you, been committed to your work. I saw it as ours. The more fool I. Sometimes I feel as if I could be dead, lifeless and you'd keep going regardless because the light was good. And now this. I don't know...' She bites her lip and shakes her head. 'My father used to call it diminishing returns.'

'Oh God, Jo, I'm so sorry.' He looks stricken, sober. 'I didn't realise. I'm too obsessed with my work. You're right. You've already felt forsaken.' He goes down on one knee in front of her, his mouth contrite.

'I hate amateur dramatics, you know.' But he reminds her of herself, many moons ago, kneeling before her mother in the very same room and she almost grins. Grovelling does not suit him.

'What can I do to make you come home?'

'Want me for more than your model or your maid.'

'You have my solemn promise.'

He puts his head in her lap.

She realises as soon as she says it that you cannot command want, nor promise to deliver it. As long as she still sits for him, he will take more than he gives. As he enfolds her in his arms she is bone-white, sad, stiff. They do not kiss. She is gun-shy and worn out. She could not ask for what she really needed: his support for her to paint. The moment to speak it had slipped out of her grasp. She has given up on herself again. She is more like Jim than she has realised. He gave up on the lover who needed to be with Jo and chose his family; Jo has given up the artist she needs for the lover, the muse.

'Can I stay here with you tonight?'

She shrugs. He has made a new choice. She can tell from his eyes that he knows how serious it is.

'I'll be back before she's up.'

The room is dark. She is not ready for him. Her body is hollow, dry. The white girl is bleached and empty as a cockle shell washed up on a strand. Jim is kissing her. She tastes Fanny's mouth. He is whispering in her ear. She hears Fanny's moaning breath. He is caressing her behind with both hands. Fanny's hands are opening her thighs. She imagines she can smell Fanny's perfume. Can he? Is it still in her hair? She is aroused and befuddled.

> *There are three in the bed*
> *and the little one says*
> *Roll over, roll over!*
> *So they all roll over and one falls out;*
> *there were two in the bed*
> *and the little one says*
> *Roll over, roll over!*

They were small children. In their parents' bed on a Sunday morning. All snug and warm. Her father's side smelt woody and faintly greasy; her mother's side of vanilla and cinnamon. They would sing that song and roll over and Jo would topple out of one side of the bed and race around to the other side and climb back in again. Then it was Bridget's turn. Simple family love. She does not know how to exist in its picture. She is either outside it, peering in, or at the window, straining to get out.

Jim's hips are pinning her to the bed. As his fingertips move over her skin, the touch feels blind as if the burn has spread its smooth numbness over every pore of her skin.

'Wait,' she says. 'I want to see you.' She needs to see his expression, know that he knows it is her, not Louisa.

She leans over for the matches and he lights a candle.

'There you are, my beautiful Jo. As Venetian as a dream.' His voice is soft as sunlight. He strokes her hair from her temples.

'Hello,' she says, touched.

She leans up to kiss him and then guides him into her, raising up her hips to catch his rhythm. He is tentative, tender and grateful. It is familiar and sad. She is a spit of land that high tide used to cover but it does not any more. It misses the wash of the water, the freedom of fish, the lovers they were.

'Where have you gone?' he asks quietly. 'You're not here, Jo.'

'What is hubris?'

'What I've wallowed in all week. Enormous, stupid pride.'

She cannot help but smile.

'I need to paint, Jim. I need to have work that touches me.'

'Paint? Of course you can paint. Do I stop you painting?'

'I don't know. I thought you did. But I can see my life with my father replacing my life with you. The housekeeper. I don't know how to keep choosing it, as you do. I see everything else that needs to be done, or tidied or fixed or cooked or washed or dusted.'

'You need to want it more than life itself.'

'And not believe it's selfish to do so.'

'Yes.'

'What an odd prayer. May I learn to become more selfish. More like you.'

Jim puts his forearm over his brow and gives a sigh. Then he turns to her. 'Listen, Jo, you're still angry. I don't know how to help you. All I know is that no one looks at a masterpiece and sees selfishness. All they see is generosity and truth – the harmony and unity of being alive and at one with a total world.'

'Yes.' She sits up. 'They don't see the women who guarded the studio door, who fed the painter and washed his clothes and cleaned his bedding. I need a wife.'

She gets up and wraps a rug around her. She is too unhappy to sleep. She goes downstairs to fetch a glass of water. She thinks of the waves at Carnac, running alive and charged, picking up whatever light they could from the moon. The sleepless work of the sea.

165

The following Saturday, they meet Gabriel and Fanny outside Tudor Lodge and take a couple of cabs up to Astley's Amphitheatre on Westminster Bridge Road. Everyone is talking about the equestrian spectacle – Jo has seen the posters all over town. As they climb into their separate cabs, Fanny gives Jo a wink but they have no chance to talk. They have third row seats, with Fanny and Jo sandwiched between Jim and Gabriel, and Algernon in the seat at the end. There is a ramp extended into the auditorium and a sense of tremendous anticipation as the lights are dimmed and the fife and drums strike up. The master of ceremonies tells a few warm-up jokes before announcing a special appearance, all the way from New Orleans, by popular demand, Miss Adah Menken as Lord Byron's *Naked Mazeppa*. The lights go out and a spotlight follows the face of a young man with short cropped black hair and large black eyes. As he starts to sing badly in a falsetto, the lights come on to reveal a semi-naked woman strapped to a black stallion that begins to slowly circle the stage. The crowd gasps and hollers. They clap in time to her song.

'That's the best way to treat an unfaithful lover.' Fanny says in a low voice.

The woman lights a cigarette and as she comes down the ramp they can see that she is wearing transparent fleshings and a blue satin doublet. She begins to untie herself and perform acrobatics on the bareback horse. Then she stands up and cracks a whip over the heads of the audience and slips down again, astride the horse. Fanny takes Jo's hand and brings it to her lap. Jo is electrified. She has never seen a girl so free in her body in public. She stares agape, exhilarated. If only she was lithe and athletic, could ride a horse like a man. She remembers the solid stance of Rosa Bonheur that day at the Salon, making her look like she was the hero of her own story.

'Isn't she marvellous?' Jo whispers and squeezes Fanny's hand. 'I heard that she converted to Judaism and has been married and divorced three times already.'

'But she only looks about twenty-five. They say her father was a Negro.'

'Let's run away and join the circus!' Jo says.

Fanny tightens her grip on Jo's hand but gives the tiniest shake of her head. Jo cannot tell if it is a reproach. Her hand is suddenly too heavy and she wants to withdraw it but she does not move.

A trapeze is lowered from the ceiling and Mazeppa climbs on to it and swings back and forth, hanging upside down, reciting poetry as the trapeze is hauled back up out of sight. The crowd goes wild, bursting with cheers and whoops of 'encore!'

'I've never seen anything like it!' Algernon stands to applaud.

'Let's go backstage and invite her to dine with us.' Gabriel is up on his feet, straining to go.

'But we can't leave before the panto.' Fanny tugs Gabriel's arm.

Jim beats his cane lightly across his knee. 'By jingo, she's just what you need, Algernon.'

'Yes, and she can't write, which is perfect,' Jo mutters.

'Come on, girls. We'll go down to Simpson's.' Gabriel pulls Fanny up. They slip out the side entrance and work their way around to the stage door. Fanny waits for Jo and as the men walk ahead, she links her arm.

'How are you, my kitten? Is everything sweet with Jim?'

'Sweet enough. His brother Willie is coming to London so we can escape the gorgon for a while.'

'So you'll head to Paris?'

'Probably, but Trouville first. We want to be at the seaside again.'

None of it is what Jo wanted to say, had dreamed of saying. Their eyes, scanning each other's faces as they walk down the blind alley at the side of the theatre, are having a less timid, less tame conversation. Suddenly they are at the hubbub at the stage door, where people are holding up their autograph books.

Is that it, thinks Jo, this new formality? She is deflated and bewildered.

'Will you write to me?'

'Yes, my dear Jo. I will write.'

Later, after dinner, when the cabs drop them off at Lindsey Row, Jo wonders why neither of them suggested that they meet before she left. She does not know if the rift is from too much desire or too much fear.

V
La Belle Irlandaise, 1865

'Well, mother is exceptionally happy and I'm overjoyed to have escaped out of that great upheaval,' Jim says. 'I was beside myself with claustrophobia.'

They are standing on deck, leaning against the guardrail, watching seagulls hover and dive into the churning wake of the ferry like a letter torn up and scattered into the wind. Jo looks out over the dove grey expanse of the Channel and inhales. It is the end of August and French tourists are heading back en masse. The breeze is warm.

'And Willie seemed happy to be in London, so it's quits all round.'

'He's so manly, isn't he?' Jim tweaks one end of his moustache. Jo can see that he is less gay than he claims. 'He doesn't take any of mother's ceaseless palaver.'

'He seems much older than you. War must have aged him.'

'It's the white hair. The things he witnessed at Gettysburg don't bear thinking about.' He rubs his face with his hand.

'Did they really think Britain would come in on their side?'

'It was touch and go for a while, as you know. Corn or cotton. Which commercial gain would they rather protect. I feel so redundant, Jo. I did nothing.'

'Chin up, chum,' she puts her arm around him. 'We've two months with no obligations. You need fresh air and rest.'

'I need to start new work. A new direction. It feels stale. Every time I think I've made a breakthrough – '

'You feel discouraged again. I've seen it before. There will be another breakthrough. Trust me, Jim.'

Jo has never been so relieved to see the back of England. She resolves to not discuss Jim's mother any further. She looks at Jim's profile against the sky, then at the horizon. This trip will restore them to each other or reveal the impossibility of that ever happening again.

'I'm going to check out where the lifeboats are.' He pecks her cheek before wandering towards the prow.

Jo goes back down to their cabin to fetch a shawl and catches her hand in one of the heavy metal doors on deck. For some reason, as she rubs the back of her hand, the dull pain makes her think about the word 'breakthrough'. What would it be like to have one? Even if nothing changes for very long, or you end up going back to the same figure in the same style, it must feel extraordinarily good to have a flourish of self-belief, a new infusion of conviction.

Jim asks to sketch Jo less and less. Since the Louisa affair she has found sitting for him makes her edgy. The last portrait he had done with her and Milly Jones made her miserable. She was bored with the white frock, the languishing girl. She no longer felt confronted by aspects of herself and she needed these revelations to keep the sitting fresh, keep her vital and engaged. She kept dozing off as she sat with her head on one hand and the other outstretched along the divan. It was not finished still. Milly could not credit how many sessions it took him. 'Gawd help us, Jo, I don't know how you stick it!' she wailed one late afternoon as she tried to rub the circulation into her numb feet.

Jim and she had had an almighty row that evening.

'If you look bored, the painting will look bored,' he shouted as he left the house.

Jim has taken to drawing a self-portrait every night before he goes to sleep and his chalks, pencils, pens and inks are spread out on the shelf-table. She picks up a sketchpad and some pencils on a whim.

Back up on deck, Jo watches a young girl in a red cape and red cap playing with a wooden spoon as though it is a doll. She has tied a ribbon around its neck, painted it eyes, a nose and a mouth. She watches Jo watching her and plays more extravagantly, cradling the spoon and talking to it in a squeaky, cross voice. Jo sketches her, trying to capture the way she stands, her sturdy legs set apart and the planted scuffed boots, their laces trailing. She must be about four or five and has not learnt the stance expected of her yet. She makes her way closer to Jo, checks out what she is doing and suppresses her delight.

'What's dolly's name?' Jo asks.

'Spilly Lily.'

'What does she spill?'

'Teardrops.'

'Shall I draw some flowers in her hair? It might cheer her up.'

The girl nods and hands Jo the spoon. She decorates the back of it with curly hair and daisies.

'And the good thing is – she can swim,' Jo says.

'Can you?'

'No, but I hope to learn. What's your name?'

'Nancy.'

Jo writes 'For Nancy' and gives her the drawing. The girl runs back to show her mother and the mother smiles at Jo and nods in appreciation.

Jo begins to sketch three generations of women sitting under parasols on the deck. The middle one passes out apples to each of them.

'Excuse me,' a voice begins. Jo looks up. It is the girl's mother. She has a scattering of moles on her cheeks, brown expressive eyes and a girlish smile.

'I don't mean to bother you, but this is such an exquisite drawing, I wanted to thank you and offer you something for it.'

Jo laughs with surprise. 'Thank you so much. But I – it was a gift. It was my pleasure. She's a beautiful child.'

'Can I ask if you would mind doing my portrait? My husband has offered to pay for it. It's our anniversary. He persuaded me to ask.'

Jo is taken aback. She can see Nancy peer out from behind her father's deckchair. She is glad that she remembered to wear the wedding ring.

'Why, I'd be delighted to.'

They introduce themselves and agree a price. As Jo draws the woman's broad shoulders, something is forming, collecting energy, turning a wheel inside her with its own volition. It is the

171

germ of an idea. To paint a series of women, each a different age, each at a stage of living in her body fully. Jo is barely aware of the other three women beginning to stare until they gather round to watch how the drawing will finish. Later when she hands over the portrait, she looks around and sees Jim standing at the guardrail watching her. She signals to him to come and look at the drawing but he turns and looks out to sea. Her minor victory fades and she goes down to the cabin.

Jim comes in looking like fury.

'It cheapens your work to sell it like that, Jo.'

'Why? It's not as if I have a reputation to protect.'

'No, but those sort of transactions should be discreet. It's not as if we're that hard up.'

'Why didn't you want to see the drawing?'

'You're changing, Jo. I want to say hardening, but that's not quite right.'

'You mean I was always hard, you just didn't see it.'

'No, that's what you mean.'

They check into the Hôtel le Lion d'Or as Mr and Mrs Abbott. The hotel is a pretty yellow building on the seafront. They have a large room on the third floor, with a wooden balcony and a sea view. Jim goes out with his easel right away while the weather is fine. Jo watches a flotilla of small fishing boats and a steamer heading towards Le Havre in the distance. A small, crowded bac chugs in towards the harbour, probably from Deauville. She unpacks their trunks and then stretches out on the bed. She brings Fanny's letter out of her pocket and re-reads it, even though she knows its every word. When she thinks of her she imagines an eternal line of substantial, bold women, from witches to queens, full of open and frank goodness.

Dear Pretty One,

This is to wish you *Bon Voyage* (the only French I know apart from *Fin* and *Vin*!). I will miss our times together. Trust that I will continue to think of you every day and dream of you each night. As you know, I have not the fancy words for love and all that nonsense, but I have a fondness for you that I have never known. That is God's honest truth, my pet. I love my Rhino still, although he has taken to calling me Elephant which makes me less than content. Remember, please, that you are a delicious morsel and do not come to any harm.

Your loving friend,
Fanny

Jo has fallen asleep by the time Jim returns, his face flushed.

'You'll never guess who is here, Jo! Gustave Courbet! I met him on the beach.'

'You're joking.' She turns lazily and closes her eyes again.

'We've been invited to dine at his hotel tonight. My God, he's done a portrait of some Hungarian princess here and swears that there's a line of grand ladies at his door every morning.'

'Braggart.' She yawns and folds her arms behind her head. 'I may just stay here. The sea air has me knocked out.'

'Oh come on, Jo.' He hops from foot to foot and pleads with his hands. 'Think of the commissions! Please, my darling. You can help me fend him off. We've half an hour to get dressed.'

'Pray tell, does he ever *get* dressed?'

'Oh I doubt it. That's too much artifice for "the natural man". Do you know he was sporting a blanket with a hole cut out for his head as an overcoat? He's a sight for sore eyes!'

Jo laughs. 'Give me a kiss, first.'

He obeys and then springs up and claps his hands.

'To think there are models two a penny here and buyers with them. It's splendid!'

Jo says nothing.

As they stroll along the promenade Jo's chest expands with the old joy of being in France. Hearing the rhythms of the language, smelling the change of air make her want to open her mouth and let out a high operatic note. It is wonderful to be out of London, away from its packed streets, its rattling omnibuses and cloak of smog. The weather is still balmy and small groups of people are sitting on wooden chairs on the beach, watching the sunset. It is a broad, sandy strand, unlike the pebbled front at Brighton or the shingled beaches of Essex. The edge of the town spreads into grassy dunes with green headlands rising beyond them.

Jo enjoys the walk among the Trouvillais, looking at the ladies' fashions, the cut of their dresses, the width of their bonnets, the folds of their bustles. She will walk like a Frenchwoman one day. How can they wear the plainest garment and yet walk with such poise that it looks like the last word in design? She is wearing the new getup that Fanny helped her make – a peacock blue dress, a jade green hat and green boots. She has changed the way she does up her hair, showing more of it below her bonnet, and notices passers-by staring at her.

'They're all wondering where this new princess is from.' Jim raises his eyebrows and rolls his eyes at her.

'The Land of Bad Salad!'

'And a fear of garlic!'

'An abhorrence of Roquefort...'

He wields his cane in the air. 'And a terror of absinthe!'

The Hôtel Casino is an imposing, pastel pink building opposite the two piers with tricolours fluttering from its rooftop. They pass in under the enormous arched hotel entrance with its illuminated fanlight window and are guided towards Monsieur Courbet's table.

'Ah, Whistler!' Courbet rises to meet them. He is already in his cups. 'And Madame.' He kisses Jo's hand.

'Miss Jo Hiffernan,' Jim says.

Courbet waits till they sit down before he rocks unsteadily into his own seat again. Jo can feel the room's greedy gaze swivel onto them. She knows that Jim and she can make an entrance.

'But I feel I know you,' Courbet addresses Jo as she removes her bonnet and tidies her hair off her face. 'Of course I know you from Whistler's magnificent painting of *The White*

Girl but didn't you come to Brasserie Andler once – you wore a patterned red and black velvet scarf.'

Jo is startled. He had barely shown any signs of noticing her that evening.

'Yes, that's right. It's good to meet you, Monsieur.' She does not exactly know why she is cool towards him and protective of Jim.

'I've ordered oysters. And shrimp salad. And champagne. They know me here – ' He sweeps his hands down his front as if to excuse his tightly fitting jacket, his worn trousers and a white shirt with no collar or tie. 'They've given me an apartment overlooking the sea. It couldn't be better.'

'The light is tremendous – you don't get that pure red gold at dusk in London,' Jim says, watching the sun's glittering path on the sea. He places his violet gloves by his cutlery and shakes the white linen serviette flamboyantly onto his lap.

'Yes, you must get out in it, mon ami. I'm out in all weathers and swimming twice a day. Truly invigorating. Do you swim, Miss Hiffernan?'

'Not yet. Jim is always saying he'll teach me but – '

'Oh, it's segregated on the seafront but I know some hidden coves I can show you, fifteen minutes' walk away. The sea has had all summer to warm up.'

'The bathing machines are a nuisance. A ridiculous prudishness,' Jim says.

'An eyesore and a rip-off. Women can walk on the sand like any man. And be seen coming out of the water, *quoi*.' Courbet pours the champagne. 'When we were young, men didn't bother with suits at all. We jumped into the river Loue – now that was chilly – straight off the karst of the Jura.' He raises his glass and shouts: 'To clear skies and new ways of painting them!'

'Hear, hear!' says Jim, tasting the champagne. 'And to vain women with husbands rich as Croesus!'

Courbet seems to encourage every eavesdropper openly and even warm-heartedly. He signals to the *maître d'hôtel* who brings a basket of bread. The staff wait on them with great

175

eagerness and it is clear how much they adore and indulge him like the happy subjects of an eccentric king.

Jo studies Courbet for the first time. He is a handsome man in his mid-forties with black hair silvering at the temples, prominent cheekbones and a black bushy beard. His brown eyes are gentle and full of spark. A set of wrinkles radiates out from his eyes and his brow is lined. He is stout but he glows with ruddy health and looks less badgered and bloated than when she last saw him.

'You've hurt your hand, Mademoiselle.' He misses nothing. His attentiveness takes her off guard.

'Call me Jo, please. It's fine, really. I caught it in a deck door on the ferry.'

The skin on the back of her hand has purpled. She had not spotted him noticing. He appears able to absorb ten things at once. He is undeniably the bachelor and the eyes of every woman in the room are glued to him.

'And tell me, Whistler, the oysters are good, aren't they?'

'Delicious, thank you.'

'But surely their pleasure is too brief,' Jo says.

'Brevity is pleasure's triumph, I would argue.' Courbet looks at her from the side of his eyes and then mops up his plate with a crust of baguette.

'Fantin tells me you're on this art for art's sake bandwagon. Is that it, Whistler?' he asks.

'That's right. And if you lived in England, sir, you'd adopt this approach too.'

'Why's that?' He leans forward on his elbows and wipes his beard with his serviette.

'They like their paintings laden with patriotism or pity. The broken soldier, the poverty-stricken wife and children. It's all clap-trap. Art has to be independent of all that.'

'Well, I never painted a picture even as big as my hand to please anybody.'

'Me neither!'

They shake hands fiercely across the table.

'Bravo!' Courbet shouts. 'More champagne! France is full of silly bleating sheep too, you know. My aim is to create living art – whatever name you give it. Listen, artists make art for all kinds of reasons but mostly to get ahead or to get sex. Excuse me, Jo, but I speak plainly, what. We're all desperate to escape death – it's as simple as that – become immortal on a canvas. Or annoy the establishment and create an unholy row. Why do you paint, tell me, Whistler?'

'To show how I perceive and feel. To get a sensation of colour. Like music. It's aesthetic and intellectual.'

'Oh, that's airy-fairy to me. What's Darwin got to say about it, eh? How the deuce did we manage to evolve with this desire that no-one understands intact? Of course, I don't read Darwin or anything else unless my name's on it – oh my dear Proudhon – he did my reading for me.'

'We heard he passed away,' Jo says. 'I'm sorry, you – '

'That he did. God rest his soul.'

It is the second time he has cut her off mid-sentence. Jo bristles, her compassion evaporating. Despite its vehemence, she is wearying of the Courbet performance.

'But his book came out in a blaze of glory.' Courbet rattles on. 'All Paris was jealous and agape. Did you read it?'

On the Principle of Art? No, but I must,' Jim says without enthusiasm.

'You must,' Courbet continues with hardly a pause for breath. 'He was a genius – do you know what he called the newspapers? "Cemeteries of ideas". Isn't that formidable? I miss him.'

All of a sudden he seems to cave in, implode like some mighty whale that has found itself beached. Who was it wrote 'the sea-shouldering whale', Jo asks herself. He has fallen quiet and gazes out of the window as though he has forgotten that Jo and Jim are present. None of them speaks. The sun has gone down leaving tags of cloud flushed orange and pink. The small white lights of the fishing boats begin to dance on the bay. Courbet pats his stomach. 'Oh I am too fat! I am too old!' He packs his pipe with shreds of fresh tobacco and puffs at it

177

sombrely until it catches alight. The sad lion without his circus tent, Jo thinks and something softens in her.

A statuesque woman with Spanish eyes and complexion sidles past their table. She lowers her fan and says in a happy, teasing tone, 'Until tomorrow, Monsieur Courbet.'

'Yes, indeed, Madame Guix. I shall look forward to it.' He bows his head, smiles and rallies again. *'Bonsoir.'*

Courbet signals to a waiter. 'Dessert, Jo? Something sweet? Crème caramel? Apricot tart? Chocolate gâteau?'

'No I mustn't, thank you.'

'Oh anything we mustn't do we must see if we must. Life's too short for mustn't. Would you like it or not? It's straightforward, no? Ah, but the straight is never forward with ladies, I've found. Eh, Whistler?' He laughs at his own joke. 'It's round and round and back and forth and then they say something quite out of the blue.'

Jo squirms under his scrutiny.

'We'll both have a slice of gateau,' Jim says placing his palms flat on the table.

'No, I'll not, thank you all the same.' She'll not have two men making up her mind for her. 'I'm full.'

Jim and Courbet fall about laughing.

'What did I say?'

Courbet thumps the table, rocks back on his chair with a prodigious ho ho ho that is infectiously disproportionate.

'Tell me!' she pleads.

'Ma chérie,' Jim says, wiping his eyes, 'what you said means "I'm pregnant" in French.'

She covers her mouth and her shoulders shake with laughter.

It was Spenser. 'Spring-headed hydras and sea-shouldering whales / Great whirlpools, which all fishes make to flee...' It comes back to Jo just as she is falling asleep to the boom and the shush of the sea, where monstrous scolopendras, monoceroses and sea-satyrs are gathering further out in the deep.

The next day begins with a mackerel sky and its ribbed patterns of high, thin cloud. The morning sun is warm and there is no wind. Jo and Jim walk along the promenade, Jim armed with his easel and box of paints and Jo carrying Palgrave's *Golden Treasury of English Songs and Lyrics* that Algernon gave her, a parasol and a picnic basket. They stroll past the Malakoff Tower at the far end of the town and meander down to the beach. While Jim sets up, Jo climbs over the rocks that have emerged at the shoreline and are covered in fine, lettuce-green seaweed and circular colonies of orange lichen. The tight clusters of periwinkles and cone-shaped limpets make her think of her father and how he would have relished collecting them for dinner. She remembers him showing her how to poke a pin inside a steamed periwinkle and pull out the corkscrew body, and its gritty, rubbery taste. When she next writes to him, she will suggest that they go to visit West Cork later in the year. There is so much she wants to know about Ireland. She peers into a rock-pool, the colour of a pink blancmange, and studies the small yellow and russet sea snails and translucent crabs scuttling to hide. Anemones purse their glossy red lips, then spread out their tentacles. The surface remains imperturbable.

While Jim paints, Jo reads, both absorbed and silent, letting the occasional thought be said aloud.

'Listen to this, Jim.' Jo pauses to read him her favourite lines. '"I sent my soul through the Invisible / Some letter of that After-life to spell".'

'Who wrote that again?'

'The Rubaiyat of Omar Khayyam. It's from 12th-century Persia. It opens my mind out, like drifting in the universe with no ties to earth, no gravity.'

'I want that kind of spaciousness in this picture. It feels as if we are at the edge of dissolving into something and yet our bodies are as solid as ever.'

'Being near the sea, perhaps our bodies remember that they are mostly water.'

'Mine is mostly air. Is it munchtime yet?'

179

'No, but the holiday appetite says it is.' She digs into the picnic basket and hands Jim a tranche of baguette with a wedge of Brie and a jar of black olives. He opens a bottle of local wine and Jo brings out glasses and serviettes smuggled from the hotel dining room.

Jim removes his eyeglass, leans back on one elbow and stretches his legs out. He pushes his hair off his brow. 'I'm beginning to feel everything slow down.'

'It takes a few days to hear the silence again, doesn't it?'

'Why do we get so frantic?'

'Each time we come back from a trip on the continent, we promise to get more fresh air, take more day excursions to the zoo or the forest – '

'And there never seems to be the time.'

Jo eats her sandwich and empties her glass of wine. She lies back against a rock and dozes under the parasol, listening to the seagulls and oystercatchers gossip and children squealing some distance away down the beach. How glorious to have time to think, to not think, to not move lists of things around in her head. To be quiet. To be still. To not chase her own tail. Then the sounds start to lose their anchor and meander in and out of that hovering, sweet daydreaming place of the afternoon nap that is neither fully awake nor asleep. Her body is suspended and warm, her breathing slow. After a while, she rouses herself and makes notes for a poem on the flyleaf of her book. Then she finds herself making a sketch of the headland, the waves, idly, faintly, as if it did not matter. She keeps the drawing out of Jim's sight.

That evening they go to Café Tortoni that Fantin recommended for moules marinières and turn in early. They are astonished when they wake to find that they have slept without interruption for ten hours. They have missed breakfast and so ring for coffee and bread and eat out on the balcony, watching women come back from the fish market. Maybe Jo could sketch them tomorrow morning, let Jim go out to the beach alone.

Something is niggling her. She wishes they knew no-one in Trouville, that they could have been more alone. She does not want the enervating demands of society and society portraits on either of them. At that moment, Courbet calls 'Salut!' from the street. He is wearing a fisherman's cap and paint-spattered smock. With his easel and box of paints strapped to his back, he resembles a large upright beetle. He stops and leans on his tall staff.

'Have you got your bathing costumes? It's a superb day for a dip. What's keeping you?'

'We'd love to. We'll meet you in half an hour at the tower,' Jim calls. Then, as Courbet ambles on, he mumbles, 'I can't spend all day nattering and clowning about. Please see to it that I work, Jo.'

They walk along a narrow sheep path over the headland. A young woman is spinning wool in a field where her grazing flock are scattered. Jo thinks that maybe France has retained more of a farming life close to the towns. They ramble down among the heather and bracken to a sandy cove where the water looks as green and clear as a gem. Jim wipes the sweat from his brow and begins to take off his clothes as soon as they reach the beach.

'Avanti!' he hollers and runs in a mad dash into the sea and dives into the jade crest of a breaker. For a moment Jo tenses. Jim almost drowned the last time he bathed.

'Comme l'eau est bonne,' he calls.

'Please don't swim out too far,' she calls back.

Courbet strips off, pulls on his costume and walks slowly towards the water. He is a walking black barrel and his rolling gait seems to command the beach as he commanded the dining room two evenings before. He splashes his face and head noisily. Before long he has dived in and swum out further than Jim.

Jo takes longer to change, wriggling beneath a bath towel. She tucks her hair up under a bathing bonnet. She will not risk going in beyond her waist, she tells herself. The water is chilly and then warms as it hits her calves. She sits down and lets the baby waves roll up over her legs. Jim swims closer and then crocodiles on his hands in the shallows towards her.

181

'Stand up. I'll lead you.'

She hesitates as she stands waist-high and contemplates the water. 'I can't do it.' She is ramrod rigid. He reaches for her hands. She cannot imagine how to lie on its surface. Surely she will sink at once?

'Lie straight with your head up and kick. I'll pull you. Now, before the next wave breaks.'

She is nervous and juts her chin up, but she manages to give a couple of kicks. She springs up before a wave engulfs her.

'It'll take a few days to get used to it. That's good, so far.'

'I'm scared stiff.'

'It might be calmer later and you can float and get your buoyancy, *ma puce*.'

She smiles. He has not called her that for months. Can a flea swim? Can a flea feel trapped in its body? What does a flea that is suffocating say?

Their costumes are spread to dry out on the rocks. They are semi-dressed, Jo in her undergarments and skirt; the men, bare-chested, in their trousers. They have set up their easels, a good distance apart, as po-faced as duellists.

'Let's both paint Mademoiselle Jo and then compare,' Courbet jests.

'Let's paint the view.' There is a note of defiance in Jim's voice.

'Anyway, I'm on holiday, chaps,' Jo says, leaning back on her towel with her book.

'Fine, as you wish,' Courbet says brusquely. 'I don't offer to paint merely anyone, you know.'

Monsieur Courbet is clearly someone who is used to having his own way. But as she casts him furtive glances she can see that he is more relaxed out of doors and the dark energy he emitted that night at dinner has vanished.

The men begin to sketch the tumble of rocks at the base of the headland that form the curve of the cove and the boats at sea. A cormorant lands on an outcrop of rock and surveys them like a hunched and disapproving priest. Grey and white terns and turnstones peck and dart at the incoming tide. Courbet takes an age to draw his pencil outlines of the scene. Jim has already started applying paint. Jo stares at the waves catching the sunlight as they crest and then churn up the sand as they froth and foam out over the beach. Wrinkled tide marks and a line of broken white shells show where high tide has reached earlier. She considers how she would paint the scene.

She watches as Courbet dabs at the canvas, layers on paint with a palette knife and then wipes it half off with a rag and even his thumb. He sings as he works. He has a good tenor voice but the ballad seems to be his own and its ridiculous rhymes make Jo laugh. She goes back to her book but the words dance and dangle out of sense.

Then Courbet announces that he is finished and tries to peek impatiently to see what Jim has done.

Jim refuses to look at him or his canvas. He raises his palm. 'Amuse yourselves. I need more time!'

Courbet opens a bottle of white wine he has chilled in the damp sand near the rocks. Jo offers him a glass but he drinks from the bottle. She declines to join him.

'Look, this is how you do it.' He has this habit of starting midway through an idea. He points his arms out and opens them in a breaststroke. 'Copy me.' Jo follows him. 'It's the legs that are the tricky part.' He lies down on the sand and works his legs like a frog. She giggles. 'Come on, you try, Jo.'

'I'm not doing that!'

He sits up and lights his pipe. He draws on it as he studies her. 'So,' he whispers, 'will your Jim lend you to me, do you think?'

'Pardon me?'

'I'd like to paint your portrait, mademoiselle. Isn't that clear?'

'It's not up to Jim.'

'Isn't it?' His handsome eyes gleam.

'Besides, I heard there was a queue of two hundred ladies at your door.'

He rolls his head back and laughs his big belly laugh.

'There are, my dear Jo, but you are – '

183

'I'm almost done,' Jim calls in a nervous voice. 'It's sketchy, but I can show you.' He turns his easel towards them. A flood of emotion passes through her.

'Ah, very well, Whistler, let's see what you have.' Courbet approaches him as a dog approaches another, with a sidling walk and a suspicious look on its face, its nose long. Then he drags his easel closer and parallel to Jim's.

Jo can see at once that Courbet's seascape is more real. Some parts are as exact as a photograph. The grasses on the headland are just the right yellowed green; the rocks are an implacable impasto black layered with intricate emerald seaweed and pale smudges of guano; the sea is a watery, luminous aquamarine while the sky is a soft white rising to a deeper blue.

But Jim's is more true. The diaphanous sea and sky merge more gently, the colours more subtle, the edges shifting into one another under much thinner washes of paint. His has the glints of where blue invents green, the gold of the sand becoming whiter at the drier edges. It is a muted mood or memory of the view but still unmistakably the same scene. A tender afterimage perhaps, Jo thinks, rather than the image itself.

'Formidable,' Jo shouts.

'Not bad,' Courbet almost sniffs at the canvas and then scratches his beard. 'But *mon ami,* where do you see that strange frost on the sand? And for me, that mauve is interfering with the sky's blueness.'

'If I paint a smoke-blue sky edging into lavender, it's not so that people can forecast the weather, it's so that they can experience the colour.' Jim's voice tightens. 'The sky is never constant. Twilight is already present.'

'What tosh!' Courbet slaps his thigh. 'That's like saying that black night is the same as broad day.'

'The stars are still there, we just can't see them. Did you paint the stars in your realistic picture, Monsieur Courbet?' Jo asks.

He paces the beach between the two canvases, relights and sucks at his pipe. Jim takes a step back and puts his hands on his hips.

184

'Your headland is almost sculptural and your light on the sea is pretty, Courbet,' Jim says with a note of generosity.

'I detest pretty. I don't know...' Courbet pauses. 'Your horizon is too low or your sky too high. But it has something.'

Jim lights a cigarette and exhales forcefully. His mouth is grim.

'The way the tide is eating at the sand – that is a remarkable texture, isn't it, Jo?' Courbet concedes as he stares at Jim's work. Does he really imagine she will collude in patronising Jim?

'It's something new,' Jo says. 'The public haven't caught up yet.' She sits down on the sand, hoping that the tension will shift.

'Believe me, you can't win,' Courbet says. 'If you give them too much realism they call it excessively ugly. I've said to them, "Show me a goddess and I'll paint one." Still they prefer an impossibly flawless young nymph to a real-life milking maid with strong calves and calloused hands.'

'You've done a lot to challenge that, *mon vieux,*' Jim says weakly. *'The Bathers,* for instance.' He comes to sit down beside Jo.

'Is it true that Napoleon once struck it with a riding crop in the middle of the Salon in 1853?' Jo tries to move to a less controversial topic.

'I was delighted,' Courbet chuckles as he stands over them. 'That beautiful Céline from my village was too buxom for them. They found her an affront to womanhood. She is what womanhood looks like.' He mimes grasping a pair of full breasts and then hips in his hands. He looks directly at Jo. She looks away.

'The ideal crucifies the real,' Jim says.

'For us ladies more than anyone.' Jo fans herself with her book.

'The Bonapartists have nothing but insults for my work. They tried to buy me off, you know.' Courbet picks up the wine bottle and swills it back. 'If only I would be less quarrelsome, they said, they'd put me in the International Exhibition. Do you know what I said?' He begins to laugh in anticipation of

185

his own punchline. 'I told them I didn't consider myself part of their government, that I was a government too, *quoi*. You should have seen his face! A Monsieur, no, pardon me, *Count* de Nieuwerkerke, the director of the Beaux-Arts.'

Jo digs her toes into the sand.

'But we all thought you'd well and truly buried Romanticism with *A Burial at Ornans*,' Jim says drily.

'It's vampiric,' Jo says with a forced laugh.

'Needs a stake through the heart,' Jim says, eyeing Courbet.

'Death to Doric columns and knights and damsels!' Jo says.

'Exactement,' Jim says.

'Have a drink, *mon ami*.' Courbet hands Jim the bottle of wine and Jim takes an ample swallow. His face, however, fails to relax.

Then Courbet announces that he has an appointment to paint an elderly baroness at two o'clock back at the hotel. He packs away his easel and materials, pulls on the rest of his clothes and heads cheerfully up the path.

Jim crosses his arms. He is disconsolate.

'I never wanted to be involved in a painting race. It was imbecilic of me to participate. He sucks everyone and everything into his vortex.'

'He must be the most arrogant brute I've ever met.'

'His blasted realism eats away at me, Jo. Part of me wants people to admire the great likeness – my vanity would be assuaged – but it's not what intrigues me in the end.'

Jo looks into his troubled eyes. 'It's not wrong, it's just different, Jim. And he isn't universally understood by any means. He sings a tune with words while you...you hum and make sounds that are nicer than words, for the words that can't be found.'

'I'm whistling in the dark and he's a bad influence.' He screws up his face.

'He doesn't know everything – he just thinks he does.'

Jim draws a scribble in the sand with his fingertip. 'He befuddles me. I can't make head or tail out of what he says half the time. I wish Fantin were here.'

'Yes, me too. He could moderate. The way he used to with Alphonse. Dear Fantin.'

Later they are sitting on their hotel balcony after an early dinner, having a glass of Calvados, Jim smoking a cigarette, his face flushed from the sun.

'You're Miss Rosy tonight.'

'Luckily I don't tan. I'll be fresh and white as bread tomorrow.'

They hear a shout. 'The sea's calm – it's high tide. Perfect for learning to swim, Jo.'

'I'm afraid we've just eaten, Courbet,' she calls.

'Tomorrow perhaps,' Jim says.

'How about a midnight swim tomorrow? A marvellous plan. I'll come at 10pm. Plenty of time to digest. Or would you care to dine with me – a local painter called Boudin is coming. A marvel, Whistler. You absolutely must see what he's doing. I ran into him quite by accident yesterday. The sea's in his blood like the mountains are in mine.' He opens his arms wide and embraces himself with merriment. He then salutes them and is off, headed down to the beach, his togs rolled under his arm.

'What's in your blood, Veeslair?' Jo teases in Courbet's accent.

'Gin and tonic water.'

'Good grief, it makes you hesitate to visit your own balcony of an evening.'

'He has his eye on you.'

'Nonsense!'

'I can tell. You're flattered. I know you so well.'

'And I know a painter's eye. Besides, he's as old as my father.'

'That can be an enticement.'

'Maybe, but I draw the line at bad table manners.' She mimes scoffing food with her hands.

Jim begins to laugh, then takes a sip of his drink and smoothes out the tips of his moustache. He looks at her for a while with a hint of something like caution in his eyes. She winks at him and soon she can see his longing return. She falls asleep early that evening. They have not made love for weeks and the holiday has already become more like hard work.

A cold front blows in from the east bringing rain and cloud for a few days. A gauze of grey hangs over the headland. The season feels over, the resort unanchored by the foretaste of autumn. The bathing machines stand forlorn like time-travelling relics from another era. Jim paints the melancholy scene of the empty beach from the hotel window. Jo is restless. She reads her volume of poetry but finds the words blurring in layers of lint in her head. She wonders if she could get out her paints and start something new. But that person on the ferry with an urgency to paint the world has lost her way. She does not know how to fully admit it and so she buries her and pretends she was never there. She takes out some notepaper to write to Fanny. She knows it will help to clear her head.

> My dear Fanny,
> Thank you for your sweetest farewell note. I keep it with me and it warms me when I read it. I cherish memories of our times together. You make me feel as if I can take on the world – and win. You have always been so wise and I need a dose of your wisdom now. We have met the great painter Gustave Courbet and he wants to paint my portrait. I am half-thrilled but can never show Jim. Whilst he once admired and respected Courbet, he now feels hampered by his style and belittled by his temperament. Monsieur Courbet is the most ebullient fellow I have ever met but loathsomely conceited. To sit for him would betray Jim and all he stands for but I am more than curious to see how Courbet would portray me. Although I am worried that Jim would see it as some kind of revenge for him painting Louisa, I am tempted. It would be the first time I have sat for anyone else for four years. I have just realised as I write this that Jim is the painter of my life. I am caught between

them as a flame between two draughts. Did I mention that Mon. Courbet is frighteningly handsome, though corpulence itself?

Oh, how I miss you. Please write with your news of Tudor Lodge and give my regards to Gabriel, Algernon and the furry menagerie.

Yours as ever,

Jo

Later that afternoon, Jo tries to coax Jim to come out for some air – rain is never as bad when you are out in it, she tells him, but he prefers to keep painting and repainting, making and unmaking the view until he gets it right. She takes a long walk under her umbrella up along the promenade. The town is showing the winter self most visitors never see. It has a shut-up sense to it with the awnings wound in and the tables and chairs stacked up on the damp terraces. As she climbs over the headland, she passes an old woman bent double with a bundle of sticks on her back, leading a goat. They say good afternoon to one another. Jo has the impulse to help her, imagines the harshness of her life, her labouring journey home in her sabots and the lighting of tonight's fire with sodden kindling.

She is on edge. She can see more rain coming in from the sea in ragged grey columns like warriors from the cold north. She remembers their trip to Carnac and misses the wilder, more lonely coast of Brittany. She realises as she walks what has been niggling her. When they met Courbet first at the Hôtel Casino, he remembered her at once from a very brief meeting at the Brasserie Andler. He clearly had a talent for keeping faces distinctly in his head and yet when they had met him in Paris, he had claimed to not know Whistler at all. She twigs all of a sudden that it was an intentional putdown in front of Baudelaire, the rest of the crowd at his table, and her. I will miss nothing, either, mister, she tells herself. You will not have one over on us.

The next evening, Courbet appears at the dining room in their hotel and asks if he may join their table. He has had his beard

189

and his hair trimmed and is sporting a new black tailcoat over checked trousers, a lilac-tinted waistcoat and black, shiny shoes. As he orders his entrée of hare ragout, Jim whispers to Jo, 'He must have a new lady friend.' She nods and feels a twinge of – what is it? – she cannot believe herself – something quickening like inquisitiveness – and she can picture a big-boned and fleshy girl combing Courbet's hair, dressing him and now waiting voluptuously on his hotel bed. She has a clear vision of her lying there, naked, her legs relaxed, her dark, Spanish face satisfied.

'I've decided to stay longer so I sent for some clothes from Paris. How's the work going, Whistler?'

'A bit hampered by the rain – '

'But why? You go in for that sort of mellow misty blur, no?'

'Come on, you fellows,' Jo begs, 'can we have five minutes without a tirade on art?' She cuts decisively into her joint of beef and a squirt of blood reddens her plate. There is an uneasy silence and Jo regrets what she has said. But as Jim refills their wine glasses, he gives her a grateful smile.

Courbet's change in attire has not improved his eating habits. He gobbles ferociously, messing up his beard and wiping his plate to the last drop of gravy with a crust of bread with a strangely intense concentration as if he has not eaten for days. He tells them that he took a boat up the river Touques to paint an exquisite waterfall in among some moss-clad rocks and came across a group of women washing clothes on the banks.

'Oh dear, I'm back discussing art. I am incorrigible, aren't I? I'm happy to discuss you, if you wish, mademoiselle,' Courbet says with a long look at her. 'Two days should do it,' he goes on, addressing Jim.

'Do what?' he asks.

'Her portrait. What do you say, Jim? Can I borrow your superb redhead or is she copyrighted by the butterfly signature?'

'I see that the gauntlet is on the tablecloth, gentlemen,' Jo raises her hands in a gesture of dismay.

Jim lays down his knife and fork. 'It's entirely up to Jo.'

'I don't work under a contract, Monsieur Courbet,' Jo adds firmly.

'What are you, scared, Whistler, eh?' Courbet taunts. 'I'll show you up, is that it?'

'That is not it, sir. Realism barely influences my work.'

'I'm talking about truth in nature, here. The natural girl. That's the purpose of art, as far as I'm concerned. To reveal her as closely as possible to the human eye.'

Jim's voice hardens and he interlocks his fingers. 'There is not truth in nature, only in art. That nature is always right, is an assertion as untrue as it is one whose truth is universally taken for granted. Nature is very rarely right. It might also be said that nature is usually wrong.'

'Very well,' Courbet glares at Jim and rubs his beard in his serviette. 'It's nothing. Forget I asked.' He sticks out his chest and stretches out his arms.

'If you can paint her as an object of beauty, then go ahead. But not as some fanciful truth in nature.'

Courbet seizes the edge of the table and for a moment it looks as if he is going to explode and overthrow the table and everything on it. The dining room is stunned into silence as if by a clap of close thunder.

'It would be a great honour,' Jo says quietly and firmly. 'Thank you. I shall think about it.'

Jim looks at her with some consternation. Then he says to Courbet in a warning tone, 'Head and shoulders only.'

Jo cannot stop a rush of fury.

'I believe those terms are mine to define, Jim.'

Courbet swings back in his chair and tears his serviette from his throat and roars,

'That's settled then! Come tomorrow afternoon at 2pm, Jo. I rarely work before lunch. Of course, you are welcome to come too, Jim, if you wish.'

Jo looks down. 'Head and shoulders only.' The words ring with the swift, hot anxiety of being cut down to size that she once felt with Anthony Mulligan. She is not Jim's property, will not be portioned and measured with a draper's tape. She will not be curtailed. Her foot twitches with the need to kick something. Courbet has succeeded in dividing them.

191

The sun suddenly appears from behind a buffer of cloud in an intense funnel of brightness just before it sets. They watch it vanishing into the sea as if it was a rare performance that slows the waiters' movements and quietens the eating and talking of the diners. A sense of withheld applause hangs in the room and they sit hushed in the brink before the afterglow shimmers on the mirrors, the glasses and the cutlery, and then the golden gloom strikes their skin and their eyes with its kind goodbye. Without any haste, the waiters begin to light the candles and the gaslights.

Jim walks Jo to Courbet's hotel the following afternoon. The wind has dropped and the sky proffers a scant blue. Jim says he would rather stay outside, paint the harbour and the lighthouse and wait for her. He hesitates before turning away. Neither of them has mentioned her agreeing to pose for Courbet the night before as if to discuss it would enflame it further.

As she climbs the broad curve of the garnet-marble staircase, her hand following the brass banister and her feet sinking into the pink and gold floral carpet of the landing, the hotel's elegance wraps around her. She has washed her hair and put on her favourite ink blue dress and bonnet. She is Judith entering the camp of the enemy, the den of Holofernes. She will strike if he so much as lays a finger on her.

Courbet is jovial and genial. 'Excuse the luxury,' he says with a wave of his hand. He offers her water, wine or elderflower cordial. She accepts a glass of cordial. She glances around the high-ceilinged room with its intricate gold stucco patterning the walls and gathered in a rose around the chandelier. The white and gold furniture has been pushed into one corner and about twenty to thirty canvases are lined against the walls which are covered in a mouse-grey silk. The pink carpet is protected by white decorating sheets. She notices that the bed is in the adjoining room to the right, the double doors shut. She pictures a woman lying in there, able to hear every word, and has a moment of self-consciousness. The easel and a table

192

spread with tubes of paints and brushes dominate the centre of the room.

'Don't look so timid – I'll not eat you.' He laughs.

She is not aware of appearing timid. She intended to be steely and stately. He sits her at a table that he has covered with a rumpled piece of white silk. He asks if she would gaze into a small oval mirror. She sits with her one hand on her lap, thinks of Jim on the pier below the window. Courbet grunts and sings and moves about the room, sketching and erasing the outline and repositioning the easel.

'It's too static. Let me see. Jo, do what you'd do if you were alone with the mirror.' His tone is peremptory.

She holds the long-handled mirror up to the light and turns her head from side to side. Her colour is good, her hair shining, and her eyes sea-blue and clear.

'That's more natural. Don't worry about what I think. Fix your hair.'

She pretends to pin her hair up into the usual style. His eyebrows knit and wrinkle the bridge of his nose.

'It's too set. You're too ready. Unready yourself. Ah, *le diable,* this is the problem with working with professionals!' He guffaws. 'Imagine you've not done your hair. Let it down.' She does what he asks.

'Bring it around your shoulders. Feel its thickness. Look a little past the mirror. That's it. Think of your first love.'

Jo was not expecting that. Anthony Mulligan. The name rises in a quick violet flash before she can stop it. The rat. The cad. Treated her like a bloody dishrag, like dirt itself. Suddenly she is full of the same shyness she experienced the first time she sat at Rathbone Place.

'Oh, *merde,'* Courbet says swiftly. 'Wrong instruction. You've gone cloudy, *ma fille.* I'm sorry. Let's see...imagine you're swimming. That's it. Your hair is floating around you. You're a lily. A sea lily, if such a thing exists. You've never felt so bodiless, light, with the warm water caressing your limbs. That's it, drift,' and then he breaks into song and she is drifting, drowsy, lulled by his voice, his odd ballad:

193

> *When at night she dreams of being free*
> *To the sea she floats,*
> *She can breathe underwater so easily,*
> *Beneath the sailors' boats.*

'What a beautiful girl,' he mutters. 'Why do I eat so much, drink so much? The young turks are at my heels and I can't run as fast as I used to. Ah, but nothing can beat this. No one has painted you the way I will. Just wait till you see, Jo. Everyone will want it. Everyone will want you! You'll be the envy of all of Paris – as I am!' He chortles and she watches him out of the corner of her eye as he seems to pounce on an area of canvas, pace back and forth and then pounce again with renewed gusto.

'Did you always want to be an artist?' she asks after a while.

'My father tried to make me a lawyer but books boiled my head. Art is the only thing I've ever lived for – I drove myself so hard to get it. I had to convince him that it was a serious career and my only choice. And you know, deep down he is an artist, too. A sculptor, perhaps. He was always making things – useless, unusable things – inventions to improve farming. Locals would call him a *"un cudot"* – do you know this word?'

'No.'

'It means "a dreamer". We've a storehouse full of his dreams at Flagey. One day, the Louvre will be full of mine.'

Heavens above, he must be the haughtiest man in France, she thinks. She resolves not to engage him in conversation any further.

'And you, *ma belle Anglaise?'*

'Irlandaise,' Jo says.

'Ah, *Irlandaise!* I've always thought Catholics were more attuned to art. And to the body.'

'There's more of it in our churches certainly.' This has not crossed her mind before.

'Protestants prefer to use words for spiritual aspiration or cold marble.'

'But surely there are a great many Protestant painters.'

'Name one.'

'Rembrandt.'

'Ah, good.'

'Frans Hals.'

'Excellent. Emotional depth and crispness of detail. But you have to look at Caravaggio or Velázquez for passion and abandon. They made the appetites of the body spiritual as well as carnal.'

'Well, the English are more terrified of the nude than the French, it's true.'

'Your students flock to the ateliers of Paris – to learn how to handle form. Through the body itself, not from ancient Greek marble. And to shed that lily-livered neo-classicism. The English try to elevate the poor nude above the base response of the senses. But I ask you, who has ever seen a woman with a smooth and hairless *mons veneris?*'

She laughs and feels her face and neck redden. But she does not want him to think she is a prude. 'Yes, you're right. The National Gallery even censored Bronzino's *An Allegory,* you know. They required less nipple on Venus's breast and more sprigs of myrtle to cover Cupid's tail.'

'But Proudhon told me that we're descended from apes not cherubim for crying out loud!'

Jo is laughing with him.

'Did you hear about the Baptist who gave a nude statue a bashing at the Crystal Palace? With the handle of her parasol! This is what we're up against.' She sits up to look at him, forgets for the first time that she was meant to hold her pose.

'So, where did you study art, Jo?'

'At night school and my own hours of looking. I worked as a copyist for a while. We had to copy Old Masters for a rich gentleman. I love to know how great paintings work. So I go inside them for hours.'

'Try José de Ribera. You go too deep inside his works and you might never come out again.'

'He's in the Prado, isn't he? I was on my way there last year and had to turn back.' She notices that she did not say 'we'. She wonders why for a moment.

'His *Jacob's Ladder* inspired a painting of one of my favourite themes – sleep. And what about you? Do you paint?'

'I don't. I mean to. But it seems to have given me up.'

'If you paint things as well as you can look at them, you can paint. Take a prepared canvas from over there. Paint me the cove. I'm curious.'

The church bell strikes. 'Oh, goodness, what time is it?' She had meant to be reticent but has been caught up in his garrulousness and his ideas.

'Is it five?'

'Already? I have lost track of time. Jim's waiting. Can we stop please?'

'I don't know if we can.'

His voice is slightly mocking. She wants to see his expression but the late afternoon sunlight floods the room and he stands as a tall dark silhouette against it. She shields her eyes but cannot make out his face.

He moves towards her. His eyes are too serious, yet soft. He is fully lit.

'I don't want to keep you.' He casts her a look that belies what he says. 'But I do want to keep talking to you. Is that wrong? I want to get to know how you think.'

'I have small thoughts, Monsieur Courbet.'

'But they are your own and I like that. I like that very much.'

She turns away and begins to pin up her hair and put on her bonnet.

She finds Jim at the edge of the pier painting the sandbanks of the small harbour where a few fishing boats lie stranded sideways, their hulls caked in barnacles flashing in the sun. A flicker of apprehension strikes as she walks towards him. She waves.

'How was it? He didn't eat you?'

How strange that he used the same expression as Courbet. Did they both see her as a cream cake? 'No, he drowned me in words.' She tries to suppress the excitement that she must radiate.

'And the portrait, is it any good?' He watches her closely.

'Oh, who can tell as yet?'

He scoffs and gives an awkward, brittle laugh. 'You mean he didn't knock it off in one sitting?'

'He'd like me to go back for a few hours tomorrow. Would you mind?'

He shrugs. 'The sooner it's over the better.'

They walk along the promenade to their hotel. Jim is smoking in that fretful way of his, inhaling and exhaling like an animal working out its frustration. She can tell she is losing him. Oh their playfulness is still there, but it has become the play of siblings: teasing, childlike, rehearsed. They dip into nicknames and familiar sayings and can complete each other's sentences but whereas once it made her feel safe, it has begun to stifle her, feel too snug.

They pass the shops where the shopkeepers are winding in the striped awnings. Families are gathering their belongings together on the beach. A mother calls to a young boy to come *tout de suite* or they will go home without him. He is filling a tin bucket with water and pouring it out, over and over again.

A sense of despondency comes over her. It occurs to her that people are the only things we know we are losing before they are lost. If she thinks about losing her favourite kid gloves, then that is not the moment she will lose them. And if they are lost, she will not know until after it has happened. She does not hold her gloves more tenderly on the day she loses them, or look at them more deeply to try to remember all their features, the way she looks at Jim, the way she wants to hold on to him.

Jim buys a newspaper to read before dinner. They go on to the balcony and order a Pastis.

'Heavens! Listen to this. Chile has declared war on Spain.'

'What's happened?'

He flicks opens the paper and puts on his monocle to scan the inside pages.

'It's about Peru's unpaid colonial debt. Peru's refusing to pay. A ship came in to collect coal at Valparaiso and the Chileans refused to deliver it.'

197

'I'm sure Spain took more than it ever gave Peru. Hasn't Chile been independent for ages?'

'Since the 1840s. Spain wants it back. Its empire is crumbling. Queen Isabel II's fleet invaded some islands off Peru last year. They've now blockaded Valparaiso and the British Government has lodged a protest.'

He is engrossed in the article, agitated.

'Sometimes I yearn for a life of action, doing more out in the world. Simple choices of right and wrong. Not the ambiguities of tonal harmonies, subtle textures. It's all so damn indulgent.'

'It seems that artists are the ones who doubt the use of art more than anyone else.'

Jo takes his arm as they go down to the hotel dining room and order grilled sardines and tomato salad. Jim is still restless, drinking his wine as if it is water.

'Take the evening off.' She touches the back of his hand to steady him. 'Let's go for a walk. You'll get some perspective tomorrow. Relax. Nothing can be done about the world's wars tonight.'

'We could go on saying that every night.' His tone is bellicose and bitter. He finishes his glass of wine and refills it. 'I never know when a call to duty is just an evasion of a greater duty to myself.'

'Believe me, I know.' She thinks of all the dutiful decisions she has made as a daughter, a woman, a housekeeper, a bookkeeper, a lover, instead of making time for her own painting. When will she ever summon the determination to start to say no and say yes to her self? She swallows her glass of wine and wants its easy oblivion.

'Courbet isn't twisted by doubt and indecision,' Jim goes on. 'He's like a factory line.'

Jo thinks of the canvases lining the walls of Courbet's apartment – more in two months than Jim has painted in two years.

'Maybe he's just more of an artisan than you. Like a shoemaker.'

198

'He believes he invented realism. Really. It's infuriating.'
His voice is slurring. He bangs the table. 'What about
Caravaggio? He rebelled against tradition and authority and the
ideal of beauty in his time.'

'Yes, he spoke about him today.'

'He did? To you?'

'Yes, we talked about how painting on the continent differs
from painting in England. He supposes that Catholics are more
attuned to painting's sensual power.'

'How absurd. He would.'

He looks glum. She realises that she should not have
mentioned it.

She tries to deflect him. 'And surely Géricault's *Raft of the
"Medusa"* is an example of a form of realism in France?'

'My point exactly. He thinks he's winning the race but he's
merely circling a track behind the Dutch and everyone else.'

'Come on, Jim. Finish your meal. It's almost cold.'

He has lifted the newspaper again. 'Chile?' he says as if it is
a new idea he is trying to articulate.

'I don't understand why this has upset you so much. Why
the sudden interest in the world's affairs, Jim?'

He does not seem to hear her.

Jo returns to Hôtel Casino and sits for Courbet for a few more
hours the next day. Even though he has all the windows open,
she is too hot in her petticoats and dress. She wishes she could
have worn a lighter dress and her espadrilles. There is none
of the contemplative stillness that she shares in a sitting with
Jim. Courbet talks and sings and guffaws and grunts, balls up
paint-encrusted rags and tosses them into a shabby box in the
corner of the room. He tells her that he plans to mount his own
exhibition in Paris through his patron Alfred Bruyas. He regales
her with stories of his trips to Montpellier and how spoilt he is
by the *famille* Bruyas. He makes her relax and startles her at the
same time. He is vulgar and then uniquely delicate, earthy as
wet soil and then sparkling with insight.

'I didn't see the sea until I was twenty-two,' he tells her. 'How strange it was for a valley dweller to come face to face with the horizonless sea. I felt as if I was carried away; I wanted to take off and see the whole world.'

'My father would take us to the seaside – English seaside towns in Kent but that didn't count. I don't think I really saw the sea until I saw it in Brittany at Carnac last year. I was twenty. I will never forget my first sight of that stony space with so few humans and yet such signs of their presence.'

'Twenty. Last year? Ho hum.' He strokes his beard, tries to pull in his paunch. 'My friend Baudelaire called it man's looking glass. The sea. "With a gulf no less bitter than the mind".'

'Baudelaire once told me you had scant regard for poetry.'

'He did, did he? Well, it seems dishonest to me to speak like an aristocrat. Most ordinary people do not have a notion.'

'My father has been a working man his whole life and read Shakespeare, George Herbert, John Donne and William Blake with a passion. What could be clearer and simpler than the metaphor of the sea as man's looking glass?'

'Oh, I am the first to contradict all my own dictates.'

'My father sees the appreciation of poetry and art as his right and his inheritance. I can thank my lucky stars for that.'

'I suppose I find it hard to believe in metaphor.'

'I don't believe I could understand the world without it.'

He wipes his hands on his smock. 'Let's throw in the towel, Jo, and go for a swim. I've done all I can do today. It's nearly five. I won't be needing you again to finish it. What do you think?' He stands back and beckons to her. She tries to hide her nervousness as she comes up to view the canvas.

Good grief, she thinks as she stares at the portrait, he has caught the determined chin of her mother's, her own chubby knuckles, the uneven pink mottling of her cheeks. She is not sure she agrees with such realism, she realises with a rush of indignation. But he has painted her eyes full of sorrowful beauty, her mouth as sensual and her hair abundant and gleaming around a thoughtful countenance. It is the closest portrait she has ever seen of her face. For a moment she imagines that he has been reading her mind, has entered the bemused and complex passageways and wandered in them at will. She struggles to speak at first.

'So...I...Well, I must say it is striking. You can see that I – or she, I mean – she's not dreaming about herself but is elsewhere. Yes, I...I like it very well. My brow, especially. You can see I'm thinking in there.' She stops and swallows. She is nearly overcome. This is a version of herself she has not seen before. 'Thank you.'

He bows extravagantly. 'No, I should thank you. It's been a rare pleasure.'

There is an awkward pause as they pull back from the intense concentration of the sitting and the success of the painting itself. Then Jo turns and gathers up her light shawl and her embroidered drawstring purse and pulls on her gloves. As he opens the white gilded door for her, and they walk down the staircase together, she knows that the white girl has gone.

Jim is no longer on the pier, nor in their bedroom at Hôtel le Lion d'Or. She explains to Courbet that she will not be joining him at the beach but he fails to listen.

'Come on, what harm can it do? The weather may change tomorrow. Look at the sea, will you? It's like a pond. The best looking glass I've seen yet, in fact. Leave word with the hotel reception that you've gone to the cove. Jim's probably on his way back.'

She fetches her bathing costume and towel and walks with Courbet to the cove. Every step she takes after him on the grassy path over the headland, she tells herself, *everything is chaste, everything is chaste.*

'Ah, the fresh sea air! The good it does you!' He whacks the weeds and nettles lining the path with his long staff.

They pass two young lovers entangled in the long grass. The girl hurriedly pulls down her skirts. Jo thinks of that first kiss at Hampton Court with Jim, how much she wanted him. Nothing can happen with Courbet, she insists to herself. She detests him. His pomposity, his stubbornness. Each step she takes in his shadow, she strikes another blow against him. His

201

monumental gluttony, his glib stupidity about poetry. What an unsettling man!

When they come over the crown of the headland they can see Jim down on the beach below in front of his easel.

'Ah, Monsieur Le Monocle!' Courbet cries. 'Time for a swim!'

Jim has painted Courbet into his seascape as a lone, dark figure that stands looking out past the reaches of tawny sand towards the golden dusky sky. There is something undeniably ominous and mournful about it.

'Oh there I am!' Courbet laughs when he sees Jim's painting. 'That will increase its value in Paris, *mon ami.*'

Jim looks at Jo sourly and arches his eyebrows.

Courbet is already changing into his togs. There are barely any waves. The water is lapping in small ripples at the shoreline. The sea looks like thinned warm honey in the early evening light.

Jim strips off completely and runs into the water. Jo changes and joins him. The water is glassy as she swishes through it. A white flat fish skims and flutters away along the sandy bottom. Jim swims back and takes her hands again so she can learn to float and kick. He tells her to do the breaststroke legs but her body keeps sinking. He holds her hands high and is pulling her along. Then there is a hand on her belly holding her up and looks around and Courbet has swum underwater beside her. He stands up, smiling, his eyes alive and cheeky. It is the first time he has touched her. She feels stung.

'Now let go, Jim. I've got her,' Courbet says. 'Move your arms, Jo.'

Courbet almost propels her through the water with his hand. If Jim is peeved, he does not show it. He does the breaststroke alongside her and she begins to synchronise her arms and legs. She glides through the water with Courbet keeping her afloat.

'This is heavenly!' Jo is laughing.

'Don't laugh. Concentrate or you'll duck under,' Jim says.

'She's doing fine.'

But Jim is right. She misses the timing and her chin dips and she swallows a gulp of saltwater. She chokes, panics, and stops and staggers. Courbet quickly seizes her waist and straightens her until she finds her feet.

'That's enough for one day.' Jim is treading water.

'But I was just getting the hang of it.'

'Don't be such a spoilsport, Whistler. Let's try again, Jo.'

Jim says nothing and turns and swims towards the shore.

'Nothing has happened,' Jo tells herself but when Courbet touches her again, it is as though the sea has become a huge erotic entity through which their charged bodies can touch. She practises again, with Courbet wading beside her, holding her up.

'Point and then turn the palms outwards and push the water away. Make your own path. That's it. Keep breathing.'

'Don't let go, will you?'

'Not on your life.'

But his hand supports her less and less and then pulls away. As she moves forward several more strokes on her own, her body seems to stretch and move differently than it does out of water. Her elbows and knees tuck and flare in time. Her breasts and belly relax into the buoyant horizontal and it is easy.

Then just as quickly, she flounders, her limbs a lead weight, and she sinks. Courbet reaches to pick her up again and she clasps his shoulders.

'You were swimming! Bravo!'

'Glory be, I was! It was marvellous. I've joined a whole new kingdom. Thank you so much!' She is lithe and light in his arms and suddenly embarrassed. His face is too close. She looks down, her feet finding the sandy floor. As she wades towards the shore, she notices that Jim has already left.

Jim is standing in the middle of the hotel room, smoking furiously. The ashtray is full, the air choking. Jo's hair is dripping down her back in tails. Her cheeks and lips are taut with salt. She goes to the bathroom and rinses her face and hands. She starts to heat the water for a bath and begins to undress.

Jim comes in and watches her. 'You were ridiculous, do you know that? Like some bloody tantalising siren out of the worst Frederic Leighton painting. What are you playing at?' His voice is fuming, his hands thrashing at nothing.

'Oh stop it. It's a bit of fun. I can swim – did you see me?'

'I saw more than I wanted. What else has he taught you, eh?'

'Nothing.' She has never seen him so incensed.

'I may as well pack my bag and baggage and go.'

He leaves the room. She follows him.

'Don't, Jim, please. We were clowning about, that's all.'

He stubs out his cigarette and lights another. 'I need to get away. Make something happen. I don't know. I've had enough. The joy has gone out of it. Maybe I should go to Chile. Be useful somehow.'

'You're over-reacting.' She goes towards him. He backs away.

'No, Jo, something's changed. Don't you think I know that face of yours? All its expressions? Every shade of emotion. There's a new light in your eye and it isn't for me.'

She winces. It unnerves her that Jim has recognised her desire almost as soon as she has acknowledged it herself. This man must really love her, she thinks. She softens.

'You're precious, Jim. I didn't mean to hurt you.'

There is a look on his face that she does not recognise. His eyes are hard black stones. He turns and looks out of the window. His voice is low when he speaks.

'You've dropped the vase. The one we pass between us. It's shattered.'

'No, Jim, you dropped it. I've been repairing it for months. Since Louisa.'

'So, what do we have left, Jo? Cracks. Broken crockery edged with glue?'

'He won't need me to finish the portrait. We can leave if you want.'

204

'I'll decide that.'

He blows out a column of forceful smoke, sits down and looks at her with a kind of cruel amusement. She is frightened of him for the first time. She glances at the door.

'I forbid you to see him.'

'Oh? And how do you intend to do that?' Her voice is rising. 'Keep me prisoner in this room?' She is being punished for something she has not done. 'Listen to yourself, for pity's sake.'

'I have always said you looked like a bit of a whore,' he says.

She is too stunned to speak. She closes her eyes, covers her mouth. She leans against the dressing table and grips its glass edge. She is being tugged down by a powerful undertow she had always known was there but has managed to avoid. Nothing can ever be as it was again.

'Well, come now, Jo, I wasn't your first, was I?' His lips are twitching with sarcastic rage. 'Well, was I? Who was he? Tell me.'

'I am warning you, James Whistler. Don't go any lower if you know what's good for you.'

'Well, I wasn't, damn it, was I?' He is shouting, his face distorted.

She will not reply, will never speak another word to him again. She brings a hand to her neck.

'Do you hear me?'

Her voice is quiet and even. 'I was fifteen. I fell pregnant. We were to be married. He left me. There.'

Her knees weaken and she slumps down and rests her back against the dressing table drawers. She does not know why but then she curls up in a ball on the floor, a spasm contracting her belly.

He comes to kneel beside her. He strokes her head and she flinches. 'Oh my poor Jo. I had no idea. I am so sorry.'

He cannot ask about the baby, please God, she says to herself. Do not let him ask. Not now. She wants to hold Bridget's hand, hear her voice.

'I didn't mean what I said. Forgive me, angel.' Jim spreads his palm on his chest.

She cannot speak. Neither of them moves. There seems to be no sound anywhere. She feels transparent.

'Jo? Are you all right?'

Her thoughts are tangled and turbulent, her stomach knotted. She is down in the jet black abyss, inside its lightless core. She has looked over its rim before, but she has never witnessed it from within. There is no way out. She is utterly alone. Panic spirals and seems to spin her around. Will she be able to haul herself out? Is this the beginning of the swirling lost world of madness?

'Shall I order some tea?'

Does she want tea? She knows that she should want it for Jim's sake. To show she can come back, can love him. His voice is a ladder. She takes it rung by rung. It takes all her strength.

'A warm cup of tea, my darling?'

She keeps climbing. She must focus on her hands and feet, lifting her slow limbs.

'That will make you feel better. Come on, sit up. You're starting to scare me.'

His hand rests lightly on her shoulder.

'Yes. Tea.' She nods her head as if she is not sure her words have come out. She begins to push herself up. She lets him take her in his arms. They sit huddled on the floor holding each other for a long time.

'And the baby, Jo? What happened to your baby?' he asks.

'Stillborn. Gone. After seven months.' Her voice is hollow, her heart is hollow. 'Gone.' Finally she begins to cry. She crumples against him and he rocks her back and forth.

Neither of them sleeps that night. Jo listens to the waves clasping and unclasping the shore. The sweep of the lighthouse beam through a chink in the curtains makes a thin bar of light travel over the wall. She watches it, waiting for it to recur and vanish again. Something inside her has been freed. Something she did not know that fell in a veil between her and Jim and coloured all her interactions with other men has slipped away. She has not told anyone but her sister about the baby, and its spoken clarity has swept through her body in a clear, rinsing emotion. She does not want to picture the dim, musty confessional of her childhood but she does. *I have sinned: I have carried a sin that was not mine. I lay it down here in the dark for you.*

VI
L'Origine du Monde, 1866

Whatever has got into Jim's head, no one can say. He has become utterly possessed with news of Chile and asks Willie for military advice about going there to defend it from Spanish attack. Jo has only ever seen him this fired up about a new painting with a new aesthetic direction. She asks Gabriel and Algernon to talk some sense into him and they ask anxiously what happened in France to make him cancel plans to go to Paris and abandon work towards the next Salon.

'Don't worry, Jo,' says Algernon. 'It's a romantic whim. He's too devoted to you and to his work to leave it all.'

'It's no longer a devotion that feeds him, I fear.'

For Jo, it is as though part of him has already left, departed on a steamer from Le Havre when she was not looking. Chile is like a beautiful, unknown, exotic woman, who offers the challenge and the romance Jo no longer can. Jim takes himself off to socialist meetings and lectures in a working men's club in Red Lion Square and finds a band of young men idealistic enough to set off on a stormy and dedicated adventure overseas with him. He will take his easel and paints of course, he says – you never know. His fervour reminds Jo of the collective enthusiasm of the Salon Des Refusés, but with this passion, she and Jim's friends remain outside it. He stocks up on travel books and maps of Chile and is vague about how long he will go for. Finally, he ignores a letter from Fantin urging him to reconsider and books a ticket from Southampton to Panama and carries it around to show people as if he has won a prize.

When they came back from Normandy, Jo returned to her father's house in Calthorpe Street and Jim visited less and less. In her being mended, something has been broken between them. Jo recognises that being around Courbet seemed to sap Jim's confidence in himself as an artist and a lover. He is suspicious of her, even though he works to disguise it and has no basis for it. They have sex rarely and in such a rushed and shallow fashion that she has to force herself to feel aroused. Since meeting Courbet, Jim has seemed more and more of a boy to her. She often thinks of that afternoon in the sea at Trouville when Courbet lifted her into his arms and she became a girl again, a carefree, pretty girl.

They had gone to Courbet's hotel briefly to say goodbye. He invited them up to his apartment, was eager for Jim to see the finished portrait, but Jim said they had a diligence to catch in ten minutes at the pier. He was fidgety and rude. Courbet was effusively sad to see them leave. As he waved them off with both arms, framed by the massive entrance, he looked like a medieval lord who had mistakenly ambled into the nineteenth century. Jo's eyes welled up at the thought of never seeing him again. His teasing, testing wit had made her feel she was his equal and that he could see her as she yearned to be.

She had turned her head away from Jim and swallowed hard as they climbed into the carriage. There was a screech of oystercatchers flying low over the water. She took a last look at the turquoise and red wharves and the breaking surf. The diligence carried them past quiet, autumn fields. The low sky was a strange kittenish grey-pink as if a storm was building in the mild air. The landscape and weather conspired to make her feel more and more indistinct.

That night she dreamt that she was in Courbet's white and gold hotel room, sharing his bed. There was a knock at the door and he called for them to come in. A couple of artists and their mistresses entered the room expectantly. Jo was horrified and said in a firm voice, 'I want you to myself.' But Courbet only laughed and beckoning them, he winked and said, 'The more the merrier.' More and more artists filled the room. Some wanted to watch, others wanted to join them in the bed. Jo started to scream at them all to get out. Courbet simply chuckled, his large naked body rippling with mirth.

She woke upset and chastened and went downstairs to light the fire. Mary had not arrived yet. It was still dark and she could hear the rain drumming on the windowpanes. Farringdon Road was still quiet. She remembered that it was the year's darkest day – the solstice – the day the Celts would celebrate until dawn with bonfires, dancing and singing away the darkness to welcome the reborn sun. There was an ancient stone chamber tomb her father told her about. What was it called? Where the first beam of the solstice sunrise would strike the gap under the lintel and hit the centre of the altar stone with perfect accuracy. She knelt down and turned and blew at the embers from the night before. The kindling caught a spark that glowed for a moment and then died. She took a sheet of newspaper and spread its headlines across the mouth of the hearth. The chimney sucked and pulled the paper inwards with a crackling sound as if the house itself was breathing. Then the flames ignited and shone through the newsprint lighting up the word 'Valparaiso'. She scrunched the paper and tossed it into the fire.

'Let's be together in sad and singing weather,' are Jim's farewell words at Waterloo station on the last day of January, 1866. She recognises the line from one of Algernon's poems.

'I pray so, my darling boy.' She holds him to her tightly and then lets him go. He waves his broad-brimmed hat from the window. She watches until the train has pulled away and then stands there uncertainly on the emptying platform, her eyes welling. What is this ridiculous war, she asks herself, and how did its lance reach from so far away to pierce her heart? How much easier it would be if all the women were waving off their men to the same front. But, she thinks as she puts her hands in her pockets, this is Jim's single, particular battle. And she sighs when she thinks of how she loves exactly that – his doughty, determined, singular spirit. And what life is she left with? What of her spirit? As she walks unsteadily along the platform she knows that she has to wake up to her own purpose. She needs a departure but does not know where to go.

When she pushes through the turnstile, her eyes blurring, she sees Fanny standing by a flower seller at the exit. She raises her hand and then shrugs and tries to smile. Fanny hands her a posy of crocuses and snowdrops.

'Bet you need a cuppa, old girl,' she takes Jo's arm. 'I know the perfect place for two ladies to take afternoon tea.'

'I shall miss him.' Jo struggles to stifle shedding tears. 'But you know, Fanny, he left me months ago.'

'I know, love. And yet you and Jim will never really lose each other.'

Jo spends most days at Tudor Lodge. Her father is outraged by Jim's hare-brained scheme and looks at her with such concern that she would rather avoid him. Jo tells him that Jim has left her enough money to last three months if she is careful.

'So, he'll be home by spring then?' he asks.

'Yes, Da.'

'Fair enough.'

She mopes about, drinking tea, chatting to Fanny and Algernon, reading poetry and trying to decide if she is truly on her own, or holding still, waiting for Jim to return and for their love to start ticking again like an old, reliable clock. London is disorientating without the focus he gave it. She has lost a best friend in losing a lover and her habit of sharing her thoughts and her everyday experiences with him is hard to shake. She catches herself thinking, what would Jim make of this grubby little Tuesday or what would he say if he tasted this mouthwatering, toasted coconut macaroon? For the first time in her life she is not sure if she knows anything at all about love. To have felt so certain for so long and to be left so uncertainly and swiftly, has rendered her self-conscious and diminished in confidence.

She helps Fanny feed and clean up the mess of the growing zoo and forms an attachment to a baby kangaroo. But she soon grows tired of this limbo. She needs work and learning. She cannot seem to commit to her own direction. She has lived most of her life so far by following her instinct and she is not sure what message it is giving her.

She has the strangest recurring dream. She is swimming without water. Oddly, it does not hurt to move along the ground but it takes immense effort. Dry swimming. Her body seems to

212

slowly harden without touch, harden and turn in on itself. She cleans her father's house mercilessly to make her feel as though she exists. Her distaste is doubled and her pleasure halved. The city seems tiresome and small without Jim's eyes lighting on it, lighting it up. She tries to remember the exact golden yellow of the broom that day as they walked to the beach at the Bay of Biscay. Had the young green shoots begun to break through the charred earth again?

Fanny is generous and patient with Jo's listlessness. She makes her a striking new dress in amber velvet and they go hunting for gloves and a bonnet to match. She gives her manicures and bakes her complicated cakes with too much cream. They are silly and affectionate with each other but they never mention the time they touched. They do not need to. The acute desire between them has stretched and lengthened into something else.

Late one evening when Gabriel and Algernon have gone to a private view at the Royal Academy, Jo and Fanny are sitting by the fireside looking through *The Queen* for new designs. Fanny seems preoccupied. When Jo asks her what is wrong, she is surprised to learn that Fanny's one regret is that she cannot have children.

'It might have taught me to love,' she says lightly.

'You? Love? Never!' Jo teases. Then she sees how troubled Fanny is and goes to sit beside her. 'Come now, dearest, you are the most loving person in the world. We can all see past the gruff and bluster, you know. You would have made a great mother. I am sorry, my sweet.'

'You too, Jo. Do you want children?'

Jo wants to confide in her, can feel sweat prick her palms at the thought of it. But just then a wombat shuffles into the room and Fanny gives it a firm kick in the snout. 'Out, Admiral! You know the rules. You've dug up the garden so that it looks like the King's Cross underground station and now you want to start in here.'

The moment has passed. The jab at Jo's heart lessens.

'I do want to create something. I'm not sure that it is children,' she says.

'What's keeping you?'

'I know,' Jo shrugs. 'Now, I've the chance to truly see the answer to that one.'

'Let's wrap up and go outside and watch the fireworks.'

A letter arrives from Paris bringing the change Jo needs. She writes back at once with her old vibrancy making her fingers dance and her eyes alert.

My dear Fantin,

It made me so happy to receive your letter and news of you, your new love and your latest still life paintings. I would be delighted to come and visit you as February, as you know, is London's grimmest month. You ask how I am and I must say that I can hardly answer. In a quiet, bemused chaos, I suppose. I feel like I am at the end of a brilliantly sunny day and seeing the sun begin to tinge everything a soft but slightly sad pink. My skin would be tingling from the sun's heat and I would watch the sun till the last minute before it slipped down below the horizon. It is funny to feel this melancholy just as spring is coming in on the plum branches outside my window. I keep expecting Jim to appear at my side in bed at night or when the front door opens, I think, that'll be Jim, now. We were so much part of each other's daily routine for so long that I miss him dreadfully. Sometimes I start to prepare his favourite dish and then remember that he is not here to share it.

My mind has been grasping for a reason for his impetuous passion for a war that is not his. Oh Fantin, I too wish that you had been here to warn him against it. He has made me the full beneficiary of his will, but do not breathe a word of this to anyone as gossips will have a heyday. All I know is that he wanted to get out and get on and his art was at an impasse – the most serious one yet. Get out where, get on how, he did not know. Chile gave him the answer. You would have thought he had won a grand commission he was so exhilarated.

You ask how things fare with us. I feel left behind but the truth is that our leaving one another began some time ago. We still love each other deeply. Sometimes I think Jim is the 'man' of me and I am the 'woman' of him and we fit together. I remember once after a quarrel he wanted to swim out into the Bay of Biscay and never return. This quarrel is mostly with himself. I cannot imagine how he will manage with the food and the heat, let alone the fighting. He was never cut out to be a soldier, as you well know. Thank you for being a dear and loyal friend to us both.

Yours,

Jo

Fantin is there to meet Jo at the Gare du Nord. She is so gladdened that she has to lower her face to hide a rush of tears. They embrace exuberantly. He is all dapper in an expensive black wool overcoat, a mustard-striped waistcoat and a gleaming top hat with mustard trim. They go to a café off the main square to have a drink. She tells him how three drunken men harassed her on the ferry and because the weather was devilish she was seasick and unable to stay below deck.

'My poor Jo. You'll have to wear a veil when you travel alone. Look as though you're in mourning – no one will bother you.'

'A splendid idea and not far from the truth.'

'Oh forgive me. That was insensitive. Let me get you a brandy.' He stands up to head to the bar and says over his shoulder, 'Courbet's joining us shortly. I hope you don't mind.'

'Oh, no, I – ' Jo gasps and stutters. 'I need to freshen up.'

'Oh ladies. I didn't think of that. We'll leave word with the owner and come back in an hour. How's that?'

'I'm surprised Courbet's been prised out of Brasserie Andler.'

'Haven't you heard? It's been shut for demolition.'

'And his studio?'

'Safe as yet. Anyway, he was delighted to hear of your arrival and would have dashed up to Calais if I'd let him.'

Her face and neck get hot and she takes a gulp of brandy.

Fantin hails a cab and they talk animatedly about their mutual friends in London and Paris and who he has lined up for her to meet. She is too flustered to enjoy the ride down the new boulevards, to savour her homecoming to Paris. What will she say to Courbet? She has a quick vision of his dark-haired, muscled forearms, his broad barrelled chest.

'So, I saw Courbet's portrait of you from Trouville. He's made two more copies people like it so much. It's quite spectacular. You look naive and mature at the same time.'

'May I always be!'

Ah Fantin, she thinks, those benign eyes and that swept-back ginger hair. How odd to see him without Jim at their side.

'You're very present as you, if you know what I mean. What was it like?'

'To not be "The White Girl", you mean?' She begins to laugh and mimics Courbet's accent. 'He said I was too professional. And I doubt if I was grateful enough to be chosen by The Great One.'

'Oh Jo, I'd forgotten what a breath of fresh air you are!' He presses her arm. 'He has a reputation, you know.'

'Oh he brought that with him to Trouville too.'

'He works hard though.'

'He drinks and eats hard too. He's very fortunate to have such intense focus and certainty when he paints. His eye is so decisive.'

'And modest with it,' Fantin adds in an undertone.

'Ha! That's a good one!'

'And do you ever see Alphonse?' Fantin asks.

'Not at all. A sore point.'

'Our little *société* is indeed fragmented.'

216

It is still the same tiny room in the rue Laromiguière with no room to unpack and nothing to unpack into, yet it is magnificent and the greying sky over the slate rooftops of Paris never feels as glum as London's greasy grey. She stands for a moment and watches the lowest bank of cloud fragment and catch the wind and the lamps come on in the maids' rooms in the attics nearby.

Later, back at the café, Courbet is hunched at a table in the corner, nursing his pipe and a glass of milk. He leaps to his feet when he sees them and encloses Jo in an enormous bear hug. She is alarmed to see that he has lost weight and asks if he is unwell. He takes her hand and peers into her eyes, 'I'll be well, now, seeing you. It's a stomach upset. It's upset that it's had to leave me!' He pats himself robustly with both hands where his paunch used to be and lets out his habitual and reassuring belly laugh.

'And you, winter agrees with you. Glimmering pallor – lovely, lovely.'

She presses her nails into her palm to control her blush. 'Au contraire, I miss the daylight. The only thing I like about winter is the clothes. I'm not stifled.'

'And Whistler's off to be a big gun? Bizarre, no?'

Fantin shrugs and Jo does not reply. As Fantin goes to the bar, Jo follows him with her eyes, then makes an engrossing study of her fingernails.

'I find enough battles to fight right here with recalcitrant buyers and bent brasserie owners,' Courbet says.

Fantin passes Jo another brandy.

'I'm taking Andler to court. He says I owe over 3,500 francs for the past eight years,' Courbet snorts.

'But everyone and his mother drank at your table,' Fantin says.

'Most of them never had a sou. Did you sell *Hommage, Fantin?* You look as if you did.'

'Handsomely,' Jo smiles with some pride.

'And what will keep you out of mischief in Paris?' Courbet asks Jo.

'I want to attend an atelier. I'm doing a series of drawings on the seven ages of woman.'

'I recommended Atelier Suisse on Ile de la Cité.' Fantin offers Courbet a cigar and they both light up.

'Yes, I followed Delacroix there and Pissarro and Cézanne followed me. It's always full. And tell me, Jo, are you looking for sitting work, may I ask?'

She is not sure if he is taunting her. 'If it's paid. Yes, I may be able to fit it in,' she says lightly.

'I'll mention you to a few people, then,' he says, without looking at her.

This leaves her slightly crushed. She had not realised how much she wanted to pose for him again, to be around him. It is months later, she supposes to herself, he will have a string of new models. He had painted her portrait and was done with her. She hopes her disappointment is not visible. Her face always shows too much. She finds a handkerchief and pretends to blow her nose. The handkerchief reminds her of Jim and suddenly she is overcome with missing him, the 'we' they were, his 'shall we, Jo?', his eyes giddy with fervour. Paris is all at once full of strangers, ragpickers, pickpockets and scavengers and she has that fearful wave of homelessness she sometimes suffers. She misses London, coming up the Charing Cross Road, the curve of the red buildings of Shaftesbury Avenue ahead. Fantin can see she is fatigued and suggests that they leave.

'You won't have a bite with me?' Courbet asks. 'The shrimp salad won't be as fine as in Trouville but...'

'Some other evening, I'd be delighted,' Jo shakes his hand.

'Tomorrow then. Come to Brasserie des Martyrs. Around 6pm. You know I skip lunch.'

As she leaves with Fantin she finds she is furious with herself. She will not put herself in this position of being no more than a sitter again. She must find her own way to be in this city, to become an artist and look for her own muse.

The crooked, narrow cobbled streets and irregular buildings of Montmartre have survived Haussmann unscathed. The button and boot shops and the poky bars are still there. Jo has heard of the Brasserie des Martyrs but never visited it. There is a young lady the same age as Jo seated at Courbet's table. Jo ripples with apprehension. She should not have come. Courbet greets her cordially and introduces the blonde-haired Madame Lydie Jolicler. She is highly fashionably dressed, with expensive taste and looks as though she is going on somewhere fancier later. Jo feels outdated and out of place.

'Oh, but you're even prettier in the flesh,' Lydie says as she greets Jo.

'Lydie is from near Ornans where I grew up. I kidnapped her from a carriage passing through one night and made her play the piano at a local concert we were putting on.'

Lydie laughs coquettishly. She strokes her beaver fur collar. 'It's true. I was livid at the time. I missed the theatre at Besançon.'

Her face is flat and heart-shaped with a small nose and mouth. Her expression changes from one moment to the next. She is almost stern as she turns directly to Jo and says, 'But, this is a good man, a true friend and an exceptional artist. He repaid me as he promised he would with an exquisite portrait.'

Jo does not know how to respond. Courbet straightens his grey satin waistcoat.

'He has three sisters – I've met them all and he's a loyal brother to each of them.' The chandeliers are lowered and lit and the light flickers on the gilt mouldings around the walls.

'If she wants to know about them she can read Champfleury's book,' Courbet says with a note of impatience.

'Yes, his friend wrote a novel based on the family, you know.'

'My one-time friend, I think, Lydie.'

She gives him a tiny look of reproach with just her eyes and Jo has to choke back a giggle as it dawns on her that Madame Jolicler has been engaged to vouch for Courbet's upstanding character. She stares at the painted panels on the walls to distract herself but a tiny smile plays on her lips.

'He comes to stay with my husband and me when he needs to rest and recharge.'

Courbet is about to speak but stops himself. He barely looks at Jo. It strikes her as wrong that he is so docile. She catches sight of them in one of the long mirrors and smiles to herself. The composition reminds her of Jim's painting of her as a prostitute with two men on the terrace of the Rose at Wapping – only in this composition two women are negotiating over a man.

'What's so amusing, Miss Jo?' Courbet asks.

'I'm happy to be back.'

'The whole room is happy. Can't you see them looking at you?'

Her shoulders soften and she begins to relax. She orders chicken liver pâté, roast duck with a mushroom and sherry sauce, fried potatoes and almond tart with cream to finish. She eats with relish and is too caught up in Lydie's vivacious charm to notice Courbet's table manners. He leans back in his chair and lights his pipe.

'You must come and visit us, Jo, when Paris is too much. It's in the foothills of the Alps.' Lydie touches Jo's hand. 'The air makes you ten years younger overnight.'

'And if it makes me twenty years younger, all the better,' Courbet says with a guffaw.

'But first,' Lydie continues merrily, 'there are new department stores to show you. They are the last word! And you must visit the House of Worth.'

The Atelier Lévy takes up the top floor of a former Huguenot silk-weaver's house. The south-facing skylights along the sloping ceiling allow excellent light, especially in the morning. There are twelve students, and among them, Jo has met a wealthy young woman called Sophie Arnaud. Today, Monsieur Lévy introduces Marielle, a beautiful mulatto model. She slips off her cream silk dressing gown in a perfunctory way and rubs her hips and belly casually before lying down on her side along a yellow chaise longue. Jo is more nervous than the first time she modelled before a room of artists even though Lévy had praised her drawings of her mother, Bridget, Fanny and young girls on the streets of Holborn. The atmosphere is more relaxed than in the London studios, with more chit-chat among the students. But this is the first time she has drawn a nude and can barely look at her. It has taken her years to be on the other side of modelling and now that she is sitting in the dream she carried for so long, she can barely believe it exists. It reminds her of swimming – she must trust that she will float.

Lévy is a spry, intense fellow with a bald, oval head and a fastidiously thin moustache. His wiry eyebrows run in a thick line across the bridge of his nose which moves down when he leans in to peer at work or arches up like an agitated caterpillar when he is stressing a point about style: 'Line is more important than colour and no colour is as important as black. Everything lies in relation to the dark solidity of black. The shadow. The abyss.' He speaks in time to his step, marching about the room, pointing and gesticulating with his cane as he quotes his favourite painters and recalls their masterpieces in astounding detail. He provides such an engaging one-man show, with such passionate eloquence, that at times Jo has to tune him out to focus on her drawing. 'Don't be afraid of the dark. All happiness depends on our ability to survive suffering, after all.' Sophie mouths his phrases behind his back but it is clear that the class respects him enormously.

As she draws, Jo finds herself thinking of all she learnt from Jim's style quarrelling with the way she has watched Courbet paint. After a while she has stopped seeing only the nudity and has begun to see the beauty of the lines of the model's body and wants to work out the challenge of how to show the fuller left breast, the slight pucker of the right nipple, the lighter shades of skin on the model's palms and soles. What is the difference between showing her with her eyes closed and conveying that she is asleep? Can she make the face slacken? She finds that she has to forget both Jim and Courbet to concentrate on her work and make it her own. If she imagines either of them looking over her shoulder, she is done for.

221

'Elasticity, Mademoiselle Hiff.,' Lévy says. It sounds almost like 'If' in his accent. 'The skin moves. It's always moving. Even in death.'

It was her old problem of being too static. How hard it is to portray stillness without it looking inert. He is right. It must breathe. If, If, If... The curve of the thigh; the dimple below her hipbone; the neat fuzz of her pubic hair; her lean, lanky calves and neat ankles. She imagines a baby curled at her breast. Also asleep. How that would alter the drawing and alter the breast. She needed to find a baby. The drawing needed it. The stage of being a mother.

She approaches Sophie at the end of the class. 'Excuse me, I need to ask you for a favour.'

'Fire away, Mademoiselle If.' Sophie scans her with her wide, mobile eyes.

'I need a baby.'

Sophie laughs. 'I certainly don't!'

'To draw, I mean. Do you know of anyone who'd let me come and make sketches? Or a mother and child?'

'Of course! My sister has a two-month-old baby boy. A darling. She might pose too. She fancies herself as a bit of an actress but has no talent whatsoever – don't say I said so – far too over-dramatic. Leave it with me.'

'I can't really pay much.'

'Not a problem, my dear. She married into more money than she knows what to do with. And she's had plenty of practice already. Can I invite you to have lunch?'

Later Jo walks back to Fantin's with a little ardent cog running inside. She is grinning to herself. She has no edges, is dissolving into a liquid happiness, the images she wants to create gathering large around her like parts of herself she has never shown or been able to be. Today the streets of Paris are her streets. She cuts through Jardin du Luxembourg where men in overcoats and hats sit reading the newspaper and students study in the white wooden chairs scattered along the paths and under the trees. She goes in search of the bas-relief wall fountain of Leda

222

and the Swan, behind the new Medici Fountain that Lévy mentioned to her. She stands and stares at it for a long time, sketching the limp neck of the swan, the flailing arm above Leda's head, her powerful torso. She will remake it. Her Leda will avenge Zeus.

She walks down a long wide avenue of horse chestnuts beginning to come into bud above the line of majestic marble statues commemorating queens and other illustrious women. Who was Clémence Isaure and what did she hold up in her strong left hand? A torch or a sword? It reminds her of that dynamic self-portrait of Artemisia Gentileschi with her hand raising a paintbrush towards a canvas and her whole body engaged as one forceful diagonal behind it.

The dun-coloured bare branches of a poplar are picking up the sunlight and shining it back. How happy to be that exposed, to shine back, to weather the season, she thinks. What does it matter what she achieves in the world's terms, as long as there are moments like these? She is the poplar and the poplar is her, if only for a split second. It is a joy, this living, after all, she thinks. The seventh woman in the series will be a tree-like crone, her mouth a gnarly knot, the creases around her eyes spreading out to let in the sky.

When she gets back to the rue Laromiguière there is a box addressed to her containing one arum lily. There is a card from Courbet. Will she come to his studio at 2pm to see a new painting? Her mouth is a white lily, just opened.

She will.

And she does. She does not have time to stop for lunch. She sidesteps a woman with a broom whisking the dust from her doorway and the section of footpath outside her building into the gutter. Perhaps because Jo is rushing like a true city-dweller, her long skirts sweeping the pavements, a man stops her and asks her for directions. When she replies that she does not know, he asks her what part of France she is from. She is speaking like a native. It tickles her.

When she sees Courbet's building ahead on the corner of the rue Hautefeuille, her step quickens. It is so hard for this flammable body not to want to burn, she thinks as she walks. Climbing the ornate Louis XIII staircase, she imagines a grand, light-filled studio, a room as luxurious as in the Hôtel Casino.

Nothing has prepared her for the scene that greets her when Courbet opens the door and ushers her in. The place is in complete disarray with canvases and dirty clothes and rags and pipes and newspapers and beer glasses littered everywhere. He waves his hand at a small group of other spectators and says gaily, 'Associates and apprentices, this is Jo!' She is deflated by the presence of the crowd and under the familiar acidic whiff of the oils and the tobacco smoke, there is the odour of something else she cannot name. Courbet stands at the easel putting the finishing touches to a large canvas of a deer and a stag by a woodland stream. Ample light comes pouring in from the large skylight above him. Another small window looks out onto the street. The high-beamed, arched ceiling is the only sign left that the room was once the apse of a chapel. Courbet offers her a misshapen chair but she shakes her head. Huge rolls of white canvas encroach from the corners. Various implements – a hammer, a mallet, screwdrivers, pliers and a saw – hang from nails banged into the wall. She tries to not look around but rather to concentrate her attention on the painting. As a landscape, it is extraordinarily serene – all light and delicate handling of the glade's greenery and a gentle subtlety in the alert stillness of the wild animals. The only thing that offsets the balance of the canvas is the figure of Courbet, the hunter, on the right, knocking the composition off with its angular, dark dominance. He makes a couple more deft daubs with his palette knife and stands back with some satisfaction. It is then that she sees something lying on the floor and gives a horrified cry. It is a dead stag, its white tail unbelievably fresh and fluffed up, the fur on its flank still a chestnut gleam and its antlers pointing towards her.

Jo turns hot then cold as a spell of dizziness overcomes her. A shutter closes. Red shadows flash and fragment behind her eyelids. She can hear a voice but cannot seem to identify its source or direction for a moment. She cannot remember falling

224

asleep, so what is this slow, queasy awakening, this mental heaviness? Then she comes round and finds she is lying on the floor with a ring of trouser legs and shoes standing around her. She has not fainted before. She is exposed and ridiculous, absurdly female.

'Give her air,' someone says.

'You're all right. Here, a drop of water.'

'Open the door.' She recognises Courbet's voice and sits up. She wipes her hand over the sweat on her brow. She should have eaten earlier. Courbet opens the small window.

'I am fine. Really, it's nothing.' Her voice is gluey.

The other visitors say their goodbyes and Courbet waits until she can sip some water before speaking as if afraid of startling her further. She tries to stand up, but Courbet touches her arm softly.

'Please wait a moment. You're as white as a sheet. And I didn't think you could get any paler. They've taken the beast out. I didn't realise it was still here. A butcher's stall near Les Halles supplies them for me. It was a bit rank. I'm sorry.'

'The figure is wrong.' She is bold because she is still almost outside her body. 'The hunter.' She nods towards the painting.

'So wrong it made you faint. My! I've never had that kind of visceral response. It shall go at once.' He pretends to get up.

'Wait – '

'No, you're absolutely right and everyone else is too damn sycophantic to tell me. I've dithered about it, taken him out, put him in again and that should have been a sign – I never dither. He belongs in another painting and in fact I stole him from an earlier portrait.'

'He's a fine figure – I – ' Shyness stops her.

'Is he really? Is he not cursed with always being in the wrong place? Or at the wrong time?' He is opening and closing his big hands and will not meet her eye.

'If he holds back any longer he may be too late.'

He looks up, hopeful as a boy. He leans over and kisses her. She puts her arms around his neck. Then he lifts her up and

225

carries her to the small bed behind a wooden partition at the other end of the studio.

He starts to undress her slowly, carefully, as if she has been wounded, kissing her bare neck, her chest, her shoulders as he reveals them. She tries to reach up and touch his face and to undo the buttons of his shirt but he stops her.

'Let me have you. I need to hear you cry out for me.' His voice is guttural and urgent.

She wavers on the edge of panic. She has not lain so passive with a man and let her body be taken before. She does not know if she can be so helpless and sees herself elongating along a dark tunnel like vapour. Her chest tightens and she glances uneasily around the small, untidy room, then back to his face.

'My, what a luscious girl you are.' He is soft with emotion, his eyes glassy. He seems bigger and more well-built than before as if desire has broadened and defined every muscle. He turns her on her front and unlaces her corset. She can feel his breath on her back as he lowers down her undergarments. Wetness begins a slow stream down her inner thighs.

'The shade of you, the scent of you, the shape of you, are all sweeter than I imagined...than I dared imagine.'

A shiver of fear and pleasure shoots through her. He plays with her, caressing her buttocks, dipping his hands down between her legs. It is easier to surrender lying this way with her face hidden. Both his hands find their way under her and knead her breasts, pinch her nipples. She does not know what he will do next but likes the measured, authoritative manner in which he discovers her. Then she wants to see him and attempts to turn but he presses her down with tender firmness.

'I've got you. Don't I know what is good for you, my little one?' He is licking her ear, talking to her, telling her how much he wants her. She wishes he would touch her. She begins to push her hips up towards him. He growls. She can feel his cock against her. She is ready to burst, feels as if she will climax without his touch. She squirms and lets out a groaning sound. He raises her on to all fours and strokes her clitoris. She is so aroused across her pelvis and groin that it takes a long time for her to climax, but when she does, it is full and complete, roaring out of her throat and bolting from inside her like something wild getting free. He eases his cock inside her and she rocks back against him, as though she could fuse her molten hips to his hard, tense frame.

He falls back, finally sated, his breathing forced.

He pulls her to lie on top of him and holds her.

'My God, never in all my life have I heard a holler from a woman like that. If only I could paint that!'

She smiles. She likes the new way to enjoy her body, to feel strong and greedy and open to being taken.

'A man could change for you, Jo.'

She smiles, says nothing. She knows it is the afterglow of sex talking but she is moved. No matter what she says, every woman wants to be the one to tame the untamed, she thinks. And then, she considers as she stares at the holy ceiling, they miss the wild man they have lost and he misses him too and must go out and find him in someone else.

'Let me look at you, my redhead beauty.' Courbet rolls over and leans up on one elbow. 'Hmmmm...sumptuous.' He kisses each breast and kisses a trail down her belly to her sex. 'Ah, I'll call this the Prophet.' He nuzzles between her legs. 'I can't leave this. Its smell, its taste have possessed me. What quiet neat edges...and then the roar of it. It's the most beautiful thing I've ever seen.' His fingertips touch the edge of her lips, trace where the flesh of her thighs meets her groin.

'I know what you're thinking,' she says quietly.

'What?'

'You want to paint it. You're choosing the palest cream, the hint of wet red – '

He looks up. 'No, Jo, stop. Believe me, having you is better than painting you. This is now. Now as your lover I am looking at you, wanting you. You're the one who cannot be here...is thinking of the next painting. The job. The work. Be here with me.'

He's touched a sharp, sore spot. 'I'm sorry. You're right. Thank you, Gustave.'

She strokes the crown of his head and feels a hot tear roll down her cheek.

'Let's eat!' He does not wait for her reply and is already up, seizing his clothes. He dresses so haphazardly, it is a novelty to watch. She is surprised that he is steady enough to stand. She would have preferred to have lain together, talked and separated more gradually. He rinses his face and hands in the basin at the washstand and dries himself off. He smoothes down his hair and his beard. She remembers the first time she saw him walk into the sea, as if he was anointing himself with it.

'I wasn't sure if I would ever have you,' he looks down at her, fresh-faced. 'But he was!' He grabs his crotch. 'He's seldom wrong.'

'Cheeky sod!' She pretends to be indignant, but she had felt exactly the same. Her cunt knew. Her prophet.

She washes quickly and tries not to look too closely at the hand towel he has offered her.

'Am I all right like this or should I change? I'm a scruff beside you. An old codger and a scruff.'

'Don't bother. You look splendidly bohemian,' she says but she is touched.

'Oh, not that!' he says emphatically. 'Anything but that! Most bohemians are mere poseurs, not real artists at all. They have a wretched disease called "artistism". They think an artist is a child, running free. An artist is someone who knows where to buy paints and where to put them.'

He turns and changes his shirt and waistcoat.

As they walk towards Café Momus, Jo is ravenous and happy. She is relieved that she did not think of Jim at all and then she feels a hint of shame. Courbet, the cock of the walk, is singing his heart out.

The next morning, the concierge brings Courbet his coffee. The mixture of resignation and pride on her face intrigues Jo. Her back is bent into the letter 'C'. She greets Jo inquisitively and jokes with Courbet. The vertical lines carving her cheeks seem to disappear when she smiles. Her unhurried manner and quiet poise make Jo think that she has made peace with her age and the life she has led. Jo hopes her own face will tell that story when she is old. Would she agree to sit for her if she asked? She will mention it to Courbet.

As she gets ready to leave, Courbet insists that Jo sees something first and he slides out a canvas to show her. *Psyche and Venus,* he explains, was rejected by the Salon last year. 'What's so offensive against morality in that?' he asks as he swivels the canvas around to face her.

It is a portrait of two nude women in bed, one kneeling above the other who is still asleep. It is shockingly direct. The women look full of might but the drapery seems too purposeful to her.

'Of course,' he goes on, 'I had to call it that or it wouldn't have been considered at all. What do you think?' He is watching her closely. An almost fearful shadow crosses his face.

'I like the sleeping figure very much. Dare I say, the sheets almost seem like another person between them.'

'They are! A priest and an archbishop. The chap who was going to buy it demanded that I insert that absurd drapery – I should never have agreed but the 16,000 francs had a hand in it, I must admit.'

'So you can be bought,' Jo teases, 'in spite of all your boasts of independence and free will.'

'To change a public's taste, its way of seeing, is no small thing, Jo. Painting, when you think about it, is a state of frenzy, a continual struggle, a way of going crazy.' He begins to cough and bang his chest. He taps his pipe on the table and refills it.

'So why is the painting still here?'

'Oh, now he says he never agreed to the sale – it's another court case, I'm afraid. A deplorable waste of time.'

He stands and studies her with a dancing light in his eye. 'And you, have you ever...' he pauses.

'Ever what?' she asks though she knows fine and rightly what he is going to say. She realises that he did not want her opinion of the work of art at all.

'Have you, well...ever loved a woman?'

'Yes, but that's not what you mean, is it?' She is racing him, enjoying their speed, like skaters who have forgotten their fear of falling. She moves playfully towards the table and collects her bonnet and jacket. She pauses, looks at him. 'Men are not as necessary to a woman's pleasure as they like to believe.'

'And you may not believe me when I say that that can be a relief. It thrills me to see a woman aroused by another woman.'

She goes towards the door and says over her shoulder. 'I understood that men dislike feeling superfluous.'

'No, for me to see that hidden side of her that I'll never access ...I...I like it when something unknown reveals itself. It's a privilege.'

'We're always searching for the inside of some experience, to feel what it is like inside someone else.' She places her hand on the handle of the door. She has the rush of the memory of Fanny's touch, meeting the mirror of her own shape that summer afternoon. 'Something always remains unknown.'

'Yes, perhaps, that's why we keep wanting to paint it. To get further in. To be allowed.' He is crushed with embarrassment. 'I do imagine – no, you wouldn't – you – ' He twists his hands like a hawser.

'What? Say it.'

' – you with a woman, letting me watch.'

She swings open the door. 'Letting you paint, you mean. Adieu, Monsieur Courbet.' She waves and dances down the stairs.

As she walks back through the morning streets towards the Latin Quarter, she wonders where 'Psyche' and 'Venus' are now and feels an unexpected barb of jealousy. She would do it better, more convincingly, she finds herself considering. Why does going further than he thinks she will, give her such acute pleasure? As she crosses rue Saint-Jacques, she imagines that she is connected to a clandestine sexual tributary running beneath everything she sees in the street: the high dimples on the cheeks of a shop-girl; the raffish man playing the tin whistle who tips it up at her as she passes by; the lingering eyes of a bank clerk, all make her energy soar as if she will never need to sleep again. It reminds her of the underground rivers in London, rivers like the Peck, the Fleet, the Tyburn and the Effra and how she once saw water gushing out through great cracks in the middle of the Caledonian Road from a hidden source. She searches the faces of passing men and women to intuit if they too are day-dreaming of pleasure, or counting down the hours until they can strip off, be adored, released into someone's arms. She wonders if all the other stuff of life – manners, clothing, work, shopping, eating, waiting at bus stops – was all there simply to serve, to make ready for these moments of extreme delight, of naked delirium, of the joy of the touched, touching body. She is bursting with the greed of it; its softening eyes; its opened face.

For the first several hours, Jo is contented and serene, enjoys her class and arranges to meet Sophie's sister, Camille, the following day. But by the afternoon she is anxious and unsettled, unsure where it is stemming from until it blooms into the most overwhelming lust. She regrets that they did not agree to meet – does he assume that she will come around to his studio at 5pm? She is perturbed by the casualness of it all, realises that she prefers something more spoken. Jim would never let her out of his sight without knowing exactly how many hours he had to wait to see her again. She realises that she is less wild and liberated than she would like to think she is, after all.

Try as she does to banish Courbet from her thoughts, every gesture seems redundant without his eyes seeing it, each movement aches to touch his body again. It reminds her of when she was swimming and foundered, returned clumsily to the element of air, the unrelenting pull of gravity in her feet, the secret skill lost. She goes back to Fantin's to see if Courbet has sent any word. Nothing. Fortunately, Fantin is at his studio and does not witness her distraction.

Later that evening, she is embarrassed to find herself in the rue de Poitevins outside the brasserie run by le père Laveur, Courbet's new dining haunt. She gives the windows a sidelong glance and catches sight of him at a table, swathed in smoke, surrounded by a ring of exuberant friends. She has not enough nerve to go in and hurries by. She buys some baguette, ham and mustard and goes home but finds that she has no appetite. Later in bed, she dares to touch herself for the first time, climaxing to the remembered sound of Courbet's dirtiest voice saying, 'I want to use you' and the image of him towering over her, slathered and charged as a cavalry horse, his pupils wide with dark, fulfilling joy.

She wakes early the next day in an unthinkable state. If she could have sex with him just once more, she tells herself, then she would be cured. She itches as if she is in heat. She has heard other women describe their hunger this way but this is the first time she has experienced it. She is beside herself. Recklessness bolts through her: she will get up and march straight to his studio. She wants his large hands on her, handling her. She gets dressed in a flurry of exultation and then she falters. She changes her dress and bonnet and checks herself in the mirror. No. She tells herself in an admonishing voice to resist...resist... She will not go to his studio... She will meet Camille and her infant and spend the morning drawing them as planned. She experiences a streak of ire that he can make her so distraught and scolds herself as she takes the stairs: *Remember only your art. Forget only your heart.*

Camille lives in a narrow townhouse with its own courtyard entrance and back garden in the rue Soufflot. She still carries the extra weight of pregnancy and like Sophie, has big, inquisitive eyes, but her face is rounder and her hair more blonde. It is mild enough to drink tea at a small metal table in the garden where pale apple blossom is beginning to break out on the overhanging tree. Jo cuddles Georges so that he can grow accustomed to her and breathes in the scent of baby milk. His active eyes seem to follow her lips as if to grasp what she is saying. It is a long time since she has felt the soft pliable body of a newborn and it engrosses her.

Camille loves the idea of a drawing of her breastfeeding and agrees that Jo will do one as a commission and as many as she needs for herself. They move into the sitting room, which is full of carved stone statues and small bronze figures Camille's husband has collected around the world. They seem to watch and wait like a silent, benevolent audience. Jo particularly admires one with pointed breasts and her hands on her hips.

'It's from the Middle East. From about the 2nd century BC,' says Camille. 'It's funny you should select that one because it's a votive to Ishtar. She was the Babylonian goddess of fertility. You can pick it up, you know.'

Jo considers how she can bring this figure into the series. Then as she runs her fingers over it she notices that the votive has large ears, earrings even, eyes, a nose but no mouth. The ideal mother cannot speak.

Lévy has advised Jo to try sumi inkstick and inkstone and Chinese paper, to use looser calligraphic lines and more washes and Fantin has given her a goat-hair brush to test. She is eager to see how the experiment turns out and soon discovers that she likes the freedom of a new medium and using as few lines and tones as possible.

Camille nestles into the corner of the sofa and feeds Georges till he falls asleep, his mouth unlatching from the nipple. Jo works on a drawing board balanced on the arms of a chair. She tries to sketch blindly at first, looking at Camille, not the paper, to limber up and erase the interval between seeing and recording. She reaches a peaceful, absorbed plateau during the session and as Camille falls asleep too, she has the drawing she wanted. She can remember after the death of her baby how, for a long time, she could not look at mothers and infants without extreme physical pain burning down her torso. She imagined she had become transparent and needed to hide the poverty of her glass body, its failed fecundity. For months the street

233

corners of London seemed to ambush her with perambulators and babies' piercing wails.

She is pleased and consoled to discover that sitting in the radius of Camille's direct and mesmeric love has gently, almost imperceptibly, diluted some of the hurt she has carried since she was fifteen.

As she leaves Camille's with her new drawings twilight is falling and the sparrows begin to signal the calamity of nightfall from the rooftops and window ledges. She realises as she follows the indigo Paris skyline that art happens when you do not notice what you are holding, what you have let go, what is touching what; things connect through you, as if in spite of you, in spite of – or was it because of? – past wounds. Then she thinks of Courbet and realises that when sex is so good, it creates a kind of art that touches both ways and that is why people believe in it, arrange each detail in their life to make it happen again and will sacrifice everything for it.

Fantin is making a pot of tea when she gets home. He gives her a big grin.

'So you amused yourself well the other night? Someone new, may I ask?' He strokes his ginger beard playfully.

'Someone old, actually. But it's not serious.' Jo slices a lemon for the tea.

'Anyone I know? You're blushing. It must be.' He tilts his chin to the side.

'Please don't press me. It may be over already.' She closes her eyes as if that can protect her.

'It's Courbet, isn't it?'

She knows her face betrays her. 'Yes.'

He claps his hands. 'You are scandalous, Jo. And fantastic! Into the lion's den.'

'I will keep my head.' She hopes he cannot tell how skittish she is as she lifts the teacup to her mouth. 'And can I show you a set of drawings?' she asks. 'I seem to have found a model.'

'Who is coming out of her shell?'

'I still need it to curl up in sometimes.'

That night she dreams that she is rowing a small boat across a wide ocean when the cresting waves on either side of her transform into silver fish that rear up and stand on their tails and lift the boat magically into the air and carry it forward. She sleeps on with a new kind of ease and certainty and wakens with the image clearly surrounding her and the lasting feeling of being buoyed up and transported. If Jim gave her a grammar to understand art, Courbet has given her the courage to use it for herself: to really speak it.

The next morning a red rose is delivered with a note.

> My dear Jo,
>   It would be my great delight if you would join me this weekend on a trip to a hotel in the country. Platform 4, Gare de L'Est at 11am on Saturday.
> Gustave

Courbet has dressed for the occasion, kitted out in new grey and black trousers banded in horizontal stripes and a green velvet waistcoat. He tells her that he is taking her to a small hotel in the pretty, medieval town of Nogent-sur-Seine, south-east of Paris. She wonders if that is where he takes all his mistresses. He is attentive and talkative on the train and apologises for having neglected her – he has been finishing a new commission for a Turkish collector called Khalil Bey he wants her to meet. A former Ottoman ambassador in St Petersburg, no less. A fellow who loves gambling and painting and undressed women. He owns a Delacroix and an Ingres. She says she would love to meet him, view the collection.

He is more relaxed outside Paris, more like the Courbet she knew from the cove at Trouville. He leans out of the train window like a dog as if to drink in the wild scents of the country air and the fresh haze of green on the burgeoning hedgerows.

She is reserved with him at first and does not admit that she has been waiting in a kind of fever, a mayhem of wanting. But by the time they climb the stairs to the bedroom she is desperately aroused and cannot hide it.

They are hard and voracious with each other for several hours. She trusts him more this time and lets herself follow his lead. She does things she has never done, never dreamt of doing and in more and more bizarre positions. She is lewd and base and does not care. He loves to lick her, loves the taste of her, the smell of her. He whispers to The Prophet, things she cannot hear, as if her sex has a personality of its own. He laughs heartily with the noise of her orgasm, and slips inside her. She is so relaxed she can barely feel him and strains her pelvis up to draw him in deeper. They judder against one another and then coil together in the moist warmth of their bodies and drift into sleep, as meek as lambs.

Afterwards, he does not rush to get up, but holds her, with her head on his chest. She can hear a song thrush in the tree outside.

'You've no idea how I suffered in Normandy. I was so jealous of Jim. And yes, probably troubled by his ideas – I don't have art theories, I have instinct, *quoi*. I felt quite stupid and of course I was stupefied by wanting you and knowing I couldn't have you.'

'He was very touchy about his work. And about you.'

'I don't want to use you all up at once.'

She is painfully aware that he has not seen her for three nights but she says nothing.

'I'm not husband material, Jo. I must get that out in the open. Art and marriage don't go.'

'Who said anything about marriage? I'm not in the market for a husband.'

'Excellent. Kiss me.'

She does and the minutes disappear into the falling sand of another hour.

As she dresses, Jo begins to sing a folksong called 'Cill Aodáin' that her mother used to sing. She thought she had forgotten the words and they seem to pour through her body from another place and time, curled on her mother's lap or before that, rocked on the sea, wrapped in a shawl on her back, her face tucked in from the salt wind, the blowing mist.

Courbet watches her, smiling, listening, then he hums along. He starts to invent his own ludicrous lyrics in a song about a black bear and a white pussycat that leaves her tune far behind. When he boasts that he could have had a career on the stage she falls about laughing.

They take a walk along the riverbank, and Jo marvels at how green the Seine is here and how fast-flowing. The air is voluptuous; the colours are voluptuous; the faces, flowers, dogs, kerbstones, chimneys – all voluptuousness. Tall, feathery poplar trees line the path, some supporting strange globes of dark green growth in their leafless branches. When she asks what they are, he tells her that it is mistletoe.

'How does it get there?'

'They say from birds. They eat the seeds and shit them in flight and they hook into the bark and sprout.'

'So it's a parasite?'

'Yes.'

She stops to look up at them more closely. So a plant gathered in fertility rites lives off something else, she thinks. Anthony first kissed her under the pinned-up sprig of mistletoe at a Christmas party in his father's house. She had wanted that kiss, had lingered near the threshold to coincide with him passing through the doorway.

Courbet walks on and then turns and waits for her.

'I love the way you walk,' he says. 'It was one of the first things I noticed about you. Don't be offended if I say you walk like a Prussian soldier.'

She bursts out laughing and taps his upper arm. 'So much for aping the genteel ladies of Paris!'

'Your broad shoulders thrown back and all your heavy weapons at your hips. Long strides like a man.'

'Are you saying I swagger?'

'No, I'm saying you march straight ahead and don't look back. It's a walk of command. Some women walk as if the ground will damage their feet.'

'I'm not "Le Beau Navire" then?'

'No, but I envied Baudelaire that sight at the time. Let's see. Something like "d'un air placide et triomphant tu passes ton chemin". That's all I can recall.'

> *Quand tu vas balayant l'air de ta jupe large,*
> *Tu fais l'effet d'un beau vaisseau qui prend le large,*
> *Chargé de toile...*

'I regret that I can't say it with words, my little one. But I'll say it with oils, I promise you.'

'But you did make me a kind of vessel with wind in my sails when you taught me to swim,' she says. *'Les Fleurs du Mal* was the first book in French that I read.'

'What an introduction! He used to stay the night at my studio from time to time and asked me to note down his dreams – nightmares more like – he was high and raving: those images terrified me. I refused to do it any more.'

'Look at the chaffinch gathering straw,' Jo says.

'Every bird is building its nest. Will you come to my nest, Jo? I'll make you the happiest woman in Europe.'

'No, Courbet,' she bites back a smile. 'You know it has to be no.'

'Oh, you're perfect!' he laughs as if he was only testing her and grips her hand.

Her smile disappears. 'Listen, don't make me perfect. That will destroy what's good.'

'You see, where nobody knows me I can be quite the ordinary man and then I miss the ordinary things. A wife. Some kids. Bringing in the harvest, repairing a stone wall.'

'I know.'

As they stroll back to the hotel, she watches a twig caught spinning in an eddy and looks away. They can hear the sound of cataracts rushing through the sluice gates nearer the town. A beggar is sitting propped against a milestone, his feet a blistered and bloodied purple. Jo gives him a few centimes but Courbet empties the change in his pockets into the man's cap and wishes him luck. The man smiles and bows his head. His filthy patches of clothing are held to his body with bits of twine.

'When does dignity give way to defeat?' Jo asks as they walk on.

'When you can't tie the knot on the last end of string.'

'Listen,' he goes on after a while. 'I'll tell you a story and you can tell me if it is about dignity or defeat. It's the story of a man and a woman and a great passion. They were called Héloïse and Abélard. Have you heard of them?'

She shakes her head.

'Imagine the 12th century. Héloïse was nineteen when she met Abélard. He was forty-one. She was a brilliant scholar and he a famous philosopher. They fell in love and slipped off to get married secretly. But when the girl's uncle, her guardian, discovered, he ordered that Abélard be castrated. Héloïse and Abélard were separated. He went to a monastery in Brittany and she to an abbey just south of here.'

'Why do great passions not last?'

'Because they are extraordinary. Only the ordinary lasts.'

She has fallen into step with him and asks herself what makes us throw in our lot with another person. It feels so arbitrary and yet so utterly particular that it seems beyond chosen – it is inevitable.

'Did she ever see him again?'

'No.'

'It's defeat, then.'

'Well, some argue that they kept their love pure and eternal, thus turning defeat into dignity. They were re-buried together in 1817 in Père Lachaise.'

'Shall we go and pay homage to the unlastable?'

He half-smiles. 'We shall.'

She is cross with herself for having broken her first rule, to not ever again say 'shall we?' She has tried to couple them despite herself. She does not believe him anyway. Paris is only for work.

She suddenly runs ahead towards the river. She climbs a few stone steps onto the embankment and stands at the head of the weir.

He pauses to watch her, taken aback, enjoyment playing around the corners of his mouth.

'You have the look of a queen. As if everything flows from this moment of you standing up there. This is all that matters. You're like some great source.'

'I am,' she laughs. Then she thinks, as she watches the gushing water, this is hers, this energy. She must harness it, direct it.

They spend most of Sunday in bed. Their room is pungent and sticky with sweat and sex. Courbet takes her up to the violent verge of herself and she looks over it. What shocks her is that she is not shocked. She knows that he can hurt her, while she did not think that Jim could. She has her eyes open. Courbet will make or demand no promises.

They are lying naked, facing each other.

'I love your skin. The different textures and hues of it, here,' his hand brushes up her calf, 'and here,' he frisks his fingertips over her hipbone, 'and here,' he follows the line of her neck. 'The story of where daylight has touched and where only night-time.'

'And so tell me,' she asks without coyness, 'when are you going to ask permission to paint a nude of me?'

He whoops with laughter. 'I thought I'd have to woo you with a couple more weekends in fancy hotels!'

She gives him a light clip on the ear. 'You old bugger.'

They travel back to Paris on Sunday evening and Jo looks across the carriage at Courbet's dark and handsome face, more youthful now without its tightening stress. She realises that although they keep having sex, it just makes more desire for the ache in the gap between them to be closed. This is a totally new kind of appetite. She wants to discover everything he has ever done sexually and do it all again with him, for him. She wants to surprise him, impress him, yes, perform for him, open him up further than anyone has ever opened him before. And then she wonders about when that opening is done, will that be the end of their desire? And is it at the end of every desire?

Jo goes home. She wants to prove to herself that she can sleep alone. She will not be caught helpless in his strong current. She wonders why it seems easier to offer to pose nude for Courbet than it was for Jim. She has much less to lose. He can see her hunger to be more than she seemed, to be more than seen.

As she climbs the stairs to Fantin's apartment, it galls her to realise that most artists are like mistletoe, living off the tall, fine body of someone else till they have drained it of its sap. Can women achieve it differently? Can she? It is the end of April and the money Jim has left her is almost gone. She remembers what Henry Murger wrote: two abysses flank the artist – poverty and doubt. Will there be escape ladders to climb up and will she be strong enough to climb them or even recognise them when they come? She will have to return to London soon. And then what?

A few days later, Sophie waves and beckons to her as she comes into the atelier.

'Good morning and good news, Jo. Camille wants to commission you to paint a family portrait. How about that?'

'Heavens! That's wonderful.' Jo's hands fly up to her open mouth. Paris is hers again, even just for a short while. 'How can I thank you, Sophie? But do you think I am ready?'

'This is the best way to find out. Are you free to call in there later?'

'Of course.'

'She wants to help you get all the materials. She knows they're costly. And look at this mess of mine, will you please? I can't get the feet right at all.'

'Hands and feet are the real test, aren't they? My figures have El Greco hands on Poussin bodies.'

At the end of the class Jo shows Lévy her drawings of Camille. His single eyebrow twitches and jumps as he leafs through them. He runs his hand over his head as if forgetting he no longer has any hair to groom. He selects two and lays them side by side. She bites the edge of her finger. He seems to take an age to say anything.

'This is heavy-handed, sentimental even. The ink is too thin here and here,' he says caustically as he points at one of the first portraits she did that day. She can see at once that he is right and wants to take them all away and burn them. 'But this,' he goes on, pointing to a later piece, 'is well controlled, resolved – the huge responsibility and tenderness of motherhood are there in the weight of that cradling arm. This has the makings of a very good piece of work. Continue.' He dismisses her with a flick of his hand. She wants to fling her arms around him. As she steps lightly down the stairs, she tells herself that she must be achieving consistency and her own discernible style at last.

She walks to the rue Hautefeuille singing, lucid with the sense of her own adventure, her tread buoyant. She will paint every day. She will treat her art as she would a newborn that must be fed, washed, dressed and rocked to sleep or it will perish. It must be as demanding and absorbing as Georges is to Camille. Drumming through her head come her mother's last words: 'It is your gift and don't waste it.'

Gentlemen's eyes trail her and her desire builds as she turns down the rue de l'Ecole-de-Médecine. People having lunch on the street outside Café de La Rotonde throw her a jaunty 'good afternoon' as she passes under the large arched entrance to Courbet's studio. As she climbs the stairs she inhales the sweet moist scent of pipe tobacco. She is lusty again, a draining sweetness, as if all her energy is collecting around her groin and a barrage of remembered sensation sweeps through her.

She can hear the most dreadful squawking. She knocks and Courbet opens the door with a large green and yellow parrot perched on the back of his hand.

'Isn't it superb?' he says. 'A bird of paradise, like you.' The bird takes off and flies up into the rafters.

'It looks like a flying flower!'

'It's adorned with its own plumage so owes nothing to anybody. Like a beautiful woman who can do as she pleases.'

He kisses her and his touch and smell make her body hum. She does not want to let him pull away. Each hand rests in the dips at the small of his back.

A string of white shit drops from the ceiling and splats on the floor. They laugh. 'So much for paradise,' Jo says.

He has prepared the divan with a clean white sheet over the green rep and set it up against a backdrop of patterned tapestry draped between two step-ladders. The fire has been banked up with fresh logs. They burn with a faint smell of pine and cedar.

'Come here, my little one. Will you be warm enough?' He looks sheepish. 'I bought this for you. Here.' He hands her a flat, white cardboard box.

Under the tissue paper lies a heavy, turquoise silk dressing gown, embroidered with pink camellias.

'In case you change your mind.' He smiles and watches her undress for a moment.

'You look radiant, today. If I can paint all the ardour I feel for you, it will be a major success. It will be the most human nude. Like the painting by the Chinese fellow who painted such a realistic bird that he didn't add the eyes because he believed it would fly away.'

'I'd like my eyes open, seeing, please.'

The robe is the only thing of luxury in the room and she is inexplicably moved as she pulls it around her. It makes her feel braver that he has given her something he did not buy in order to paint, but something he bought to honour her, save her if she had a failure of nerve.

'Thank you. It's magnificent.'

243

He pretends not to have heard her, is arranging his paint tubes on the table next to the easel. She sits on the divan and lets the gown fall open.

'Ah, Jo, no one can compare to you. I am the luckiest man in Paris – my future is in your hands.' At that, the parrot flutters down and lands on the top of its white cage.

She eases the gown off her shoulders. He comes and gently takes it away. He spreads out her hair and fixes the sheet to fall over one thigh and shield her sex. He is leaving it up to her to remove it. She is touched. He repositions the easel so that he is almost behind her and begins to draw, telling stories of his pranks as a boy and breaking into song as he does so. She wishes she could see the tiny decisions of looking and light pass over his face but she can only hear him, so she relishes lying there wanting him, knowing that she can wait, that she is choosing the quietly building rapture.

'Can you lift your left hand up as if you're welcoming the bird?'

She can feel desire travel on invisible threads and thicken the air between them. A flicker of outrageous fantasy makes her bite her lower lip.

Then it happens. The parrot flaps and swoops across the studio to land on Jo's hand. She almost cries out. She steadies her breathing and watches its glassy black and orange eyes surveying her. The hooked grey beak looks vicious. It preens under a wing and turns, its curiosity and nonchalance quite palpable. Its claws are sharp and scaly. She is suddenly aware of the nut-like shape of her nipples. Her fear makes them harden.

Courbet is silent, working fast.

The bird is heavier than it looks and in its aloof eye Jo can see the clear, cold terror of captivity. After a few minutes, it flies off again and settles on a wooden perch nearby.

'I knew it would work,' he cries delightedly. 'Rest your arm, sweetheart. Can I ask you something?'

'Of course.'

'Can we stop now, please, and continue tomorrow? I need to have you.'

She turns to him, tilts down her chin and says in a severe voice, 'Don't come crying to me when nothing is finished for the Salon.'

'To hell with the Salon.' He is already tearing off his clothes and coming towards her.

Jo is lying on the divan and he is sitting beside her. They are both naked, calm. It seems strange to her that she can feel so candid and chaste after sex with him. He had done as she asked. He had withdrawn early. She had shown him the dates in her red book. He counted the days out on his paint-stained fingers.

He is stroking her body with his eyes.

'Oh am I up to it, my beauty, the glory of your skin?'

'Do you think eyes can touch like fingers?'

'That's what we're hoping, yes.'

'Ah, le cudot! Le beau cudot...' She reaches up, ruffles his hair and pulls him down to her.

Later she gets up, puts on the robe and looks at the painting. She wants to absorb it at every stage, map his decisions, consider what she would do in each section to complete it. She will isolate each gesture, memorise every layer. Her body looks strong and fine and it is easier to look at her breasts than she imagined. She realises how clever Courbet was to introduce the bird – it distracted her from her own body.

'I got my first painting commission today,' she says quietly.

'Formidable! From who, may I ask?'

'Camille Montaudon, Sophie's sister. A friend from the atelier.'

'My congratulations, Jo.' He spreads his arms. 'Take anything you need from here. Anything, Jo.'

Ten days later, Woman with a Parrot is finished and Courbet invites Paul Durand-Ruel, the dealer, to come over to photograph it. There are already two buyers fighting over it, including

Khalil Bey. Courbet is eager to get on with the next portrait but Jo tells him that he must wait. Jo wants to start her sittings with the Montaudon family. Sophie and her husband, Michel, had asked her to come for lunch to discuss the setting and pose. At first she strove to hide her nerves but as soon as they began to deliberate about the painting, she relaxed and enjoyed herself. Sophie said she would like flowers in the portrait and Jo suggested that they also have a few of Michel's collected figures. Jo made sketches and showed them to Fantin and Lévy for advice and Lévy advised a simpler backdrop – curtains rather than patterned wallpaper and fewer props. Courbet gave her a present of a large stretched canvas and Sophie offered to come to hold the baby. One morning in May, in the Montaudons' entrance hall, which had been transformed into Jo's studio, she began to paint Camille.

When Jo sees Courbet later that day, he tells her that Khalil Bey has bought *Woman with a Parrot* and wants to meet her very much. He has invited them to have dinner the following Saturday evening.

When they arrive at Khalil Bey's elegant, over-furnished house that gives on to Place Monge, he asks if they would mind removing their outdoor shoes and presents them with leather slippers. He is a compact, short man with an olive complexion, salt-and-pepper hair and a thick silver moustache. His impeccably tailored grey suit is set off by a spotted red silk cravat and grey-checked waistcoat. As he leads them around his extraordinary collection of art, he passes his green eyes lovingly over each painting, which he introduces as if it were family.

'Of course, buying art is like having a ravishing woman – the excitement of the chase and the possession are paramount. But then, something else happens,' he pauses and rubs his soft hands together, 'a quieter fondness develops, a warmth that comes from intimacy and a certain domesticity. But it's never dull. Sometimes I stop on this staircase and stare at the Corot and see a new light, an old meaning in a fresh way.' He

246

pauses and runs a finger along his upper lip. 'The Ingres, here, is my favourite morning painting and this Delacroix is host to my evening. How could one not be happy gazing upon this delectable Turkish bath, I ask you?'

'However, may I say that few of them appear Turkish, my good fellow!' Courbet says jovially, patting Khalil Bey's shoulder.

Jo too had noticed how pale and blonde most of the women were but would not have dared to comment.

Khalil Bey smiles and shrugs. 'If you have Ingres' vigour and vitality when you are eighty-two you will have led a good life.'

He continues and addresses Jo. 'A sense of beauty keeps us young, no, mademoiselle? And perhaps you know this unlikely beauty by our friend here.' He stops by a still-life of a profusion of white flowers by Courbet that she has not seen before. She likes how he has placed a small bird, twitchy, tentative, amidst the bank of white. He brings the same mysterious stillness and movement to his nudes too, she realises. Something alert, active and yet grounded.

When they sit down to dinner, Jo has the sense that something is being celebrated but she is not sure what. A collection of masks from all over the world peers at them from one wall: a huge African face carved in wood with woven cane hair and a hessian beard; a petite oval Indonesian face painted red, white and gold; a mask with a protruding horn and slit eyes; another with the placid, round face and long earlobes of the Buddha. Jo imagines the masks' rituals and carnivals and the faces that once carried them inviting her to try one on and come alive with dance and demons and hungry ghosts.

It is a lavish meal of roast quail, venison in a leek and shallot sauce, spiced figs in honey, followed by pears and cheeses brought in from all over France. A servant opens different wines to complement each course. Khalil Bey is charming, witty and attentive and wants to talk about the year he spent as a diplomat in Dublin. He is astounded that Jo has never been.

'It is a splendid Georgian city, alive with splendour and decrepitude. Like Constantinople. The art is quiet but the women noisy.'

'I'm planning a trip to Ireland this summer with my father,' Jo says.

Courbet casts her a quick glance of alarm. She looks away towards the green marble fireplace where a bronze mask of a muse decorates each corner.

'And you paint too, I hear,' Khalil Bey continues.

'Yes, and perhaps one day someone will give Joseph Hiffernan a show. I know some dealers and gallery owners in London. I shall send them my work as J. Hiffernan.'

'When will you permit me to view some of these works?' Courbet asks.

'They'll be private until they're public,' Jo states firmly.

'I see.' Courbet rolls his eyes with a look of mirth and, is it, admiration?

'Do you smoke, Jo?' Khalil Bey offers her a cigar. The dark rings under his eyes give him the look of a small, gentrified owl.

'Not yet. But Joseph would like to try, if he may.'

She takes a cigar and Khalil Bey shows her how to snip its end. He runs the tip of a match flame up and down its revolving sides to seal it and hands it back to her.

'Don't swallow or inhale,' Courbet warns.

'Taste it like a peat fire. Let it roll in your mouth and then blow it out. Like this.' Khalil Bey demonstrates with captivating aplomb and Jo copies him. The smoke stings her tongue like pepper at first and then softens and seems to bloom on her palate. She exhales, crosses her legs, leans back and smiles with bravado at each of them.

'A natural,' Khalil Bey says contentedly.

'I mean to travel to Constantinople, Monsieur Khalil.' Jo waves the cigar magisterially.

'You must. It needs you.'

Khalil Bey regards her with curious intent.

'You have that look now that compelled me to the painting, *Woman with a Parrot*. Most nude models are lost inside themselves, dreaming, somnolent, elsewhere. That doesn't interest me. But you have a way that is wrestling with something, engaged with something – you're relaxed and yet – how shall I put it? – uncompromised. Am I making sense?'

'Courbet chose the parrot for that reason. It let me be more fully alive.'

'And I chose you for that reason, too,' Courbet says quietly.

'Shall I show her my special item?' Khalil asks and raises his eyebrow as he studies Jo.

'A splendid idea.' Courbet smiles.

'Please do.' She knows by their looks and their tone that this is some form of initiation. She is tantalised as the two men stand up and Khalil Bey gestures towards the door.

They leave the room and go up another floor to a dimly lit smoking room, hung with damask curtains. There is an ornate Boulle games-table at its centre. She notices a dark celestial globe on a glass shelf, a wall of books and a well-worn leather saddle chair. Khalil Bey approaches a landscape of a chateau on a snow-covered hill. It is the only painting in the room. He beckons Jo to follow. He lifts the painting swiftly off the wall and leans it against the wainscot. Behind it is a shallow built-in cabinet. He opens it with care and stands back. Jo peers inside. It is empty.

Khalil Bey nods at his empty glass of port and leaves the room to refill it.

'Oh, was it stolen?' Jo cannot hide her disappointment.

Courbet laughs. 'It's yet to be painted. I've been waiting for the right model. Someone deliciously frank yet delightfully private.' He has a glint in his eye as he scans down her body. A bell starts to peal a slow midnight over the Paris night.

'How private?' she asks and as she does she realises what he means and is immediately both unnerved and thrilled. It is as if the bell is ringing out from her solar plexus.

249

'The most private. Life-size,' he says holding his hands as if around a peach. 'It will be beyond its time. Intimate, unflinching and true. You are the one, Jo. Will you? Say you will.'

Jo smiles. She is again transported back to Wapping with two men in a painting negotiating a price for her. Her cache of savings is almost used up. Her commission will give her just enough for another two months in Paris. She has a flare of resolve. Almost without thinking, yes is rising, flickering from somewhere deep inside her, scrolling up; a yes that will take her further than she has ever gone; will buy her a ticket to ride a long train travelling over the dry chequered plains of Spain to the Prado; and on eastwards through Europe and south all the way to the Bosphorus Strait where something else will begin. She will learn a new tongue, practise a new walk, respond to a new sounding of her name. She will become the leafless tree shining back, open and avid with joy.

She turns to him.

'Mademoiselle If has two conditions: firstly, no face,' she says, her voice trembling, her index finger straight in the air.

'If you say so,' he says, nodding. 'And the other?'

She clears her throat, stands upright. 'Secondly, I get half the commission. Or no deal.'

Courbet's mouth falls open and then he bends over with laughter and stamps his feet.

'I am serious, Courbet.' She crosses her arms.

'Oh, Jo, let's not talk business. This is art.'

'Half the fee or I leave.' She turns to go. Her life is pivoting on the spin of her heel.

'All right.' He shrugs. 'Agreed, agreed.'

She puts out her hand. They shake and he pulls her into his arms. He lifts her clear off the ground.

'The Prophet has spoken,' he says.

She is laughing, her body's pleasure distilling into clarity and boldness, red as a matador's cape. This is the fire she has stolen, the trail of bright flame, her own power.

'I know what you must call it,' she says as he sets her down. 'You must call it *The Origin of the World.*'

Epilogue

The gallery is quiet and still. Tom Mathison, the gallery owner, is setting out bottles and glasses in a back room. Jo stands back and looks at the hang. Yesterday she asked Tom to re-hang each portrait two inches lower. Yes, it is better. She walks past the work, left to right and then back, passing through three years, four cities. The paintings and drawings are recalling her, giving her back the days spent with Fanny, with Bridget, with Camille, with her father's friend Molly in Cork, with the women she met in Constantinople – a dancer called Hamiyet, Elcin, her maid and Afet, Elcin's grandmother. She has a flush of accompaniment, of fierce pride. Her first exhibition. Solo. The word is a song. She is brimming with the need to sing. It is ready. She stands in the centre of the room, shuts her eyes and opens them and looks again, trying to see with the discerning eye of Matthew Hill, the cool eye of Monsieur Lévy. In one hour everyone will arrive. There is no turning back, no more effort. No need for it, no time for it. Suddenly the enormity of the moment makes her shudder and she feels sick. Their eyes are on the pictures, scratching like scalpels, their words tearing at the canvas and paper with razor-sharp beaks. She cannot do it. She wants to snatch them all down, cancel everything and disappear. She moves towards the door, her hands numb, her head dizzy and a screw twisting in her stomach.

'Jo, are you all right?' Tom calls.

'Yes, yes, I'll just get some air.'

She steps on to Berners Street away from the imposters, those paintings she wants nothing to do with. They are not the paintings she carried in her head. They will never be. She could keep walking, go through Russell Square, meet her father walking down from Clerkenwell and turn him back. If she hurries.

'Congratulations Jo!' She turns to see Fanny and Gabriel walking towards her, Fanny holding a corsage of lilies of the valley and rosebuds.

'Where do you think you are off to?' Fanny calls. 'The fancy gallery is that way and you're in it.'

'It's no good, none of it is any good.'

'It's the nerves, my girl. It would be no fun without them.' Fanny smiles and reaches over to pin the corsage to Jo's dress.

'But I am not joking. I want to call it off.'

Fanny rubs Jo's upper arms excitedly as if she has not heard what Jo said, cannot see the anguish on her face.

'Doubt the doubt, Jo.' Gabriel takes her elbow and turns her back towards Mathison's. 'In two hours you'll be high as a kite. Is Jim here yet?'

'No.' Jo takes a deep breath. Fanny and Gabriel are acting as though she is an artist and her misgivings are perfectly normal. She begins to realise that she will have to act her way through the evening. She must pretend she believes. Is part of the game the willingness to bluff?

'Listen,' Gabriel begins, 'I remember my mother used to say that some days when she looked at her offspring she was sure she'd done a good job and other days she wasn't. Your job is over now, the paintings have to stand up by themselves.'

'Come on, let's get on with it.' Fanny tweaks Jo's cheeks to bring their colour back and steers them both inside.

Jo's arms are water. Fanny and Gabriel circle the paintings. They turn, smiling. They do not need to say anything. It's in their eyes.

'They are stunning, Jo,' Fanny says. 'I see my past and my future in my face, in all the faces.'

Gabriel is still standing in front of one of the paintings from Constantinople, his fingers stroking his lips. 'Well done, Jo. You've captured something so light in their faces and so robust in their figures. The backgrounds are dream-like impressions but the figures are solid. This is something new. Something bold.'

'They look like they know their worth and the world doesn't. That's what I like,' Fanny says.

Then Fantin arrives, her father, Bridget and Gerald, Stan McGovern, Algernon, they are all arriving, flowing in, smiling, carrying flowers. They mill in a happy throng with Jo at the heart of it. She seems to be real, to be really here and this is a room full of her work, the angles and curves of her own dreams. She is full of love, satisfied love, buoyed on belief, naked, with every stitch on.

Will Jim come? She looks at the door. Tom is moving through the room with a tray of glasses of red wine and raki. Jo finds that she can look at the work again, over people's shoulders, she can see exactly where she will go next, can sense the thirst to start something new, something too hard to do, something bigger. The next work is always the best. Who said that? Jim. She turns around and there he is framed in the doorway, in a black floppy hat, a black velvet jacket and blue cravat, swinging his silver cane.

L'Origine du Monde, 1866, is a strikingly frank painting of a woman's vulva. It may or may not use Jo Hiffernan as its model although she was certainly the model for Courbet's portrait, *La Belle Irlandaise,* 1865, and is known to have been in Paris in 1866. *L'Origine du Monde* was commissioned by Khalil Bey, but sold privately after his bankruptcy in 1868. It was rediscovered in an antique shop in 1889. It was resold and in 1955 came into the possession of the psychoanalyst Jacques Lacan; it is now in the Musée d'Orsay.

While some of the historical details are taken from the letters of Whistler and Courbet, the novel is a work of fiction. It is a tribute to the time Jo Hiffernan posed for these outstanding artists and imagines what else she contributed to their lives and their art.

Jo had left Courbet by the autumn of 1866. She returned to London and, even though they were no longer lovers, she looked after Whistler's illegitimate son. Later she lived in the south of France and is thought to have worked as an art dealer. She returned to attend Whistler's funeral in Chiswick in 1903. None of her art is known to have survived.

ACKNOWLEDGEMENTS

Many enormous thanks to Nina Rapi, Michael Langan, Jo Beecham, Jennifer Russell, Godfrey Offord, Angela Gardner, Kerry Kilner, D.J. Roberts, Karen Widdicombe, Uriel Orlow, Mikhail Karikis, Stephen Wilson, Margareta Kern, Marcus Kern, Oreet Ashery, Maureen Harter, Peppe Orru, Luciano Martins, Louise Smyth, Urs Kiefer, Uli Kiefer-Smyth and Jo Hemmant.

I am also indebted to the Writers' Residencies at Can Serrat, Spain, the Tyrone Guthrie Centre, Ireland and the Bundanon Trust, Australia.

Special thanks to Anka Wolbert, who came in time.

Holland Park Press is a unique publishing initiative. It gives contemporary Dutch writers the opportunity to be published in Dutch and English. We also publish new works written in English and translations of classic Dutch novels.

To

- Find out more
- Learn more about Cherry Smyth
- Discover other interesting books
- Read fascinating columns in our Anglo-Dutch magazine
- Check out our competitions
- Join the discussions
- Or to just make a comment

Visit www.hollandparkpress.co.uk

Bookshop: http://www.hollandparkpress.co.uk/books.php

Holland Park Press in the social media

http://www.twitter.com/HollandParkPres
http://www.facebook.com/HollandParkPress
http://www.youtube.com/user/HollandParkPress